NATURAL ENEMIES

SPIRIT SEEKER BOOK 2

JANNA RUTH

SPIRIT SEEKER BOOK 2

NATURAL ENEMIES

JANNA RUTH

First published in New Zealand in 2021

2nd edition in 2025

Copyright © 2021 by Janna Ruth

www.janna-ruth.com

ISBN 978-0-473-58854-0 (Paperback)

ISBN 978-0-473-58855-7 (eBook)

For all Story Seekers,
young and old

1

Wulf Bachmann has survived. The legendary commander of the spirit seekers has returned home from fighting a volcano, and he doesn't like what he sees. Which is mainly me.

"Let's talk about this inside," he says, with a not-so-promising scowl.

I steal a glance at Aeola in the sky as I follow him to the gate. The sylph looks nervous as she hangs out above the tree line. I mouth, "Later," only to bump into Wulf, who's holding the door for me. "Sorry…"

"Were you talking to that spirit?"

Caught red-handed, I find myself blushing. "What?"

His eyes narrow. "You were clearly communicating with…" He interrupts himself with a sigh. "Later." His inviting gesture is a little too adamant to feel welcoming.

Great. Not even five minutes in and I'm already in trouble with the commander. Bunching my shoulders, I head into the dark gateway. I make sure to reach the opposite gate before him, so I can return the favour of holding the door open. Wulf takes note of it with a chuckle.

Everyone but Miriam is soaking up the early spring sun in the courtyard. Leon sits against the mighty trunk of an old oak tree, the only tree in the courtyard, warming his face. A bandage still covers his eyes, but he looks at ease. Close by, Camille and Lukas are sparring with a pair of practice staffs. I glance at Wulf and see a smile spreading on his face. Instantly, my heart softens towards him. He's clearly missed his team and this place.

We're almost halfway across the courtyard before Lukas notices us. He freezes on the spot, earning him a direct hit on the shoulder from Camille.

"Gosh, Lukas, I'm sorry," I hear her say, but when he doesn't react in the slightest, she turns around, too. As soon as Camille catches sight of Wulf, a high-pitched squeal escapes her mouth. She drops her staff and comes running straight into his arms. "You're back!"

Wulf's laughter rings through the air as he embraces Camille and whirls her around. Camille is crying for joy, squeezing Wulf as tight as she can.

"You're alive." Lukas comes closer. He looks absolutely awestruck, as if he just saw Wulf rise from the dead. I guess, in a way, the commander has.

Wulf lets go of Camille and clasps hands with Lukas, pulling him close. "Didn't you read the debrief last night?"

"We were... No." Lukas' face softens uncharacteristically as he's somehow caught between laughter and tears. "You're back."

"I am," Wulf says, patting Lukas' shoulder. "Your form was looking good, by the way. You kept up your practice."

Lukas looks as if he's about to pass out. A rueful grin appears on his face. "Not that last hit."

I stare at him in wonder. That's the most submissive I've ever seen him. Guess I found out who holds Lukas' reins.

Meanwhile, Leon has got to his feet. "Is that you, Wulf? I'm not hallucinating voices, am I?" He laughs nervously.

I step to his side to lead him closer. "He's really here."

"I am." Wulf comes our way, instant concern on his face. "What happened to your eyes?"

"Had a little rough-and-tumble with a sylph," Leon quips. Relief floods his face. "I can't believe it. I thought I'd never see you again." He huffs. "Not that I've seen you yet, but you get the gist." Out of breath, Leon stops his rambling.

Is there anything more heart-warming than men showing their emotions? Though Wulf's face briefly tightens at the mention of Leon's accident, he immediately puts his hands on his shoulders and squeezes them. "We're both here. That's all that matters."

All this ruckus has lured Miriam from her lab. She quickly strides over to us. "I just saw the message," she says as soon as she's in earshot. "Did you teleport home?"

Wulf lets go of Leon and shakes his head, grinning. "I took the first flight I could get." For the flash of a moment, his face freezes. It's so quick, I wonder if I imagined it.

They embrace, but Miriam's curiosity gets the better of her. "It said the mission was a success. Does that mean..."

"He caught a volcano spirit," I announce matter-of-factly, as if I've already had a whole run-down. It still amazes me how anyone can do that. It would be a bit like taking on the Erlking and his rolling storm of sylphs all by yourself, only instead of strong winds, you have fire raining down on you.

Modesty turns the tips of his ears an adorable red. It makes me realise that he's only eight years older than me at most. "I managed to catch him, yeah." And yet, he's been a celebrated spirit seeker for the better part of a decade.

"And that's"—Lukas announces, pointing at Wulf with both of his index fingers—"why this guy's a legend." He shakes his head as if he can't believe it, even though he just claimed it himself. At least his confidence is returning. "You single-handedly beat Vesuvius. What the hell, man?"

Wulf raises his hand and declares rather earnestly, "Not single-handedly. We were a team."

"But the others came back before you," Camille interjects. "They said you helped them escape."

"And some of us died," Wulf adds, now completely sombre. "Even so, I wouldn't even have lived long enough to complete the mission if not for everyone else." He's clearly been through a lot, maybe even lost some dear friends, but for his team's sake, he puts it aside, forcing a smile back on his face. Looking around at each of them, his gaze finally comes to rest on my face. "Looks to me like you've got a lot to tell, too? I heard you had a big battle with a sylph called the Erlking? I hopped on the plane as soon as the report arrived. You can't tell how glad I am to see you all alive and... well, in reasonably good shape." His eyes flicker to Leon with concern.

Leon can't see him, but his fingers search for mine. When I grasp his hand, he claims, "All thanks to Rika here. You haven't met her yet, right?"

"We had a quick chat outside," Wulf replies politely, scratching his nose. His eyes let me know he hasn't forgotten about Aeola yet.

Camille steps in to explain. "We met Rika in February. Not sure if you read any of the reports, but there was a huge sylph attack in Central Station. It still hasn't opened yet, though they hope to have trains running again by the end of the month. Anyway, we later learnt that the Erlking led the attack, and Rika helped us defuse the attack before the sylphs did too much damage. We haven't tested her NAV yet, but it wouldn't surprise me if it were as high as yours or—"

"Even higher?" Wulf completes her sentence, not sounding particularly convinced. His eyes bore into me. He knows exactly how good my natural attunement is.

"She was living on the streets," Lukas adds, apparently eager to share that embarrassing detail about me. "You should have seen her when she arrived here. Run-down clothes, matted hair, half-brown, half... I don't know if that even was a colour. Reeking of coffee..."

I'm convinced Wulf doesn't need to know all these details. Fortunately, Camille is of the same opinion and interrupts Lukas before Wulf can fully digest the wealth of information and turn away in disgust. "She's been a real asset. She has a way with spirits unrivalled by anything I've ever seen. And without her... we would have stood no chance against the Erlking. She's the one who fought and caught him."

Naturally, Lukas stresses, "With our help."

Wulf studies me, as if he's still trying to imagine how I must've looked before I met the spirit seekers. There's no smile on his face for me. "A way with spirits, hmm? You mean like casually hanging out with them outside the citadel?"

Here we go. Tensing up, I take a deep breath and await everyone's judgement. Sure enough, everyone turns their attention on me. Confusion battles revulsion on all but Leon's face.

"You're hanging out with spirits?" Camille asks to confirm.

I fold my arms and shrug, letting go of Leon in the process. "They aren't all bad."

"What are you talking about?" Lukas exclaims loudly. "Of course they're all bad. We just fought a bunch of them off while they tried to destroy Berlin."

I won't take it, not from him. "And we would have lost without her help." I fixate on Wulf. "Aeola is my friend. I saved her life; she saved mine."

"I can't believe it," Lukas mutters and takes a little walk. He stops several times to say something but is lost for words for once in his life.

Meanwhile, Camille is still battling her confusion. "How long has this been going on for?"

"I met her before I met you." It's true, if barely. I saved Aeola from drowning in the Spree before we headed to Central Station in search of shelter. "She's been with me all this time."

"And you never thought to mention it?" Camille sounds more than a little hurt.

"A sylph in our citadel..." Lukas is muttering to himself.

Miriam looks at me as if I've just hurt Camille. "You should have told us about her. This is a serious security issue."

"But it wasn't," Leon interjects, a feeble attempt to help me. "It was obviously okay in this case." He's reaching out to me, gently running his fingers across my elbow. I feel horrible for being incapable of reciprocating the touch he so obviously longs for.

"Okay?" Lukas screeches. "Did you forget the storm of sylphs we had to fight off? Where do you think they came from?"

It's all too much. Apart from Leon, everyone is staring at me as if I ordered that attack, even Wulf, who shouldn't have the slightest idea what Lukas is talking about. Defensively, I take a step back. "So what if I'm friends with a spirit? Who, by the way, did *not* attack any of you. You've always been so anti-spirit I knew I couldn't tell you about her, but she's a friendly spirit. The Erlking would've killed me if not for her. She went up against her own family. For me. A human."

I turn to face Wulf, the one responsible for this mess. "Welcome back, I guess."

Before anyone can voice any more concerns, I turn around and walk away with long strides.

"Rika," I hear Leon say, but I don't heed his call, knowing that he can't come running after me. Instead, I keep walking until I'm safely in my room, the door shut behind me.

My heart thumps heavily in my chest, and my whole face twitches in an effort not to burst into tears. I'm so mad, I could scream. Everything was perfect yesterday. They all celebrated me then. Now, I'm the worst again.

Stupid Wulf. Why couldn't he have stayed gone? Without him, nobody would've ever learnt about Aeola.

I swallow hard, my head spinning. Did I really just wish him dead? That man just survived a two-month-long ordeal under a volcano, fighting off Vesuvius, risking his life to save not only his team, but millions of people.

Dejected, I sit on the bed. It's easy to see why Lukas idolises him so much. Wulf is a hero, the best of this generation of spirit seekers. In comparison, I'm just a girl from the streets who happens to talk to spirits.

A knock sounds on my door. For a moment, I'm tempted to pretend I'm not here, but then I let out a sigh and rise from the bed. "Coming."

I almost reached the door when the thought it might be Wulf crosses my mind. Unconsciously, I rub my face, testing for tears, and gratefully finding my cheeks nice and dry. My hands are midway to my hair when I stop myself cold. What am I even attempting to do here?

Fuelled by my previous anger, I unlock the door and rip it open. "What?" It's not him but Camille. "Oh, it's you." I'm not disappointed, am I? No, I'm glad it's her. She likes me, after all. At least, she used to.

"Can I come in?" Camille asks, now nothing but deep concern in her eyes.

Flustered, I gesture into my room. "Sure."

As soon as the door closes behind us, she launches into it. "I'm sorry if we scared you away. I think everyone was a bit overwhelmed by Wulf's return. We thought he was dead." She seems a lot more fragile now that the first joyful shock of seeing him has worn off.

I cross my arms and keep my distance. "I'm glad he's not."

"Me too. Very glad." Camille steps forward, and I keep still only because it seems silly to back away from her. "How are you?"

"Me? I'm fine. Why wouldn't I be?" Well, maybe because I'm standing here in the most defensive position, ready to go to battle against my friend. With a sigh, I relax my arms. "I'm good."

Camille doesn't believe me. "You don't look good." Disappointed, she shakes her head. "I thought we were beyond this. You know you can trust me. I've always had your best interests at heart."

And now you know I can't be trusted. "It's not that easy. My friendship with Aeola was still developing, and you all... Everything I've learned here is so different from what my mum taught me when I was a kid. She taught me to respect spirits, showed me how they lived, and..." Oh no, I'm rambling. "But that doesn't matter right now. Why aren't you downstairs with Wulf? You must be so happy he's alive and well."

"I am," Camille confirms, but she takes my hands. "Right now, you need me more than him. I don't want you to feel like you don't belong here anymore."

"But I don't." I bite my lip. I want to belong here, but I don't see how it's possible. "Your commander's back."

"So?" Camille puts her hands on my shoulders and tries to look into my eyes, which, admittedly, is challenging, since I keep avoiding her gaze. "It doesn't matter that Wulf's returned. You're part of this team as well."

It doesn't feel that way at the moment. "He wanted to kill her, Camille."

"Who?" A moment of confusion passes over Camille's face.

"Aeola, my sylph friend. No questions asked, no warning. He just went straight for her. I barely managed to protect her from him."

Camille looks like she's about to faint. She's only able to respond once she's straightened her shoulders. "Right. Well..." Part of her obviously agrees with him, or she would've assured me already. "I think that you have a special way with spirits, Rika. Something I've never seen before. Honestly, I don't think anybody has seen this before. So, can you understand that it'll take us some time to process?" As I'm starting to sag, she hurries to add, "But I believe you when you say this spirit is your friend. If she truly did what you said, then we all owe her. It's just that Wulf and sylphs..." Camille rubs my arms, biting her lip as if there's more to say about that. After a while, she steps back. "Let him settle in first. He's someone you can talk to, I promise."

Maybe she's right. Maybe all this will be resolved after we've gotten the awkward truth bombs out of the way. "You should go back to him. I bet he's got a lot to tell you guys. For the record, I'm glad he didn't die."

"You're not coming down?" Camille asks, seeing right through my dejection.

"Maybe later. I'm on dinner duty today." Yeah, celebratory dinner duty. Can this day get any worse?

Camille doesn't push me. She nods and smiles gently. "Okay. I'll see you, then."

As soon as she's left, I drop back on the bed and run my hands over my face. Just when things got better, they fell apart. I had a place in this team because of my ability to see and hear spirits. Wulf can do that as well as I can, plus he's a highly skilled seeker. A living legend.

A lump forms in my throat, and I blink back tears. Time to face the truth; they no longer need me.

2

Dinner is about as delightful as I thought it'd be. The moment I reappear downstairs to prepare the food, Miriam waves me away. "We already ordered pizza for at least twice as many people. Come, sit!"

She scoots closer to Camille on the couch, who bites her lip for a second, before returning her attention to Wulf. The commander is sharing the other long couch with Leon, while Lukas occupies the single chair, glowing with attention.

He doesn't mind me one bit, instead prompting Wulf, "You caught it alone?"

"It's really not such a big deal," Wulf says. Though he chuckles, his eyes aren't meeting Lukas', but flitting around the room. "I didn't really have a choice. To be honest, I couldn't bear losing anyone else, so I sent them home." His eyes come to rest on me as I squeeze in with Miriam. Quickly, he turns away again to look at Lukas. "If I have to be completely honest, we were woefully underprepared. The spirit was far beyond our capabilities."

"And yet you did it!" Lukas grins. He leans forward to clasp Wulf's hand. "Greatest of all time, right there."

Obviously, Wulf is so great, he's even got modesty down to a T. "Not even close."

Lukas won't have it. "Sure you are. So, tell us, how did you get him on your own?"

Wulf sighs. He came here so fast I doubt he truly had time to process his mission. "Alright, alright. But I'm warning you, there was a whole lot of luck involved. The hardest bit was finding Vesuvius. That deep in the volcano, it was a maze, and I got myself well and truly lost, which is why it took me so long to get out of there."

Everyone in the room seems to hold their breath, hanging onto every word Wulf speaks, and then there's me, thinking about how I can skilfully remove myself from the situation. Just then, the gate buzzer comes to my rescue.

"I'll go get the pizza," I announce, jumping up before anyone else can even think of it.

Outside, I breathe in the fresh air. Is it just me, or was that room stuffy?

I only think about the fact that pizza usually costs money when I'm already halfway through the gatehouse. Well, I can't let the poor delivery guy wait while I go back and forth. I also don't want Wulf to see me begging for money after Lukas blurted my past to him. Opening the door, it is.

As it turns out, Miriam already prepaid for the pizza, and all I have to do is take the huge pile off the delivery guy. The smells of at least three different toppings and melted cheese assault my nose. I wish Aeola was there to share in it, but she's wisely keeping her distance from the citadel.

I deliberately take ages to get back to the common room so I don't have to hear more about Wulf's volcano adventures.

"Finally," Lukas exclaims. "Did you get lost or what?"

Before I can even think of a retort, Wulf gives him a stern, "Luke, watch your tone."

I almost snap at him that I can take care of myself, but I'm too baffled by Lukas' instant apology. "Sorry. Didn't mean it that way." His eyes tell a different story, but apparently he's on his best behaviour around Wulf.

Camille gets up to help with the pizzas and distributes them around the table, while Miriam gets a couple of beers and sodas out. I watch as Wulf guides Leon to the slices and makes sure he gets a drink. They've got this quiet ease about them, contrary to Lukas' loud mouth. Even now, with pizza in his mouth, he can't keep quiet.

"Nymph water on staffs, that's genius. I bet those salamanders didn't know what hit them." He chucks down his bite with a gulp of beer.

I have no idea what a nymph water is, but it seems like I'm the only one failing to understand, so I keep my mouth shut.

"It wasn't my idea," Wulf admits. "Tove came up with it. She'll be one of the greats one day."

"Well, she'd better step up her game because she didn't catch Vesuvius," Lukas boasts, as if it was him who'd caught the volcano spirit. "Tell us, how did you know where to find his nest?"

The pizza in my mouth tastes like cardboard and is about as chewy. Don't they have anything else to talk about? I don't want to know how a group of spirit seekers went all the way into a volcano to smoke out the spirit living there.

"Let him eat, Lukas," Camille chides the younger spirit seeker. "I'm sure Wulf will run us through it in all detail, but not tonight." She and the commander exchange a quick smile that reminds me how important he is to her.

"Yeah, yeah, but come on!" Lukas whines. "This is a once-in-a-lifetime battle. They're going to teach it at the academy, and we've got the legend sitting right among us."

Alright, I've had enough. This is ridiculous. No man should ever be put on a pedestal as high as this. So he defeated a big bad spirit. He's still just human.

I finish my second slice, listening through Wulf's modest denial of his status. When he starts on yet another retelling of his deeds, just as Lukas wanted, I get up and leave the room. Nobody even notices. Lacking the courage to go outside and search for Aeola, I return to my room and get ready for bed, only to glower at the ceiling.

Downstairs, I hear the faint sound of laughter. I always knew how much they missed him, and that I'd never be able to replace him, but this is an exquisite form of torture. No matter how wonderful he seems to be, he's as anti-spirit as they come. After our battle with the Erlking, I'd hoped to introduce the others to Aeola, but that's out of the question now. In terms of spirit-human relationships, we're back at square one. Or maybe even negative one.

The next morning, I skip breakfast in the hall and eat leftover pizza under the oak tree in the courtyard. My heart yearns to look for Aeola and talk this over with her, but I'm too scared Wulf will bust us again. It proves to be an excellent decision when I hear his steps coming up behind me before I've finished eating.

He squats next to me, elbows propped up on his thighs and a crooked half-smile on his face. "Is that your usual breakfast style?"

Maybe he meant it as an inviting quip, but all I hear is him making fun of my past. "Don't worry, I know how to eat at a table."

Wulf frowns slightly before understanding dawns on him. "I didn't mean it that way." The tip of his tongue wets his lips in a quick and unconscious motion. What the hell am I noticing that for? "Care if I take a seat next to you?"

I actually do care a lot, but my shoulders think a non-committal shrug suffices to bring the point across. Naturally, Wulf reads it as an invitation and stretches out next to me, leaning his back against the tree. Above us, the branches are still barren. Once summer comes around there'll be lots of shade to be found under here.

It takes Wulf a couple of moments to open his mouth again, a time in which I pointedly chew my pizza, though I couldn't tell you what it tasted like if I tried. "I'm sorry for how we hit it off yesterday. It wasn't my intention to make you feel unwelcome or anything like that."

"That's okay," I answer automatically. I've had a lot of time to reason with myself. "You've just come back from an exhausting and nerve-racking mission that almost cost you your life. You thought you'd return home, find everything as you left it, but you found me instead."

I stop my very clean chain of arguments when he chuckles. The moment I glare at him, he sobers instantly. "Sorry," he mutters, gulping down the rest of his amusement.

"What?" Yeah, I'm a little annoyed here. "I'm trying to be understanding, and you think that's funny?"

Wulf straightens his back. "Not at all. It's very kind of you to put yourself in my shoes." There's not even a hint of mocking in his voice which, by the way, has an intense timbre that somehow resonates in my stomach. "It was the choice of words that amused me. I didn't find you, did I? You're not a thing to find."

I'm not sure if that's a compliment or not. Why can't he be a bit more like Lukas and make his aversion clear instead of being so nice all the time? "But you didn't expect to find me here," I blurt out, to hold onto my grudge.

"Of course not. The SSA told me they didn't send any replacements, and none of the mission reports mentioned you."

I bite my lip, registering the fact that Camille has kept my presence a secret from the SSA.

Wulf cocks his head. "Camille explained it to me last night, but no, I didn't expect to find a brilliant new spirit seeker waiting for me on my doorstep."

Have I ever blushed this hard in my life? What the hell is wrong with me? His unexpected compliment throws me so much, I fumble over my following words. "Well, yes, uh... here I am. I mean, I'm not... Camille told you everything?" That's right. Focus on the important information.

"She told me a lot. I don't think there was enough time to tell me everything, but she explained how you jumped in to help my team at the Central Station, how you tried to make it work..." His voice grows a little quieter. "A little about your struggles."

The mention of my background gets the blush out of my cheeks. I can't help but feel judged about my time on the streets. People generally don't react that well to it, and I feel like he's already judging me enough as it is. On the other hand, I'm kind of glad I don't need to tell him myself.

"And then, of course, what you did on Devil's Mountain." He nods appreciatively. "That was quite a feat. You seem to be a natural."

"Maybe it's because I'm not just hearing but listening to spirits." I don't know why I can't just take his compliments, but apparently I'm hell-bent on ruining any kind of reconciliation he might try for.

Immediately, Wulf's stance stiffens. He takes a deep breath, visibly swallowing whatever he was going to say. Instead, he places his next words carefully. "If I understand it correctly, you've grown up around spirits." When I nod, he continues, "I agree that most spirits aren't particularly dangerous unless, of course, they band together." Which is what happened with the Erlking. "However..."

Oh, no, I'm not going to like this.

"...they are our enemies. Even a harmless sylph can be a spy. Especially when it's a daughter of the Erlking."

I knew it. My jaw tightens, but since he tried so formidably to be civil, I return the favour. After all, Camille said Wulf was someone you could talk to. "She stood against him. When the Erlking wanted to strike me down, she stood against him. She protected me with her own body, not once, but twice. Spirits aren't the enemy. They just exist."

Wulf winces. I notice it costs him a lot to remain calm now. "You're new to this."

"No, I'm not." He just acknowledged that I've grown up amongst them.

"I meant the spirit seekers." His voice has an edge now. "You haven't seen the potential for destruction spirits bear. One, granted, but the Erlking's not the exception, Rika. He's the rule."

I have to think of the sylphs caught up in the Erlking's anger. "That's not true. The majority of spirits just want to live in peace."

"But they don't," Wulf snaps. "Spirit activity has grown more hazardous, more violent, and much more frequent in recent years." A little calmer, he adds, "They're out to kill us."

His words remind me of the ones Aeola once flung at me. "What if it's our fault? What if the spirits only attack us because we're infringing on their habitat?"

Wulf snorts. "Everywhere is their habitat. Just like it is for us." Drawing up his shoulders, he concedes, "Fine, maybe that's why they do it. It doesn't change the fact that they're out for our blood. And it's not like we can kill half of the human population to make sure they have enough space." It's clear he's given up all pretence of trying to understand where I'm coming from. "The spirits are our natural enemies." He gets to his feet. "Your sylph friend might be harmless today, but it'll turn on you tomorrow."

As he walks away from me, I growl after him, "She. Aeola is a 'she'."

With a deep frown, Wulf turns his body halfway around to me. He seems to want to say something else, but all that comes out is, "Okay," before he walks off.

3

Later that day, I accompany Leon to his doctor's appointment. After my talk with Wulf, I'm glad for any excuse to leave the citadel for a few minutes. You'd think a medieval fortress would be just large enough to keep out of somebody's way, but Wulf has such an enormous presence he seems to be everywhere. In fact, he even offered to drive Leon, but I'd already offered to accompany him, and Leon picked me.

It's the big day. Today we'll find out whether Leon will keep his eyesight or not. Since I still feel partially responsible for what happened to him, I'm crossing all my fingers that we'll leave with good news.

"So, I heard," Leon says, while we sit in the waiting room, "Wulf's not the biggest fan of your spirit theories." I hope he didn't pick me to come with him just to convince me to take Wulf's side.

Annoyed, I turn the other way, crossing my arms. "They're not theories. I know what I know."

"I bet he'd say the same thing."

I like Leon well enough but playing devil's advocate for that infuriatingly stubborn commander will not win him any Brownie points. "But he's wrong."

Leon chuckles. "If you say so."

Yes, I know I'm acting childish, thank you very much. "Leon, I've seen the spirits, heard them. I've felt their pain."

His fingers feel for my hand, and I relent and give it to him. I kind of owe it to him. Besides, he's not the one who deserves my ire.

"Tell me about... what was her name, Aloe?" he asks.

"Aeola."

"Aeola." Leon smiles. "I've never heard of a friendship between humans and spirits."

Sighing, I relax into the back of my chair. "Daisy had spirit friends."

He frowns slightly. "Who's Daisy?"

That's right. Leon wasn't there when I met the peculiar homeless woman who'd made it her brand of weirdness to talk to spirits. "The homeless woman who worked for the Erlking and died when she didn't... deliver." I still feel bad for her, despite the fact she tried to kill me.

"Ah." Leon nods.

Watching the tip of my feet, I muse, "Maybe if spirit friendships wouldn't be so actively discouraged, there'd be nothing unique about it. Maybe if we opened our hearts to them, we could tackle our problems together."

"Sounds good in theory," he admits. I groan and want to pull my hand away, but he holds it firm. "So, what's the deal with Aeola? Why is she friends with a human, a spirit seeker nonetheless?"

Pulling a face, I slump a little more into the chair. I'm not a spirit seeker yet. "She hates that I'm with you guys. If it were her choice, we'd be travelling the world right now, visiting all the great places, the last untouched pockets of wilderness." The thought makes me smile. Travelling is in my blood and I want it just as much as the sylph. "You know what she told me?"

Of course Leon doesn't. He waits patiently for me to continue.

"That all the spirits are trying to do is survive. We've done so much damage to the world. And we're aware of that. Climate change is not a hoax. But contrary to us, they feel it. We can still go our way and pretend it's a future problem, but they can't. Their forests are dying, their water and air are polluted. I guess gnomes will be okay in the long scheme of things, and salamanders are all for global warming, but the majority of spirits are suffering."

Thoughtfully, Leon bends forward and rests his chin on his hand. "That actually makes a lot of sense."

"I told you!"

"Mr Harting?" the doctor calls.

My heart plummets to my stomach. Leon might be the one getting his eyes checked, but I'm the one who needs emotional support. He squeezes my hand and pulls me out of my chair. "Come on. Let's see... what I can see."

Yep, still feeling responsible.

Neither of us talk while the doctor explains all the potential outcomes. We're not supposed to expect too much. Be patient. Then he darkens the room and begins taking off the bandage. The whole time, I keep holding Leon's hand. He blinks at first, his eyes clearly tearing up, even under those low light conditions.

The doctor checks the reactions of his pupils for what feels like half an eternity. Finally, I can't take it anymore. "Can he... Do you see something?"

"It's too early to say if your sight will return to full capacity," the doctor tells Leon. "But the tissue has healed well, and the pupils are reacting to light. I'm positive you'll regain most of your vision.

However, your eyes will be very sensitive to light for a while. Did you bring sunglasses?"

I produce them from Leon's backpack and hand them over. While the doctor tells Leon what to expect the next couple of days and weeks, I slowly breathe more easily. He'll see again. Leon will see again.

I soak in the warm rays of the sun, unable to stop smiling. Time and time again, I tug at Leon's arm and squeal, "Your eyes are gonna be fine," or, "You can see!"

Leon laughs, though it's obvious he still needs my guidance. "Told you there was nothing to worry about." His entire posture looks a lot more relaxed, though.

We're almost at the edge of the park that lies in front of the citadel when I see a movement in the sky. In the sunlight, Aeola's kind of hard to make out, but I know straight away it's her.

Leon takes his arm from me but holds onto my hand for a second longer. "I think I need a break. I'm just gonna stand here for a bit."

I flush, knowing that he's somehow guessed where my sudden hesitation stems from. "Let me help you to that bench, at least."

After I've settled him, I hurry to catch up with Aeola. She sweeps down from the sky and ruffles my hair. I blow a strand of electric blue out of my face and let out a breath of relief. "I'm so sorry I couldn't get out sooner. Things are crazy at the citadel." I proceed to tell her all about Wulf, including the infuriating chat we had this morning. "He won't back down. I don't think he even knows what that means. I mean, he's not like Lukas, being condescending and all, but he wholeheartedly believes all spirits are evil and need to be hunted down."

Concern wavers through Aeola. "We should run away, then. They don't need you anymore, right?"

Hearing it said out loud makes my stomach turn. My chest tightens, and I swallow hard. "I... I don't want to run away." I've always run. It wasn't until I met the spirit seekers that I learnt what it meant to fight. "This is my home. I—"

"No, it's not." Aeola's wind pulls at me, pushing me closer to her. "The world is your home. You're like me. You wanted to show me the mountains and the sea."

Part of me wants to do precisely that. My soul yearns to let go of everything and travel the world, meet other spirits and people, and learn something new every day. But when I promised her, it was in a moment of fear, and there's still so much that binds me to Berlin. Maybe more than just a few months ago.

"I can't."

Aeola's wind grows stronger and I find myself stumbling on the path. "You promised."

"Aeola, please." Something's wrong. She's never been this way, not this... desperate. "Are you okay?"

The wind lessens as her face softens. "Of course I'm okay. You don't need to worry about me. If you want to stay, that's your decision. I just don't think this is the right place for you." On this softer note, she leaves me, the wind carrying her away.

I don't try to stop her because, for the first time since I've met her, she outright lied to me.

"Everything okay?" Leon asks when I come to get him.

"Sure." I give him my hand and lead him back to the citadel, glad he doesn't press the matter.

We enter the courtyard to the rhythmic clanking of two battle staffs smashing together. Lukas is sparring with Wulf, giving me my first view of Wulf's fighting prowess. I'd always thought Lukas was quite skilled with his acrobatic moves and forceful blows, but he doesn't even come close to being a match for Wulf.

The commander moves with a fluidity that reminds me of a spirit in their natural environment, one with their element. He's in total control of the sparring. Each blow falls precisely where he wants it to, challenging Lukas. This isn't for his own benefit, but Lukas'. Wulf seems to read his intentions like a spirit, expecting each turn of direction or angle. And he barely breaks a sweat doing so.

"Pretty impressive, huh?" Leon asks softly. For some reason, amusement swings in his voice.

I set my jaw, but my eyes keep following Wulf's movements. "He's okay."

Leon chuckles softly. "Yeah." He claps my shoulders. "I'm going to see if I can find the hall on my own. You stay and enjoy."

My mind doesn't truly register his words or the hesitant way in which he walks away. It's too occupied with admiring the precision and accuracy of Wulf's fighting style. Every move feels so deliberate, directed to draw out the best from Lukas. I'm pretty sure if Lukas and I had ever got to the sparring stage, he would've dominated me. Wulf, on the other hand, would probably adjust his style to make sure I actually learned something.

I have to blink twice when the fight suddenly ends on Lukas' signal. The younger spirit seeker is huffing and sweating but grinning wildly. Wulf claps his shoulder, saying, "That was good. Really good."

"Thanks. I kept the training up." Oh yes, Lukas idolises Wulf completely. He reminds me a little of an overeager puppy waiting for a benevolent pat.

And Wulf gives him exactly that. "I noticed. Your stamina's improved."

The beaming smile on Lukas's face seems so out of place I need to shake my head. That's definitely not the spirit seeker I know.

Fortunately, he notices me then, and a scowl appears on his face. "Looks like we've got an audience."

Wulf turns his head around. When he sees me, he waves me over. Left with no choice, I slowly walk over. Wulf leans a little on that gnarly staff of his and smiles. "You want to try your skills against me?"

Just a moment ago, I was mid-fantasy of doing exactly that. Now I'm blushing again. "No, I'm not at that stage yet." I look to Lukas for help, of all people.

For a moment he seems to weigh his options: leave me hanging to spite me or try to impress Wulf. He chooses the latter. "We've only just started building up her strength and stamina. I devised a training plan for her."

His training plan was to have me follow his workout and glower at me for not even coming close to his output. But whatever works for him. It had been what I'd wanted, after all. Now I want more. "It wasn't really working for me, though."

Lukas glares at me. How dare I undermine his boast? "Yeah, maybe spirit seeking as a whole isn't really working for you, spirit whisperer."

I guess I've lost all the Brownie points I collected with him for bringing down the Erlking. Or maybe it's another attempt to impress Wulf after the commander made it clear he doesn't like my close relationship with our declared enemies.

Wulf doesn't really seem to care for it, though. He rubs the bridge of his nose before telling Lukas, "You should warm down at the gym."

Lukas hesitates a moment, but his adoration for Wulf forces him to follow his command without question. "Will do." As he passes, he has one last remark for me: "Good luck."

Wulf waits until Lukas is out of earshot before remarking, "Camille told me you two don't get along well."

"Yeah, I generally have a problem with big egos and assholes." I disregard Lukas and turn around to Wulf, only to find him staring. "I... I didn't mean... You're not an asshole or... Forget what I said, please."

He smirks, then hands me the staff Lukas used. "Let's see where you at."

"I'd rather not." While I take the staff, I find myself in desperate need to be somewhere else, anywhere really. But Wulf gets into position, leaving me little choice but to stall. "Why does your staff look so different?"

Wulf relaxes his stance and glances at his staff. "It's one of the ancient ones. Has been in use for over two thousand years by spirit seekers."

Now that's interesting. I step closer, extending my hand. "And you're so good they give you the more primitive weapon?" I swallow my words the moment I touch the wood. The difference is like night and day. The black spirit seeker staffs are weapons, exchangeable, but this... this feels like it's meant to be wielded by my hand. Similar to Daisy's staff, I can feel its power surging through me.

Only when Wulf clears his throat do I notice how close I'm standing to him, caressing the staff in his hands. Now that he has my attention, he says with a glint in his eyes, "The ancient weapons are actually the best we have. Our armourers have tried to recreate them, but none have come close."

I use the time he spends explaining to step away from him, letting my hand fall to my side.

"The SSA gave this to me for our mission under Vesuvius," he says, running his hand over the wood polished by time. "After our success, they made it a long-term loan. Now, do you want to give it a go?"

"I've never fought with it before." I grab Lukas' practice staff tighter. After the feeling in Wulf's staff, this one feels cold and lifeless. Like the powder Miriam once produced from it.

"Really? Did the Erlking fall on your staff, then?" Wulf quips.

While I thought this would be embarrassing, I didn't mean that kind of embarrassment. "No. I... Fine, let's do it." It doesn't look like I've got a choice, anyway.

"Okay, well, first grab the staff like that." Wulf shifts fluidly into instructor mode. "It's not a stick you're gonna swing at a piñata. You need manoeuvrability." He steps forward to adjust my hands.

I guess, so far, I've been mostly swinging it around wildly, hoping to hit something. The new stance makes the staff feel more balanced in my grip.

"Feet shoulder-wide," Wulf continues and takes the same position. "The staff can be used for both attacking and defending. If you want to block a hit, make sure it hits the piece between your hands." He slowly brings down his staff, waiting for me to raise mine the way I think he wants me to. Our staffs touch lightly. Then he exerts a bit of pressure. "See how this gives you stability? If I hit it here or there," he touches both ends of my staff with quick motions, causing my arms to jerk away while I stumble around on my feet, "your body can't catch the blow as easily. You can use the ends to deflect a blow, though. Like, hit my staff on either side."

Sceptically, I look at him. Then I try to surprise him by quickly stepping into his range and bringing down my staff. It doesn't work for two reasons: one, with my new handle on the staff, I've entirely overestimated my momentum, and two, Wulf moves along with me, deflecting my weapon in one fluid motion, causing me to stumble past him.

Flustered, I turn around and re-assume my stance. Wulf grins. He's clearly enjoying this. It takes me a second to realise he's not enjoying his domination but the act of teaching me. "That wasn't too bad," he says.

"Yes, it was." I let go with one hand and stand the staff on the ground. "I don't need to be coddled."

Wulf snorts. "No encouragement. Got it. Now, let me show you the basics of attacking."

By the time we're done, both my arms hurt. I'm not sweaty like Lukas, because we didn't really move around that much, just raised the staff repeatedly in various angles. I've already forgotten half of what Wulf said. The only thing I take from this lesson is that I have absolutely no idea how to use my body, which is kind of sobering.

"That was pretty..." Wulf catches himself quickly. "Well, *I* enjoyed it."

"Thanks, I guess."

"We should do that again," he announces. "But first, we need to get a handle on your NAV. If you haven't got anything else planned, I'd like to run the tests tomorrow."

Tomorrow? Tests? I suddenly notice that I have no clue how the NAV is calculated. "If you have to."

"Don't worry. I'm sure you're gonna do well."

Oh, dear. Now it's tests and expectations. Too bad I can't think of anything I could plan spontaneously for tomorrow.

4

To say I'm nervous before my NAV test would be a gross under-statement. I never really went to school like everyone else. There was a time I did, but I don't like thinking back to those months. Essentially, all it taught me was that I'm stupid and won't amount to anything. And then I went and proved my teachers right by living on the streets for eight years.

My mum did most of my schooling, but it was a haphazard mix. Some writing, some numbers, but mainly she told me about the world, spirits and people, history and culture. I don't know a lot of facts or science, but I can see the big picture and understand relationships and communities. Problem is those things are never truly the subject of tests.

Even worse, I hate what tests mean. A test will determine how well I'll do as a spirit seeker, just like a test determined I should be taught among eleven-year-olds at the age of fifteen. You do well or not on one particular day and it'll determine the rest of your life. In my opinion, society overly relies on tests when it comes to people's abilities.

Ever since I've come to work with the spirit seekers, they've told me I'll score high on their beloved NAV. But what if I don't? What if I spectacularly fail their expectations and it turns out I'm not really attuned to nature? Sure, I can see and hear spirits, but that's not all that goes into the NAV, right?

Well, apparently, one part of the NAV test is a medical exam. Wulf and Miriam await me in the lab with an unfamiliar woman. Without further ado Wulf explains, "We're going to start with medical tests before running the cognitive ones. This is Mrs Leibinger. She will run the tests, assess your physical capabilities, and do a blood test."

"With needles?" It's the first thing that pops up in my mind.

"Yeah, we usually don't do the cut and drain method anymore," Wulf quips, but he only sets my stomach aflutter and not in a good way.

Look, I know needles aren't bad... not in a sterile environment. But here's the thing: when I see a needle, I think of heroin or blood poisoning. I saw a guy die because he stepped on a used needle once. It was bad enough to get the tetanus shot with Leon, but I closed my eyes then and never actually saw the needle. Now I can see several of them lying on a tray, ready to puncture my skin.

"I just don't like them," I mutter.

Nevertheless, I step towards the nurse, who's the only one who smiles at me. "Don't worry. You're not the only person who's not a big fan of blood tests. If it helps, I'm very good at my job."

I guess it does since I find myself sitting down in the chair and looking the other way, which means staring at Wulf and Miriam with their overly expectant faces. Okay, doing this in front of them is definitely awkward. "Do you have to watch?" I'm starting to think there's a way to fail a blood test.

"No," Wulf says promptly. "We'll wait outside until you're done."

"Don't worry," Miriam says, her face brightening a little. "It'll be over soon." Then they're both gone.

The nurse rolls up my sleeve and halts for a moment. "Lichtenberg figures. You got hit by lightning?"

The memory of the Erlking makes me shudder. "Uhm, yeah."

"Remarkable." She wraps a tight strap around my arm and pokes my inner elbow with her fingers, looking for a vein. As she does so, she keeps up a constant chatter. "So, you're joining the spirit seekers? That's exciting."

"Is it?" I concentrate on the red-blinking button of one of Miriam's computers.

"I don't know," the nurse admits while cleaning the site with an alcohol swap. "I always imagined it must be cool to see spirits. Though I guess it's a bit creepy. To be fair, so is knowing that there's an invisible creature with a murderous mind around you at all times."

I sigh deeply. "Not every spirit wants to murder you."

"Oh, that's good to know." Her words are followed by a sudden jab. Then the strap around my upper arm is released. "And you'll be taking care of the rest. Thank you."

The stinging pain in my arm makes it harder to keep my fingers relaxed. I want to ball my hands or tap my fingers. Instead I concentrate on her words. "Thank you?"

"For your service. I know that fighting spirits comes at great risk. So, thank you for keeping us all safe." I can feel and hear her change the tubes attached to the needle. "You've chosen a dangerous but hopefully rewarding line of work."

I hope she's right about the rewards because the balance seems a bit skewed towards dangerous at the moment. Once she takes out the needle, I breathe a sigh of relief. The nurse puts a cotton bud on my arm and asks me to press down while she labels the three tubes. It's weird to see my blood lying there outside of my body, and I'm glad I decided not to watch it being taken.

The rest of the medical tests are fairly standard. I wonder how all that features into my NAV, but maybe it's a lot more complicated than I thought. The nurse isn't too happy with my weight, but that seems to be a general concern, not one related to my potential skill set.

Finally, she packs up. "Right. So, all of this will be sent to the lab, and we'll let you know in two to three days."

"Cool." In reality this makes it even worse. After everything that's yet to come, I won't even be getting a result, but have to fret for days. How high do I have to score on the NAV scale so they'll allow me to stay?

She's barely left the lab when Miriam and Wulf come back. Miriam goes straight to her desk, retrieving a big box of material. Wulf takes a seat at the table in front of me. This time, he smiles unnervingly, as if I've got nothing to worry about. "Let's run the tests."

Miriam hands him a pen and an evaluation sheet, and my stomach tightens. Then she hands me a tablet with a number of files. "We're going to do a series of cognitive tests. First, there'll be some videos, then a few sound files and some pictures. Once we're done with that, we'll do the VR tests. My favourite."

Slightly overwhelmed, I concentrate on the tablet in my hands. Miriam taps the first video. "Please tell us what you see."

The little video is taken in the Alps. An outcrop shows a grey stone with a greenish tinge. In front of it, a group of gnomes is busy digging out a nest for themselves. They're of a different rock type with milky white bands layering their entire body like a fashionably striped shirt. I draw a total blank for what the name of the rock could be, though.

While I try to rack my brain for rock names, Wulf clears his throat. "You don't have to identify it. Just describe as much as you can see."

"Oh, okay." I replay the video and start talking. "So, I'm not sure what type of rock the gnomes are. They look a bit like granite, you know, light grey with a lot of quartz, but they have this parallel banding instead of a grainy texture."

"Gneiss," Miriam says softly. "It's a metamorphic rock that forms when granite is put under a lot of pressure and temperature."

I can't say I've heard that one before. Looks like I need to take a crash course at rock identification. Luckily, gnomes aren't super common around here. "Right, so..." I notice Wulf is staring at me. He hasn't written anything down yet.

When I look at him, he blinks and quickly makes a note. "Please continue."

"So, yeah, they're gneiss-gnomes. Judging by the weathering, they're quite old. They're..."

"No, I meant, continue with the next video, please," Wulf interrupts me. "You've already got full points for this one."

The next video shows a group of nymphs bathing in the lake under a willow tree. "So there are three nymphs in this one..."

Once again, Wulf doesn't let me finish. "No, there are two."

I turn the tablet around and point to where a third one is hovering just under the water surface. Wulf squints and leans forward. Miriam tries to look as well, but she gives up quickly. "I can't see any of them."

Wulf leans back again and makes a longer note on the scoring sheet. "Three it is."

His quiet confirmation puts a smile on my face, and I feel a lot more confident about the rest of the videos.

For the next test, Miriam hands me a set of headphones. "We're gonna play a couple of sound files, and you tell us what you hear."

That should be easy enough. I put on the headphones and wait for the first sound to play. First there's some static, then a sound like gravel sliding down a slope. It takes me a moment to concentrate on what's being said.

Apparently, it's too long because Wulf speaks up. "Rika?"

"Sorry. Can I listen to it again?" This is harder than I thought.

"Sure. Did you hear anything?" he asks.

I nod quickly, not wanting him to think I'm a total dud. "Yeah, sure. There's two... I think it's only two gnomes discussing the rock quality and lichen?" I'm not sure if I understood it correctly. Gnomes always gnash they're teeth so hard, it's difficult to understand them.

Wulf stares at me flatly. "You're making this up, right?"

Meanwhile, I play the sound again. I shake my head at Wulf then gasp when it all clicks into place. "I've got it now. Sorry. So one of them is pregnant, and she's craving lichen. You know those spots that grow on the rock? Her friend thinks it's disgusting and ruining a perfectly good rock, but well, the baby wants what the baby wants."

I thought I did pretty good on this task, but Wulf buries his head in his hands, and Miriam pats his back to comfort him.

"Sorry," I mutter.

Miriam shakes her head. "Don't be. You're doing fine. Next one?"

We go through a couple more, though it looks to me like Wulf has already given up on me. The last sound file plays a sizzling sound like an egg in a pan or sausage on a barbecue. I listen to it three times, and each time I tear up a little more.

After a while, Wulf cocks his head. "What is it now?"

"Nothing." I wipe my cheek and blink the tears away. "It just reminded me of another salamander." The one on file had been happy, cooing about how nice and warm her rock was.

Wulf checks with Miriam who comes to my assistance. "Oh, she's probably referring to the one she caught with Camille."

"He just wanted to be warm." I'm still not over how I tricked him into the tracking tube.

"Rika managed to lure it into the tracking tube without weakening the salamander or activating the tube, making sure it stayed in perfect condition," Miriam explains, still in awe about that particular feat.

"He," I correct automatically. Then I add, "I didn't lure him. I thought he was going to be brought to Iceland. That he'd be able to enjoy the heat in peace there."

Wulf scratches his chin as he processes both of our accounts. "Most salamanders are brought to Iceland."

It makes me feel a tiny bit better, though I can't shake off the memory of Miriam's initial excitement about potentially studying such a perfect individual. "Anyway, this one's a salamander, and she's enjoying the heat of a warm summer day."

Wulf still seems to be unhappy with how the test is going. He turns around the scoring sheet with a big sigh and says, "Alright. Next up is a reaction test."

"What does that mean?" I take off the headphones and give them to Miriam.

She puts them away and gets up to retrieve another piece of equipment, explaining. "We'll fit you with some VR glasses. You're gonna stand over there, where you have some space, and then there's a simulation that will basically take you on a walk. Some spirits will appear only by sound, some by video. What we're measuring is how quickly you become aware of them."

To that purpose, Wulf puts down a stopwatch. Meanwhile, Miriam leads me to the mentioned spot and fits the VR headset on me. "Just say gnome or nymph as soon as you become aware. You don't need to tell us any details. If you happen to know which direction they are in, you can point towards it. The program will register it."

The headset shuts out the lab, making me stumble in response. Luckily, the darkness is soon replaced by bright images. If you haven't tried it for yourself, it's really hard to explain. I know for a fact I'm still standing in a room in the citadel, but my brain seems to think we're in the forest. It seriously messes with my sense of balance because I expect the floor to be soft, yet it's ungiving. The sounds make it worse. There's the rustle of leaves and a bird singing in the distance, but I can also hear the ventilators of Miriam's computers running. The only things missing are touch and smell. This virtual world looks right but feels so wrong.

"We're starting the simulation now," Wulf announces, and I spin around because I can hear his voice, but he's nowhere to be seen.

I want to tell him that I'm not ready since I still feel so disoriented, but there's already a dryad moving between trees. Raising my arm in her direction, I say. "Uhm, pine dryad over there, and... Woah." I duck just in time to escape a sylph that was flying towards me. Instead of catching myself on the moss, I feel dust and the cold floor.

My stomach turns. "I think I'm gonna be sick." I swallow down the bile before saying, "There was a sylph. They're gone now, but they came from there." Gosh, Rika, get your act together, or you're gonna blow this.

I hear a creaking behind me and look around. It's just a deer. Holding my breath, I wait with getting up until it turns around and jumps away. Carefully, I get back to my feet, arms stretched out for balance. "Sorry, this is weird."

"Can you see any other spirits?" Wulf's calm voice centres me.

I hold on to it like a balance bar and twist around. "There's another dryad in that tree, but she's resting, so you can't really see much." A rustle to my left. "And a salamander down here." I crouch down and stretch out my hand, but the salamander has no interest in making my acquaintance. He scuttles through my fingers and vanishes under a rock, which reminds me sharply that he isn't real.

"Don't be scared," Miriam announces. "I'm just going to switch up the program. We're now entering the scenario test." The world around me goes dark. The only thing I can hear are her steps. "Steady." She puts a hand on my shoulder. "I'm handing you two controllers. They will look like a staff in virtual reality. It's basically like a game: you have to try to defeat all spirits. But don't worry, they're not real. While it might feel like it, they can't hurt you." She steps away again.

Great, now I need to show off my non-existing fighting abilities. When the screen turns back on, it looks like they just reused some of the images from the previous tests. I hesitate hitting the dryad that crosses my path, remembering how she just visited one of her trees. As she runs past me, I point to her. "There's a dryad."

"Use the staff, Rika." Wulf's voice sounds a bit strained.

The scenario changes, and I "walk" along a river. Something splashes in the water next to me, making me spin around, my heart racing in my chest. Because of my sudden movement, the staff hits the nymph accidentally. It seems to be enough to see her splash into water. When the sylph from before swoops down on me, I hit her squarely in the face.

The riverside turns into a mountain scenario. Someone shoots small pebbles at me. I duck under them and look around to find a gnome. She's snarling at me, the quartz veins in her face tightening. I take some distance, and she sticks to her spot, gnashing her molars. Carefully, I approach again, only for the shower of rocks to begin.

Quickly, I step back and all but throw down my staff, but of course, the controllers remain in my hand, and now the staff hangs weirdly in my knees. "You want me to kill a gnome mum protecting her nest?"

I want to take off the VR glasses, but the staff in my hands continues to confuse me. Annoyed, I try to let go of it, only to realise that I just need to slip the controllers out of my hands. The staff simulation has a severe defect when I put both controllers into the left hand and rip off the headset with my right.

I blink at the sudden change of scenery as my brain readjusts to reality. Somehow, I'm standing two metres away from where I started, facing the back wall of the lab. Turning to the side, I can see Wulf and Miriam engaged in a lively discussion over my test papers.

"Did I fail?" I ask, a little aggressively. I'm still upset about the virtual gnome mum I was supposed to attack. The one that they must have filmed or at least studied to incorporate her in their little test.

Wulf turns to me, seeming annoyed. "You can't fail an NAV."

"But…" I just want him to spit it out.

He lifts the test papers off the table, then lets them drop back, clearly agitated. "The entire test is about your perception regarding spirits. The scenario test is scored by a range of model reactions. Some spirit seekers never notice the attacks. Some are wary, others afraid. The good ones move quickly to address the danger. There's no scenario for refusing to attack while being clearly aware of the spirit."

The hairs on my forearms stand up as I cross my arms in cautious defiance. I will not defend my choice not to be a mindless robot. "What's the problem?"

Wulf kneads his forehead before looking up at me. "I don't know if I should give you full points for it or zero."

"I'd go with full points," Miriam argues. "Her eye movement shows that she clearly perceived the spirits as soon as they appeared. The NAV is all about your perceptive abilities. She's flawless in that regard."

Frustrated, Wulf throws down the pen and leans back, crossing his arms. "I'm not sure how representative your score will be."

"Does it matter if it's not 100% accurate?" In my opinion, the spirit seekers are putting too much weight into this value, anyway. "You know what I can do. So what if the score is a little off?"

For a moment he looks stunned. Then he sits up straight again. "It matters. The entire SSA is built upon the NAV. But never mind. We'll score it as it is, wait for the medical results, and take a large error into account." He tries for a smile but it comes off as a tired exercise.

"You did well, Rika," Miriam assures me, already tidying up.

Apparently I can go now. A few hours have passed, and I'm starving. Though Miriam claims I did well, I feel like I've failed in Wulf's eyes. And for some reason, that bothers me.

5

Waiting for the results is the worst, and I don't even know why. The results won't change anything. I won't be able to see more or fewer spirits. They won't make me stronger or faster. I still have to do the training. Yet somehow, it feels like a weight's hanging over me. As if those results will tell me whether I really belong here or not.

In the meantime, I've gone back to physical training, though now that her time has freed up a little, it's with Camille rather than Lukas, and I think we're both glad for it. Wulf joins us occasionally, and I catch myself watching him more than I watch myself during the exercises.

Compared to Lukas, Wulf has this easy confidence, as if he were born to be a leader. Though Lukas is three years older than me, he still looks very much like a boy, clean-shaven and rosy-cheeked. With his thirty-one years, Wulf is a man. His face is more angular, with a few early lines giving him character. He looks like he's been through some battles and come out victorious. Don't I know that for a fact?

"Let's move on," Camille says. We've been warming up on the treadmill for the last twenty minutes or so.

"What?" I snap my head around to her. "Sorry, what were you saying?"

She frowns a little. "Let's move on to the next exercise. Core strength."

I really want to listen to her, but Wulf and Lukas have switched to weights now. Wulf is wearing a tight shirt that tightens even more when he flexes his muscles.

Camille lowers her voice. "Unless you want to stay here and watch, that is."

Blushing hard, I tear my gaze from the commander and shake my head. "No, let's go."

I follow Camille to one of the other rooms. This one has less equipment and is more of a wide-open space with mats covering the floor, perfect for stretching, and I guess, indoor sparring. Camille gets two big gym balls out of an adjacent room and rolls one of them over.

Following Camille's training regime makes me feel a bit more accomplished than the cardio and weight training Lukas forced me to do. Camille is all about core strength, and while I can't compete, I feel like I'm actually making some progress.

As we plank balance opposite to each other, she smirks at me. "So, do you fancy him?"

"Who?" I ask, fighting hard to keep my balance. The blushing of my cheeks has nothing to do with the exercise.

Camille laughs. "Let's call him Mr X."

"Not X," I groan. Leon's taken it upon himself to teach me maths, and I've already had enough of the variable X. Initially, he wanted to teach me the maths behind trapping, but we quickly noticed that I didn't even understand systems of equations.

"You'd rather use W?" Camille asks.

"I don't fancy anyone," I reply tersely. "Never have, never will."

For some reason, that amuses Camille. "You've never had a crush on anyone? You've never...?" She leaves the end of the sentence for me to imagine.

"I'm not a virgin if that's what you're asking." And no, spirits be thanked, I've always managed to avoid physical contact on the streets. I actually lost my virginity relatively young to a boy with dark locks and even darker eyes. But that was a summer night's dream in the grass that belongs to another time long, long ago. "I've enough on my plate without adding relationship drama."

Camille changes position, now planking on the side. "I guess it's difficult when you've lived on the streets for so long."

I'm still uncomfortable talking about my life on the streets, or any life before that. Never look back, never ahead. The past doesn't matter; the future will happen when it does. There's only now, only today, and maybe the next. Everything else is either too painful or too fragile. But relationships don't work that way. Those are for people with futures.

"I'm sorry," Camille says, now a lot more serious. "I didn't mean to make you feel uncomfortable or anything."

"No, it's okay. You asked whether I enjoyed watching... a certain someone." That someone comes straight to my mind, showing off his pretty biceps and deltoid muscles. "And sure, he's a handsome man." With a huff, I lower myself onto my knees for a break.

Camille turns back to the middle, still holding her perfect shape. "He is. You should see the looks we get on patrol. Tall, dark, handsome. I prefer women, but if I didn't, and if he weren't a good friend of mine, I would certainly give him a second look."

"Fine! I wouldn't exactly say no if he..." If he what? Do I really think Wulf would make a move on me? He doesn't even like me.

I'm the intruder, the rusty spot in his well-oiled team. Judging from the little I know about him, he doesn't strike me as the kind of guy who'd date someone in his team, even if he thought to look twice at me. "Forget it. It doesn't matter, anyway."

Still holding her balance, Camille moves to the other side. "Why not? He's not all work, you know?"

"He's not?" *Gosh, cut it out, Rika. There's no reason for your stomach to feel like this. It doesn't change a thing.*

"He dates," Camille says slowly, savouring each word. "Not that there's anyone at the moment. He's very much single as far as I know. You know, just in case that makes a difference."

I hate how casual she makes it sound. "It doesn't. You know how complicated it is, or you wouldn't have snuck around Miriam for so long." Yes, topic change.

Camille's balance falters, and she falls to her knees, looking wide-eyed at me. "You know?"

"The boys might be blind, but it was pretty obvious to me." A little quieter, I ask, "Are you together now? I saw you on Teufelsberg."

She lowers her eyes and takes a deep breath, then lifts her core again. "We're taking it slow, but... yes," she says, no longer able to fight off a smile.

"That's great!" I lift my body again, ready to give it another try.

I can see that Camille wants to talk more about it, but at that moment the guys enter the room, and we stop our conversation. At least, verbally. With her eyes, Camille makes it very clear that I'm welcome to sneak some more looks at Wulf.

I'm twenty-three years old, and I've never had a relationship that went beyond a week or two. I had my first kiss and sex when I was thirteen-years-old, but that was one summer night. There have been other boys, but we were always on the move. Then, when I lived on the streets, I preferred to keep to myself. Like with alcohol and drugs, I'd heard too many horror stories. Who would want a boyfriend who overdosed next week? Or got caught in a knife fight? And those were the good options.

These thoughts run through my head as I stand naked in front of my mirror and look at myself.

My life has changed, I try to tell myself. I no longer live on the streets. The people I meet aren't ticking time bombs. I might even have a future, though I have no idea how to handle that yet. The thing is, I could have a relationship now. It's a possibility, even if it's not with him. Definitely not with him.

I mean, look at me. You can take the girl from the streets, but can you take the streets from the girl? My ribs are poking out under my skin. Even the nurse made a note of it. There's a rash on my stomach that hasn't gone away for two years, and there are ugly scars on my calf from when I got tangled up with some barbed wire. Though it soaked my pants with blood, I never saw a doctor about it. The wound healed eventually, but it wasn't a pretty sight. And speaking of scars...

Twisting in front of the mirror, I look at the prominent scars running down both of my arms. Lichtenberg figures, the nurse called them, marks left by lightning. Their resemblance to tree roots or ferns would make them somehow pretty, if it weren't for the angry red of my skin.

A sudden knock jolts me out of my thoughts. Quickly, I grab a towel and wrap it around myself. "Coming!"

It's already past midnight. Everyone went to sleep hours ago. Could it be?

I fix the door with a stare. Before I can decide, though, I hear a second knock, and realise that there's no one behind the door. No, the knocks are behind me, against my window, which is a bit peculiar since I'm on the second floor.

Wrapping the towel tighter, I open the window and look outside. Nothing but darkness.

Then I pick up a whisper. "Aeola is in trouble. Follow me."

No questions asked. If your friend is in trouble, you come, spirit or not. I dash to where I dropped my clothes and put them back on. Then I grab a jacket—only bought two days ago—and unlock my door.

I don't bother with turning on the light, which is a mistake, because I run straight into someone.

"Rika?"

Oh shit, it's Wulf. Why the hell is his room next to mine? A commander should have a suite somewhere far, far away from me.

He turns on the light in the corridor and studies me. "What are you doing here?"

Look, I'm all for late-night encounters with the man I'm attracted to, but this is not the time. Actually, scratch that. It's never the time. "I... uhm. I was thirsty."

"And you were going to the hall in boots and jacket?" He runs his eyes down my body and up again, not noticing that I forget how to breathe in his presence.

Annoyed, I push those inappropriate feelings away. "Sure. It's cold down there."

Wulf snorts and crosses his arms. "I saw a sylph flying outside. Is it yours?"

He could've led with that. Dammit! Why does this guy have to have such a high NAV? No one else ever bothered me about my spirits. "No." That's only the truth, after all.

"And I'm supposed to believe that?" At least his attitude makes sure those inappropriate thoughts of mine dry up quickly.

"It's not Aeola. Can't you see that?" Okay, that's a little unfair. He only ever had a quick look. "The sylph you saw looks nothing like her. Aeola's face is much longer and—"

He drops his arms with a groan. "You think I care what she looks like? They all look the same to me." I notice how he uses her correct pronoun this time.

"But they aren't... The same, I mean. Spirits are just as individual as us..." And I'd love to teach him all about their differences, but my friend is in trouble. "Anyway, I need to go."

I want to pass him, but Wulf grabs my arm. "You're not going out there!"

Okay, all attraction is definitely gone. "Let go of me." To his credit, he does so immediately. "You can't tell me what to do."

"Actually, I can. This is my command. And you're not going out there to meet with a sylph. Especially not unarmed like that."

He's got a tiny point there. To help Aeola, I might need a staff. "Great, I'll pick up a staff downstairs before I open the door."

"Absolutely not." Anger creeps into his voice. "Rika, you're not officially one of my seekers, but I won't have you going off at night with a sylph."

"What are you gonna do? Tie me down?" Aeola needs me. I don't have time for this debate on principles.

Wulf's face darkens. "If I have to. And then tomorrow you'll pack your bags and get your ass out of here."

"Bag," I correct him sharply, as if it really matters. It only took him a week to come to the dreaded conclusion that I don't belong here. And he's right. It's just that there's nowhere else to go. The thought of losing this place and the people within makes my throat grow tighter. Maybe if I'm more honest with Wulf instead of riling him up any further, I can convince him to let me stay. "Look. I'm sorry I'm not what you're used to. You know, obedient, asking no questions..." And just like that, the mocking has slipped back into my voice.

He draws a deep breath, balling his left hand to a fist and relaxing it again. When he speaks again, he sounds strained. "That is not what I expect. What I *do* expect is exercising more caution when it comes to spirits knocking on your window at night."

Okay, time for the truth. "My friend is in trouble. I know you hate all spirits, but I happen to care for her. So please, let me help her."

"It's a trap," Wulf says, crossing his arms again. At least, my honesty has taken some of the edge off his voice.

"No!" Of course, I don't know that, but I refuse to think of spirits that way. "And even if it were... would you risk doing nothing when your friends could be in danger?"

"I'm not friends with a sylph." And the sharpness is back.

Raising my chin, I say, "Well, maybe you should try it one day." A muscle in his jaw twitches. "Throw me out if you must, but I'm going."

A door opens behind me, but I don't care who it is. With one last glare for Wulf, I take off.

"Rika!" he calls after me. I close my eyes, but no footsteps follow me. Instead, I hear him talking to someone else in hushed voices. Well, he can bitch all he wants. Aeola's safety trumps my own.

I'm almost at the gates, having picked up a staff, when I hear someone running after me. "I'm going, whether you want me to or not," I say while spinning around.

"That's okay." It isn't Wulf but Camille who runs after me, her own staff in her hand. "I'm going with you."

"You need to stop making a habit out of sneaking out at night," Camille tells me as we follow the foreign sylph along the waterside. She can't see the spirit but trusts me enough to never question it. "I told you we're a team now."

"Maybe you should tell Wulf that," I answer, slightly distracted by keeping sight of the sylph above us. "He told me to pack my bag and leave." The consequences are real, but they're worth it.

Camille keeps looking around for spirits she can't truly see. "I heard. And I talked to him. It wasn't right of him to pull that card. It's just..."

"What?" I ask, annoyed. "Don't tell me this is some sort of tough love. That he's worried about me or something stupid like that." I've had experiences with tough love, and let me tell you this: there's nothing loving about being told what to do or who to be.

"That's not it." Camille sighs deeply. "You're trusting your life into the hands of a sylph. More than one."

Exasperated, I stop and look at her. "Not all sylphs are the same. They're not all like the Erlking."

Camille looks terribly sorry when she says, "But to Wulf they are."

With an angry huff, I get back to striding along the shore. "Well, that's his problem then." I've got no time for small-minded people.

"It is." Camille hurries after me. "And you'd likely be the same if you watched your parents murdered by them."

A chill runs down my back, taking my breath away. "What?"

Camille clicks her tongue, annoyed with herself. "I probably shouldn't tell you this, but maybe it'll help you understand where he's coming from. Where we're all coming from."

"His parents..." I don't know if I want to know the details, but she can't leave me hanging now.

After a sigh, she explains. "When he was nine years old, he and his parents went hiking. They were on their way back when they got caught up in a storm. They found his parents' bodies in the morning. A horrible accident, according to the police, but Wulf saw the whole thing. He saw the spirits, saw how they targeted them."

My anger has grown smaller and smaller until it is nothing more than a pea-sized marble in the pit of my stomach. I've seen enough storms in recent weeks to know only too well what Wulf has been through.

Camille carries on in a quiet voice, "When the police heard his account, they contacted the SSA. The academy took care of him."

I blink away the tension in my eyes that usually precedes tears. "Maybe they should've got him better therapy than whacking his trauma with a staff." Don't get me wrong. I feel terribly sorry for Wulf. Watching your parents die when you're not even ten-years-old is unspeakable. But knowing that he was instantly snatched up by the SSA and has probably been in training longer than any other spirit seeker explains so much. He's been practically spoon-fed all this nonsense about spirit aggression.

"I'm sorry," I say to Camille. "I get that he's wary around them, but it doesn't make it right." Then I stop and regard her closer. "What about you? Did something like that happen to you, too?"

"No," Camille says quickly. "I've never lost a loved one to a spirit attack."

"Then why are you fighting them?"

Camille blinks and looks at me as if she'd hoped that wouldn't come up. But it has, and we both know it. "Well, for one, I'm wary about spirits. I've been fighting them for ten years now, and I've seen a lot of destruction and heartbreak. And sylphs... we've had so much trouble with them lately. We barely saved Berlin from the storm of a century. I believe you about Aeola," she quickly adds, "but it's difficult for me to trust one of them. Especially when I can't see them. All I've got is your word."

Wulf could have more, but I doubt he's willing to give it a try after what I've just learnt. "And still, you're here?"

Camille winces. "Your friend is in danger. Right now, it doesn't matter whether she's a sylph or not. If you want to help her, I'm with you." Then she claps my back, getting us to move again.

We've entered the forested area around Lake Tegel, and it's so dark I have to follow the sylph by sound only. Camille has turned on her flashlight to make sure we don't break an ankle.

"Are you sure you know where you're going?" Camille asks after a while of stumbling through the forest.

I touch her arm to will her to be silent because I've just picked up some hissing in the air. A breeze strokes my cheek. "She's ahead." The sylph who led me here vanishes, leaving behind a waft of fear.

Grabbing my staff tighter, I nod to the front of us. "Careful now."

Camille turns off her flashlight and we try to make as little noise as possible in the forest, which, you guessed it, still makes us sound like a pair of elephants in a china shop. Still, I can hear the wind rustling in front of us, and after a while, I can make out words.

"You don't deserve to live, traitor," one sharp voice says, followed quickly by another, "It's all your fault." In the moon's light, I see three sylphs talking to a hollow, fallen tree.

It reminds me of a group of bullies cornering their victim in an alleyway. "Get away from her!" I shout, making it a point to swing my staff visibly in front of me. So much for stealth.

Camille tenses next to me, ready to jump into fight as soon as I tell her.

One sylph comes swooshing towards me, much like the one from the test. "There you are."

Looks like Wulf was right about the trap. I raise my staff just enough to discourage her frontal attack, and she flies over my head, leaving my hair tousled. "Yes, here I am," I announce loudly. "And if you don't leave straight away, you're going to meet the same fate as your father." To Camille, I blurt out, "There are three of them. One is above us; the other two are around that log, threatening Aeola."

Something snaps above my head, and suddenly, Camille swings her staff, knocking away a branch thicker than my thigh. Her staff shudders under the impact, but it holds. "Go!" she shouts. "I'll take care of this one."

Just as I duck away, an entire onslaught of branches comes crashing from the trees. I don't want to fight these sylphs but they're not leaving us any choice. One of the sylph whistles into the hollow log. "Aeola, your human friend is here. Don't you want to watch as we rip her apart?"

"Stay where you are, Aeola! I can take care of these bitches." Fuelled by my anger, I bring my staff down between the two.

They manage to swoop away in both directions, blowing a shower of half-rotten leaves and twigs into my face as they do so. "Revenge!" one of them shouts and comes back at me, bringing a fallen branch with her.

"Make sure it hits in the middle" comes to my mind, and I raise my staff just in time to catch her branch between my hands. The sylph can't withstand any pressure so the branch falls to the ground as soon as it makes contact. She tries to get away, but I strike her from behind, causing a shriek of agony.

Meanwhile, Camille has got on top of the shower of wood I left her in, but she can't reach the sylph high up in the treetops. The third one is just about to attack her from behind.

"Behind you," I shout, and like clockwork, Camille turns around and slashes through the sylph. The spirit dissolves in yet another ear-splitting scream.

The first sylph comes down, but she attacks neither Camille nor me. Instead, she flies to the sister I hit and wraps her in her embrace. Snarling, she turns to me. "Don't get in our way. This is sylph business." Then the two of them blow away.

"Where are the others?" Camille asks, still poised to fight.

Lowering my staff, I say, "They're gone." I fall onto my knees next to the hollow log and peer inside. It's only when Camille hands me her flashlight I can see Aeola, huddled as far back as she can. A little softer, I repeat, "They're gone. You're safe."

"Rika?" Slowly, she unfolds and hovers closer. Too many patches of her look more translucent than the others, wounds from the battle with her father and fresh ones from just now. "What are you doing here?"

"I've come to get you, of course." When she rushes into my arms, I tell her about the sylph that led me here.

"Oh, brave Boreo," she sighs. "I didn't know he'd dare blow close to your place."

"He led me here."

Aeola smiles. "May the winds bless him. But you shouldn't have come."

Cradling her in my arms, I get up. Camille looks at me with curiosity, but I ignore her for now. "Aeola, I'll always come when you need me. Was this what you didn't want to tell me? That your sisters blame you?"

"They're just angry," Aeola explains. "It'll blow over soon. Maybe in a decade or two."

I give her a flat stare. "That's it. You're coming with me."

Shocked, she tries to escape from my arms. "Into the citadel? Where that man who wants to kill me lives? The one who can see me?"

She's got a point there. Only, I don't know what else to do. "I'll talk to him..." Camille shakes her head. "We'll hide you." Now, Camille widens her eyes in shock. Well, too late. She wanted to tag along. "On the tower where we first talked, no... that's too easy for your sisters to reach." I try to recall the citadel in my mind. "Oh, I've got it. There's a nook at the back of the citadel. You can't really see into it from the courtyard, and there's absolutely no reason why Wulf should go in there. You'll stay down there."

"I don't know." I can feel the fear hanging around Aeola.

"Please. Let me do this for you." I look up at Camille, begging her silently for consent.

Camille sighs. "He never goes there. Nobody does. She... You should be safe, Aeola."

Aeola looks at her. "She can't see me, but she speaks to me," she notes in surprise.

I press her a little closer to me. "She knows you're here. And she cares."

6

Camille and I get Aeola safely into her new home. I know that this is only a temporary solution. Sooner or later, Wulf will find out about her and give me grief about it. I also hate that I've made Camille an accomplice. So far she's been saint-like, but I don't want it to backfire on her. She shouldn't have to choose between her best friend and... well, me.

"I'll leave you two alone," Camille says, subconsciously tugging her braid. It's clear that her tolerance for pro-spirit behaviour has reached its limit for tonight.

"Thank you so much," I whisper and watch her leave, feeling like I took advantage of her kindness.

The nook I brought Aeola to is surrounded by large walls, but big enough to roam around. There's even a tree growing at the back and enough grass to lay down a picnic blanket. I know it's not perfect, but it'll do for now.

"You need to fly low," I tell her, wincing at my own words. How cruel is that? Forbidding a sylph to fly? Aeola saved my life. If she hadn't, none of this would have happened. Not the other sylphs' ire, not the fear of discovery. "It's my fault your sisters are angry at you. If it weren't for me, you'd still be free to roam the skies of Berlin."

"But then you'd be dead," Aeola says, curling in on herself in my arms. So many spots shimmer silver in the moonlight. She hasn't even fully healed from her battle against the Erlking. "And I like you more than them," she adds, surprisingly adamant.

Gently, I stroke her shape. It's a bit like catching the wind between your hands, breezy and cool. "Same." Her sisters were nasty. It seems like Aeola is the exception to the rule, just as Wulf said. But then I remember the sylph that led me to her. He was willing to help us. "What's happening in the sylph world?" I can imagine the Erlking left behind a bit of a power vacuum.

Aeola deflates, sinking deeper into my arms. "Nobody knows what to do. We followed my father for so many years. I can't even remember a time when we didn't. Now he's gone, and no one knows what happens next or who to follow. Some blame me for working with the spirit seekers; others are secretly glad I helped you defeat him, I think. No one really wants to show that, though. They're too afraid to get into trouble."

"Like you did." I sigh. This is all my fault. Then a different emotion makes itself known. "You know what? They're all cowards. The whole lot of them. None of the others wanted to be sucked into that storm! You were the only one that stood up to the Erlking." Three of them banded together to harass her, just like regular bullies, and the best her allies could do was to lead me to them. "You're the bravest of them all."

"I don't feel very brave in here," Aeola murmurs, but I notice she's perked up again.

Looking at the dark grey walls, I can understand her only too well. "You're not gonna hide forever," I promise. "It's just that, sometimes, we need time to heal between battles." I know there's more to come. Either due to her sisters or Wulf. I just wish there was a way to get everyone together without any blood... or rather wind-shed.

Things are incredibly awkward in the morning. I'm late for breakfast having slept in after a long night. Still, I feel it sharply when Wulf and Lukas get up the minute I sit down. I don't know whether Camille has already delivered her debrief, but he's obviously still angry. At least, he hasn't reiterated his command for me to leave.

"Hey," Leon says, the only one who hasn't fled, since Camille and Miriam aren't here. I hope they slept in as well. "Do you want to help me with the new trapping shipment? I could use an extra set of eyes."

I know Leon's main reason for asking me to help him is so I won't feel excluded, but I instantly feel guilty about his damaged eyesight again. "Of course I'll help." This way I'm in no danger of running into Wulf, at least.

We finish breakfast and clean up, then stroll to the storage facility where we keep the spirit traps. It's a small room, rather like a basement, though there are a couple of windows. A shelf unit contains about a dozen metallic tubes. A new box stands next to a computer desk, waiting to be unpacked.

"So, what happens with the spirit when they are trapped inside one?" I ask as I help him scan the new traps into the system.

Leon balances a tube in his hand and shows me the inside. It still looks a lot like a thermos flask. "They're compressed and stay that way until you let them out again."

I turn another tube in my hands. "And when they're released in the wild, they slip back into their shape?"

"More or less, I think." He stores two of them on the shelf, using his sense of touch rather than sight. "It depends a little on the spirit. Sylphs and nymphs can be easily compressed and take no harm at all. Gnomes are a bit more difficult. They usually come out deformed, but that's what happens to rocks. I don't think they mind much."

"How do you know?" I ask, less than impressed.

Leon shrugs sheepishly. "I guess I don't. I've never seen them. It's just what they taught us in Earth Science. They eventually regain their shape, or not if they don't wish to. You have to take into account that most spirits that get sucked into here are already weakened."

I think of the translucent wounds in Aeola's body. "You mean hurt?"

"That's not the term that's being used..." Leon starts.

Groaning, I shake my head. "This is so wrong. Gosh. It's like the entire spirit seeker language is set up to dehumanise spirits."

"Well, they aren't humans," Leon objects, before granting me the point. "But I know what you mean. I guess telling prospective spirit seekers that they're going to hurt spirits wouldn't go over so smoothly."

"No." I grab another set of tubes and punch in their registration numbers. "Better to call them 'it' and disregard anything that might make them seem alive."

Leon looks down at the trap in his hand. "So, do you think it hurts them? Going inside?"

"I don't know. It's not like I could ask." I hop off the table again. "All filled tubes are sent directly to the SSA, right?"

"Yeah. They take care of the dispo—... the release and reset of traps." He shuffles over a second package.

I fish one out and look at it. "What do you need to do to release a spirit? Like, if you captured the wrong one, for example."

Leon hushes me immediately, looking over his shoulder to make sure there's no one in earshot. With his voice lowered, he says, "You could get into serious trouble for that. All tubes are registered. The SSA keeps track of them. Once a spirit is caught, the trap needs to be reset by their technicians. If you just let it free, the tube would be useless. You'd have to send in an empty trap and have some explaining to do."

"But you could do it? Theoretically," I add quickly.

Leon sighs. "Yeah, sure. Just open the cap and deactivate it. But you'll have the SSA to answer to."

"I'm beginning to really dislike the SSA." It's true. I haven't heard anything good about them yet.

Leon has, though. "They make sure humans are protected from natural disasters as best they can. For hundreds of years. They might not be big on spirit rights, but they're not the bad guys."

Maybe I really need to get my priorities straight. People are dying from spirit attacks every day. Surely, human lives matter more. If only there weren't so many innocent spirits caught up in this. "I know." Then I remember something else. "Hey, Leon?"

"Mhm?"

"Do you remember what you said two weeks ago? Before we fought the Erlking?" Judging by the blank face he pulls, it doesn't seem like he does. "You wanted me to show you how to listen to spirits."

His face brightens with understanding. "Oh, do you think it could work? My NAV is so low I doubt I'll hear anything."

"Well, have you tried?" He's probably right. If it were that easy to improve their NAV, everyone would do it, wouldn't they?

Leon smiles. "No, I haven't. Okay then. Let's give it a try. How about right now?" He stows away the last few traps.

I like this idea of undermining Wulf's anti-spirit stance in his own halls. Or maybe I'm just happy at least one of them is keen to have his mind changed. "Sounds good to me."

We get as far as the courtyard before Wulf crosses our path. He's got his serious face on—does he even have another one? He can't have found out about Aeola this quickly. Not unless Camille told him. It just so happens that I notice her and Miriam standing together in earshot.

"I was looking for you," he tells me, and my heart sinks into my stomach.

"Were you?" Can somebody tell me why my voice is all squeaky? I mean, he's not gonna make good on his promise to throw me out, is he?

He comes to a halt and nods. "Your results are here."

I let out a big sigh of relief. "Right... What did they say?"

"As expected, they were very high." Wulf doesn't seem so keen on sharing them, though, stalling by exercising the muscles of his mouth. "Maybe we should head inside?" he asks.

In the meantime, Lukas has come to join us at a distance. As usual, he's come straight from the gym. Next to me, Leon clears his throat. Some privacy would probably be good, then again the anticipation is killing me. "Just tell me!"

"512 plus-minus 34."

Lukas looks absolutely horrified, so I take it that means they're good.

"Plus-minus?" None of the others has ever used that expression when talking about their NAV.

"It's an error margin. You can't really get the NAV down to an absolute value," Wulf explains. "Mine is 498 plus-minus 17, so technically, while yours sounds higher, the error margins overlap, so we don't actually know whose NAV is higher."

That makes no sense at all to me, but I nod anyway. "Alright. What happens next?"

"Now we inform the SSA, get you enrolled, and then you're off to Italy," he says in such a casual voice, I almost don't pay any attention to the content.

Almost. "You want to send me away?"

"I'm not sending you away, Rika." At first, he thinks it's a joke, but the laughter dies quickly on his lips. "You need to receive training. Like every other spirit seeker. You also need to be registered..."

"...and tracked," I interrupt. My head feels awfully light. At this moment, I don't feel like a human but rather like the spirits who have no other choice than to be delivered to the SSA and placed wherever the agency likes them to be.

Wulf frowns. "They're gonna put your details in the database, sure, but there's no tracking."

I know I need training, but the very thought of leaving here scares me shitless. Wetting my lips, I ask, "For how long?" My voice is already shaking.

"The training course usually takes about three years. I'm sure they'll want to fast-track you, though. So, you might be able to graduate in less." Judging by his assuring tone, he still hasn't grasped the gravity of what this news means to me.

"Three years?" My voice breaks a little. "I'll be gone for three years?"

Slowly, Wulf catches on. He delivers the following explanation much more carefully. "Three years until you graduate. Then they'll decide where you're needed most."

I remember what Camille told me once. People with an NAV of under 300 can often choose their placements, while those with higher values are spread across Europe. Berlin already has Wulf.

Unaware of my increasing dread, he keeps droning on, "If we let the office know, we can have you on a plane to Italy by tomorrow."

By tomorrow. Suddenly, I can't hold back the tears anymore. "What have I ever done to you?"

"What?" His eyes are widening. He really has no idea how much this affects me. "I don't understand."

"Why can't you just leave me be? Why do you have to get rid of me at all costs?" I no longer care that my voice is all over the place, somersaulting through my tears. "You come here and... Oh, forget it! I'll go. I'll be out of your hair."

I ignore the confusion on his face and Lukas' smugness, even Leon's worried look, and run to the main building, pushing past Camille and Miriam to get to my room. Camille is trying to say something, but I can't hear it through the static in my ears. It feels like all the blood in my body is rushing through my head.

By the time I reach my room, I'm out of breath. No, not my room. It doesn't belong to me. Barely anything in here belongs to me. The rest is just borrowed, borrowed like my time in this team.

I fall to my knees. The room is spinning around me even as I desperately try to hold onto my life. It was all a lie. I don't have a place here. These aren't my people. They don't want me here. Not really—not now—not when they've got him instead.

Why is it so hard to breathe? I need to pack. I need to get out of here.

Scrambling to my feet, I grab the old backpack that has been with me for so long. But instead of filling it with as much as it can fit, I throw out everything in it until I'm surrounded by filthy, torn clothes, an old toothbrush, tampons, and two hard-as-stone buns. "Where is it?" I shake out the bag until it finally falls into my lap: the wooden tempest Pavel made me so long ago.

I hold it so tight the legs of the spirit horse dig into my palm. The pain helps me centre myself. It helps me draw breath after breath until breathing isn't such a labour anymore.

I miss Pavel. I miss the old man who was like a grandfather to me. I miss his daughter Rosie, who made the best pierogies in the world. I miss the other kids, who never told me I didn't belong. Most of all, I miss my mum.

The thought of her makes me double over as a new wave of tears threatens to sweep me away. Why did they have to take her away? Why did they target us? And why did they make her disappear?

Wulf wants to send me away, wants to send me to people who apparently know how to take care of someone like me, who will try and tell me what is right and proper. They won't accept me. They won't see me. They don't care because everybody needs fit into their world. Be a valuable member of society. Forget where you came from. Forget what you know. Forget who you are.

I know in my heart that the only way I'll come out on the other side will be broken into pieces. I'll be so removed from what I am, I won't be able to recognise myself. They tried to do it once to me; they won't get a second chance.

The determination gives me strength. I push my clothes and other stuff back into the backpack, keeping the tempest figurine in my lap. Looking around the room, I try to decide what else to take. My head tells me I'll need more clean clothes and the money. But I don't want any of it. I don't want anything from them.

The backpack slung over my shoulder, I open the door just as Camille is about to knock. Startled, she takes a step backward. A few metres down the corridor, Wulf is trailing her. His dark, serious eyes catch mine immediately. He quickly assesses my situation, frowning deeply.

"Can we talk, please?" Camille's voice reaches me through the fog in my brain.

Blinking, I tear my gaze away from Wulf and look at her. So much compassion lies in her eyes, it makes my throat constrict. I can't answer her but my head nods, and we head back into my room.

Camille closes the door behind her, shutting Wulf out. "You've packed," she notes.

The backpack slides half from my shoulder. "I can't stay." It comes out as a whisper, half-choked at the end. And suddenly, the whole realisation drops on me. I can't stay, but I want to. I never wanted to stay somewhere before, stay with someone before. Not... not since my mum was taken away.

A gasp tells me I haven't breathed in for a few seconds. The room starts spinning again, and I stumble backwards, losing my balance. Just as I'm about to fall, Camille catches me.

She grabs my wrists and pulls me into her until she can wrap her arms around me. "Yes, you can. You can stay for as long as you want. I told you that before. It won't change now."

But it's a lie. As long as I want is still nothing more than borrowed time. "He doesn't want me here."

"He's..." She doesn't say he's an idiot because that's not what Wulf is. He's nothing like Lukas. "He's still trying to catch up. He doesn't understand how important it is that you stay here with us. That you belong here."

I belong. Together, we sit on the bed I only just started to sleep in. Camille holds me while I cry into her shoulder, letting myself believe that at least one person wants me to stay.

Someone clears their throat, causing us both to look up. I hadn't even heard the door open. Wulf is standing with one foot in the room, the other out on the corridor. He knows he's intruding on something, and yet he can't seem to help himself.

Camille glares at him, but that only encourages Wulf to come all the way in and close the door behind him. When he lowers his gaze, unable to look into hers or mine, he doesn't look like the confident, faultless commander anymore. He seems much more like a child who knows they've done something bad but doesn't understand how it got there.

"I'm sorry, Rika," he says, raising his gaze to me. "I didn't want to give you the feeling that you're not welcome here." His gaze flicks to Camille, and I think I know why it took her so long to get here. She ripped Wulf a new one.

"I think you made it pretty clear you don't want me here."

Wulf looks at me in dismay. "That's not it. That's not it at all." He comes closer until he's a metre away from us, then squats down, so he's no longer looking down on me. "Look, Rika. I don't claim to know what you've gone through to get here. This is just how it normally goes. We find people with a high enough NAV and get them trained."

"I'm not a dog." I don't want to be trained. Especially not if it means to become a spirit hater.

His eyes widen in horror. He opens his mouth, but for several seconds, nothing comes out. At last, he takes a deep breath to catch himself. "It's an education that can get you a damn good job. It's risky, yes, but it pays well and comes with a lot of other perks. Social security, sick leave, health insurance..."

"Stop it, Wulf!" Camille interjects. "You're not a recruiter. Why *are* you so keen to ship her off?"

"I'm not," he defends himself. Then he looks at me. "You've got a gift, Rika. Do you know how many active seekers have an NAV above 400? Eight."

It's a chilling number. Wulf gulps, then adds, "There were ten a couple of months ago. An NAV above 500? I'm the only one who comes closest to it." His eyes seem to bore into me, imploring me to see reason. "We need you, Rika. The world needs you."

Even Camille has fallen silent now. I get what he's saying, but it's too much. Too many expectations, too much pressure. Wulf wants me to become a weapon, a weapon against the spirits. "I can't," I tell him.

The disappointment in his eyes does something to my heart. It twists it around, squeezes it dry, and leaves it hanging cold. And I only now realise I'd given him hope. And just as he was about to believe in me, I took it away again.

Wulf gets to his feet, his gaze passing over me and settling on Camille. "I won't send her away. If Rika doesn't want to go, I can't make her. You promised her a home here, and the citadel is big, but I don't see how this will work long term." He knows as much as I do that any time here is borrowed. "For now, it's just as well."

"Just as well?" Camille frowns. "What does that mean?"

"I got a call this morning from Budapest. They've got a nymph problem and asked if I could help them out. I didn't want to say yes yet because I only just got back from Naples." His hesitation wasn't misplaced. Camille stiffens beside me. "Normally, I'd advise against it since we can't risk a civilian life, but it would make me feel better knowing Rika is with you while I'm gone."

Slipping out of Camille's embrace, I stand up, facing him. "I want to come with you."

Both Wulf and Camille stare at me. He clears his voice. "What?"

Believe me, no one is more surprised than me. Just moments ago, I was crying at the thought of leaving Berlin behind, but it's... well, it's Budapest. "I want to go with you to Budapest."

"Why?" Dumbfounded, he checks with Camille, who only shrugs, equally confused.

There's an excellent reason for this, I promise, but I can't tell Wulf that. "I... I want to... see how you work. I know you want me to stay here to keep Berlin safe. But I honestly don't think you need to worry about that. The sylphs are fighting among themselves. It'll be some time before they sort themselves out again. The Erlking has left a big hole, and there's no one to step in. And most sylphs are glad about it. I really don't think there'll be anything Camille and the rest can't handle. She's a competent leader."

"That doesn't really answer my question," Wulf says, squinting at me.

Camille stands up next to me now. "This might be a good idea. This way you can also see what Rika can do."

Wulf crosses his arms, looking back and forth between Camille and me. "I know what she can do."

"You know her NAV and what I've told you, but you haven't seen it." She steps forward. "Believe me, Wulf, you need to see it."

I'm biting my lip, waiting for his decision. I don't have the funds to go to Budapest myself. I'd never even thought about it until now. It's like I'd forgotten it exists. But Wulf has opened a door

I thought had been closed forever, and I'm eager to go through it now and find what's on the other side.

He looks at me, trying to find a clue as to why I've suddenly changed my mind. When he sighs, I know I've won this battle. "Sure, why not? You might be able to see something I don't."

I don't know what scares him more: the thought of travelling to Budapest with me by his side or the enormous smile that's spreading across my face.

7

Wulf is getting us tickets for the train. We'll be spending close to twelve hours next to each other, so that's gonna be fun. There's one more thing to take care of before we leave early in the morning: Aeola.

I can't leave her here with all that's going on in the spirit world. She wouldn't want to stay here without me, either. Taking her with me while Wulf is watching every step of mine is madness. Yet that's exactly what I want to do.

It's the wee hours of the morning, long before anyone could possibly be awake, when I make my way to the little nook at the back of the citadel. "Aeola?"

She comes to me from behind, playing with my hair and settling around my shoulders like a warm embrace. "Shouldn't you be asleep?"

Giddily, I turn to her. "We're going to Budapest."

"Budapest?" Confused, she takes back to the air. "Where's that?"

"It's a city far to the east, the capital of Hungary, and it's beautiful." I have only the best memories of Budapest. "Wulf got a call-out from the spirit seekers there, and I'm going with him."

Aeola frowns. "Why? He made you cry."

"You saw that?" I ask, momentarily sobered by last night's events.

"The wind carried your tears," she explains, "and his words."

Sighing, I lean against the wall. "Yeah, well… it's not really about him. I need to go to Budapest. She… My mum might be there." It's a small chance, a tiny chance, but it's bigger than any I've had in the last eight years.

Fortunately, Aeola understands instantly. "Then you must go." A cloud of sadness surrounds her, nevertheless.

"And you must come with me," I declare, pushing myself off the wall again. "I promised to take you travelling, and I won't go without you."

Aeola breathes gratitude into my face. "But how?"

That's the critical part. "I've thought about it. Luckily, we're going by train, so following us should be possible." I really hope it is because I don't like the other option.

"Trains aren't as fast as aeroplanes, but most of them are faster than the wind," Aeola explains. "Have you checked the weather report? Will there be a wind blowing in your direction?"

The relationship between spirits and their elements is weirdly co-dependent. Many sylphs can cook up a magnificent storm, but their power is limited to short, local bursts. I guess you can't truly tame the wind or stop plants from growing. Spirits have to go with the flow. Sylphs more than any other.

Which is why I've come up with Plan B.

"There's another way." As I pull the tube out from under my jacket, Aeola shirks away in fear. It hurts to see her so mistrustful, but I get it. I'd react the same if someone offered to lock me in a cold, dark space. "Don't freak out. Just listen to me."

Aeola wavers in the air. "Speak." The word is full of tension, like the calm before the storm.

"I won't activate the trap. I'm not gonna suck you in, nor will I ship you off to Rome or something like that. You know that." If the battle against her father has shown us anything, we trust each other. "This tube will protect you from Wulf. I can hide you in my backpack, and I'll let you out as soon as we arrive in Budapest. I promise."

She probes the air around me, tasting it until she's satisfied. At long last, Aeola nods. "I trust you."

"I know."

It still breaks my heart watching her sneak into the tube. I wish I could leave it uncovered but Wulf will notice, whereas he won't question the tube. "I'll see you tonight," I whisper, then swallow as I close the trap.

"Do you want to sit at the window?" Like a true gentleman, Wulf offers me a seat first. His tickets have got us into first class, which is a little more spacious than the rest of the train.

"If you don't mind?" I still can't believe I'm actually going with him. I mean, not that it matters that I'm going with *him*, but that I'm *going*. I'm leaving Berlin behind, even if it's just for a little while.

He shakes his head and loads our staffs and the rest of his luggage into the overhead compartment. "Not at all. I'm probably gonna sleep, anyway."

How he can pass seeing the world so easily, I don't know, but I slip gladly into my seat. I only have my backpack, though Camille insisted on packing it for me, making me promise to buy a proper suitcase and more clothes in Budapest. For a moment, I press it close to my chest, feeling the spirit trap in there, then put it under my seat.

Wulf takes sits next to me. His elbow touches mine by accident, and we both take our arms off the armrest. I try to mask the awkwardness by taking off my jacket and hanging it on the little hook near the window, but Wulf chuckles.

"What?"

"Nothing," he replies, sobering instantly. "It's gonna be a long day." He stretches out, reclining his seat.

"Sorry," I mutter and look out the window, watching people on the platform saying their goodbyes.

In the reflection, I can see Wulf studying me. Turning, I confront him. "What are you doing?"

Caught red-handed, the tips of his ears flush with blood. It's surprisingly cute, I have to admit. He clears his throat. "Excuse me. I've just never seen scars like that. They're from your battle with the Erlking, right?"

I look at the dendritic lines of the scars. "Yeah." To me, they're a sign of my victory. I've beaten the odds, beaten the deadly promise he made. "I survived."

His gaze catches mine, his mouth slightly ajar. "So you did."

I'm the first to break off our eye contact and turn back to the platform. The train is moving, creeping out of the station. People wave outside, but the only face I see is Wulf's mirrored one.

Oh, yes, this is going to be a long day.

"So, why Budapest?" Wulf asks after our tickets are stamped off about an hour later. We've already left Berlin far behind.

So far I've spent most of the time watching the countryside swish by. Everywhere trees are turning green, welcoming spring into their hearts. I turn from the window to face him. "It's a beautiful city."

He has a book on the table, a crime novel from what I can see, and a spectacle case, which surprises me. Judging by the look of the pages, it's not the first time he's read it. "I've never been there."

I know he's fishing for information, but I smile without giving him the pleasure. "You'll love it."

Snorting, Wulf leans back into the chair. "Fine. Keep your secrets."

To be honest, I feel a little bad. I guess part of me is still afraid he'll put me on the train back at the next stop, despite the fact he took me along with the most feeble justification. "Speaking of secrets, you should probably know Camille told me about your parents."

A muscle in his cheek twitches, nothing more. After a while, he says, "It's not a secret."

"It's not common knowledge either." It's only fair that he's aware I know.

"I assume it hasn't changed your stance on spirits?" Oh, boy, here we go.

Sadly, I'm not one to back down from a confrontation. "It hasn't, no."

Wulf leans forward, finally looking at me. "I don't get it. The news is full of catastrophic weather phenomena. In Budapest, they had more accidental drownings last week than in a decade. In a decade. So what if there are one or two spirits that aren't dead set on destroying us? The rest of them are."

His argument is good, don't get me wrong, but it pains me more than it changes my mind. I put my hand on his, turning my body towards him. "Because it matters. Look," I say while running my fingers over his thumb until I catch myself in the act. Hastily, I remove my hand. "It's the same kind of nonsense you see among people. A few refugees commit a crime. Now they're all violent. Let's get rid of them. All Travellers are thieves and good-for-nothing. We don't want them here. Or even worse..." I'm not going there. Wulf is clever enough to know what happens when one group is deemed undesirable. He's German, after all.

"Spirits aren't people," Wulf says and turns away from me.

Obviously I won't get him by showing him the harmfulness of othering, so instead I ask a simpler question: "How?"

His eyebrows draw closer, as I've seen them do so often in the short time we've known each other. "How are spirits not people? That's like asking why dogs aren't people."

"So, they're animals?" I ask, not letting him get out of it that easily.

Wulf shakes his head as if he said something ridiculous. "No, spirits are spirits. They're intelligent beings that use their immense powers to damage us, to destroy what we build, to kill."

"That doesn't really make them sound much different from people." Of course spirits are nothing like humans, but they aren't exactly soulless monsters, either.

"No, no. you're twisting my words. People are people, and spirits are spirits." He's grown quite agitated now, using his hands to gesticulate. "You can't even begin to compare them. We're not elemental beings. They have no flesh, no bone, no organs. As far as I know, they don't even die."

For someone who was so well-trained in spirits, he really knows little. "They go to sleep," I tell him softly. "When they're really old, they often go to sleep."

"Like a volcano?" Wulf asks, interested despite his contrary opinions.

Now that he mentions it, I know it to be true. "Exactly. Some wake up again, but many volcanoes sleep forever once their time of activity has passed. The same goes for gnomes that become one with the stone, or dryads that are so old they've grown an entire forest on their back."

He leans into his seat once again. "Well, I wish they'd all go to sleep for a very long time."

I could keep arguing, but his words carry such profound tiredness, I can't bring myself to do it. "What happened in Naples?" He told us the mission details but not what it did to him.

"I'd rather not talk about it." Wulf doesn't look at me, doesn't even tense up, but it says everything he can't. Sure, sylphs killed his parents, and he's likely seen a lot of heart-breaking scenes on the job, but this pain isn't as old as the others. It hasn't had time to scab over yet.

The train takes us along the Elbe River into Czechia. Just seeing the Giant Mountains rising in the distance makes me tear up. I've travelled them with my mother. All those sleepy villages, the ravines, and the legends have melded together into a fairy-tale-like dream. One day, I promise myself, Aeola and I will hike these mountains again. We'll go there and everywhere else I'd been with my mother, and all the places we never saw.

Arriving in Prague sets off the next wave of nostalgia. So much time has passed since I was last here, yet the city still looks the same. Sure, there are new buildings, but the sea of red roofs is exactly as I remember.

We have a twenty-minute stop here, and when I step out to move my legs, I'm almost tempted to stay. To ease back into this city and see what's left of me in there. I have to tell myself that Budapest is bigger. What I'm feeling here will be tenfold there.

Wulf keeps true to his word and sleeps through most of the trip when he isn't reading his novel. He cares neither for the boundless nature around us nor the cities reeking of history. I guess, as a spirit seeker, he's seen his fair share of the world. Still, it makes me sad that there's no wonder left for him.

By the time we leave Bratislava behind us, my whole body is on edge. It's already afternoon. Our next stop will be our last. You can't actually smell anything beyond the stale air in the compartment, but I feel like I can taste Hungary when we cross the border. That taste of a glass of red wine on a summer night, of sweet and hot paprika, of steam from a thousand thermal baths across the country.

The sky is already darkening when Wulf wakes up to check his watch. "We should be there in half an hour. I better let the Vargas know we're about to arrive."

"The Vargas?" I ask, only now thinking of the team of spirit seekers we'll meet in Budapest.

Wulf nods. "József and Iván Varga. Józsie was in my class at the SSA while his brother started a year after we graduated. They lead this team. I mean, Iván is the commander, Józsie his deputy."

"I see." I don't tell him, but I really hope the Varga brothers are more like Camille and less like Robert, or even Wulf, in regard to spirits.

It doesn't really matter because soon the train enters Budapest from the north. Spring has come early here, and the trees are already in bloom. Through the windows I can see Pest with its many-storied houses from different historical eras, all fitting into each other. When there's a gap between the buildings, you can see the hills of Buda on the other side of the Danube River and the great bridges.

It's been over fifteen years since I was last here, yet there are some small parts I recognise: a particular house here, a coffee shop there, the green of City Park, which was once the festival grounds for the 1000-year-celebrations in 1896. And then the train rolls into the station and comes to a stop.

Wulf gets up to take down his luggage and our staffs. He's in no hurry to leave the train, which is just as well because my stomach has folded in on itself, turning my insides to mush. I'm simultaneously excited and scared. Excited that I'm back and scared that it might not be the city I remember.

With some help from Wulf, I hoist myself out of the seat and follow him outside. Unsure where to go next, he looks around at the masses of people. As they're dispersing, his face lights up.

The Varga brothers could be mistaken for twins if one hadn't bleached his dark hair to an elfish white-blond. Otherwise they both have the same boyish, slender faces with full lips, high cheek-bones, and prominent, dark eyebrows. It's the one with the nat-ural-coloured, slightly curled hair, who comes forward with a big smile and embraces Wulf. So, that must be József then.

Wulf carries a similar smile as the two of them clap each other's backs. "Józsie! Long time no see. How are you?"

"Good, good," his friend answers, with only the faintest accent. "Did you have a pleasant trip?"

"It was okay, a bit long," Wulf replies, then leans forward to shake the blonde brother's hand. "You must be Iván. Nice to meet you."

The younger of the two clasps Wulf's hand and smiles. "Wel-come to Budapest! It's an honour to host the great Wulf Bach-mann." Then his eyes flick towards me. "And I see you brought your girlfriend along for the ride." His accent is a bit stronger than his brother's.

"She's not—"

Before Wulf can introduce me, I step forward and do so myself. "Jó estét kívánok! Én Rika vagyok. Örülök, hogy végre találkozunk!"

Iván's dark blue eyes light up in delight. He takes my hand in his and pretends to blow it a kiss. "Kezét csókolom!" He looks at Wulf, laughing. "You never told us you had a Hungarian girl in your team now."

Wulf is in full shock mode. I can see from his completely frozen face he didn't know. It's good to know I've still got one or two surprises up my sleeves.

8

"My mum is from a small Hungarian town," I explain to Iván as we make our way through the city. "Valkó, I think? It's east of here."

He racks his brain for a moment, then nods. "I think I've driven through it once or twice. How cool is that? Well, welcome home then."

"Thank you." I've definitely dropped into the giddy side of excitement now, grinning wildly at everything.

It's already dark in Budapest, which means all around the Danube the city shines in an orange glow. The brothers are taking us to a restaurant by the river, well visited at this time of day. They must have reserved a table because the view is marvellous. I can see Margaret Bridge, which connects the two parts of the city and the small island in between. Further to the south, the lights of the famous Széchenyi Chain Bridge with its lions sparkle in the night. On the other side of the river, the majestic Castle Hill rises, the Buda Castle illuminated by lights.

Iván holds the chair for me and I thank him again as I sit. "It's so great to be back."

"So, that's the big secret; you're Hungarian?" Despite the beauty around him, Wulf wears a frown.

I decide to smile at him. Nothing can take me down at the moment. "Yes and no. My mum was born here, but we moved around a lot. Hungary is definitely one of my homes." I know better than to talk about Travellers in this environment.

My smile must have worked because his face muscles relax a little. "Where were you born then?"

It never really mattered to me and I almost answer into my mother's arms, but then I remember she did once tell me. "In a coastal town in Croatia. I don't consider myself Croatian, though, if you must know."

"Do you speak Croatian?" he asks, more out of reflex than interest.

"A little." I'm in such a good mood, I decide to indulge him. "And Czech, German, English, Danish, Polish, a bit of Russian, French, and Spanish... oh, and some Turkish, though that's mostly insults." You get to hear quite a bit of Turkish on the streets of Berlin. It's definitely worth seeing Wulf's jaw drop. Crushing expectations is my favourite pastime. I grin at him. "What about you? Can you speak any languages other than German and English?"

Wulf straightens his back. "Italian."

"Like pretty much every spirit seeker who cared about the country they studied in," Iván quips.

His brother comes to Wulf's defence. "You don't need to speak Italian to become a spirit seeker. Wulf can actually speak it fluently."

Judging from Iván's slight eye-roll, I assume the brothers have some sort of rivalry going on. József seems a lot more severe than his little brother, fitting in nicely with Wulf on the other side of the table.

We get the menu, but Iván takes mine away almost immediately. "I know what you should get. They've got a house plate with something of everything, and Rika, we need to get you rapidly reacquainted with some spiced food. Tokaji?"

"I don't drink alcohol." I know some Tokaji has more sugar than alcohol, but I still don't trust it. "Just a juice for me... no, do they have that grape soda?" Suddenly remembering my favourite drink, I try to sneak a look at the menu.

"Márka? Yeah, sure." Iván puts it straight on the order. "What about you, Wulf? Soda or some wine?"

Judging by his look, it's neither. "Do they have beer?"

"Germans," Iván quips, and I giggle despite noticing how Wulf's ears grow red.

József clicks his tongue at both of us before showing Wulf a variety of popular beers. Iván lowers his voice and tells me in Hungarian, "I've heard rumours that, for the sake of experiment, they banned fun from their curriculum. Entire class, dead serious."

I stifle a chuckle because Wulf's watching me yet again. For his benefit, I answer in English, "But it made them effective."

"True that." Iván leans back and smiles provocatively at his brother. Then he nudges me. "So, how is it working with the legendary Wulf Bachmann?" When he says "legendary" it's with a weird inflection that makes it sound more like an insult than a compliment.

Despite his nap on the train, Wulf looks tired. "Please don't." I can imagine he's not the greatest fan of having his competence thrown in his face all the time. Especially not after whatever happened in Italy.

"I wouldn't know," I answer, a little more seriously. "I haven't had the chance to see him in action yet."

Iván gasps, finding a new thing to delight at. "Oh, you're a baby! Just recently graduated?"

Wulf and I exchange a look, silently agreeing to go with the assumption. "You could say that."

On the other side of the table, József looks like he really wants to know why Wulf decided to bring a newbie on this mission. They obviously didn't ask for one.

Before we can talk any further, the drinks and food arrive. A giant plate of delicacies is set down in the middle, offering something for everyone. I can see a selection of salami with rustic bread and an array of pickled cabbages alongside at least seven varieties of meat, all dripping juice. If it tastes just half as delicious as it looks, we're in for a treat.

"Dig in," Iván encourages me. "You, too, Wulf." He raises his glass in a toast. "Egészségedre!"

"Egészségedre!" I answer likewise, before taking a sip of my long-lost childhood drink. It tastes just like my memories, sweet and not too sour. I had some snacks on the train but looking at the plate I feel famished. I haven't eaten Hungarian food in ages. Or any food this rich and flavourful. I decide on a pickled cucumber filled with cabbage and bite into it. "Mmh." It really is juicy and sour, but in a delectable way. "This is so delicious."

By the end of dinner, I've had a bite of everything, enjoying the sweetness of the paprika and the tanginess of the pickled vegetables as much as the chock-full of flavour sausages. The twice-fried duck's my favourite. Judging by the improvement of his mood, Wulf seems impressed by the food. Or maybe it's the beer that's loosened him up a little.

"So, what about the rest of your team?" he asks József. "They don't get to eat?"

It's the first time I've seen the older brother laughing. "Oh, they ate earlier today. Iván's got them patrolling the bridges at night."

"That bad?" Wulf asks.

József shrugs a little. "Most attacks happen at night. Not exclusively, though."

"We can talk about it at the convent," Iván interjects. "For now, let's put work aside and enjoy the food. Did you try the pork crackling?" He offers the tiny plate to Wulf, who declines politely.

"Convent?" I ask.

Iván sets the plate down again. "Yeah, the old Dominican convent on Margaret Island? The one King Béla IV sent his daughter Margaret to, thus the whole naming, you know? That's our base in Budapest."

"Spirit seekers really like their old, drafty places, don't they?" I joke.

Iván laughs. "I promise you, it's more comfortable than it looks. But yeah, we're huge on fortresses."

I guess it makes sense when you go to battle with the spirits. They seem to avoid places of human crudeness. Taking a sip from my second grape soda, I look out at the dark spot between two bridges that's Margaret Island. Only a few lights shine through the darkness, giving me the impression that no one really lives there. I vaguely remember visiting the parks and gardens of the island before. For the life of me, I can't remember the convent, though.

It turns out the reason I can't remember the Dominican convent is that the whole place is in ruins. It's been eight hundred years since

Princess Margaret lived here, and throughout the centuries people hadn't really cared about keeping it in shape.

"This is your base?" I ask Iván, who's lent me his arm on our stroll here. He's a little tipsy so I'm actually supporting him more than he does me.

He laughs and scratches his head. "Just the surface. The real base is below. Come on, I'll show you." He stumbles from my arm towards one of the more intact structures.

In the former retaining walls of a smaller room, a trapdoor the size of a garage door is set into the ground. Iván punches in a combination on the pillar next to it and the door slides open, exposing a flight of stairs leading into darkness. I feel my stomach turn. This isn't good. This isn't good at all.

"Come on," Iván calls. "Follow me. I promise you won't get wet feet. Maybe!" His chuckle echoes under the earth.

My backpack slides off my shoulder as my entire body shuts down. I'm rooted to the spot, unable to take one step further. József and Wulf are already on their way to follow Iván when Wulf notices me.

"Rika?" He takes a step toward me, frowning in confusion. "Are you coming?"

"I..." My voice sounds all wrong, distant and pitchy. "I can't."

His frown deepens, but then he turns around to József and tells him, "Go ahead. I'll take care of it."

József nods and vanishes between the crumbling rocks.

Slowly, Wulf comes closer. "What is it?" I only manage to stare at him, and he cocks his head to search my face. "Talk to me, Rika."

"I... I... can't go..." The very thought of setting one foot below the earth is messing with my head. I can do subways, even those insanely deep ones in Budapest, because they're still open in some way. But once the trapdoor closes over my head… I can't even think about it without feeling my throat tighten. "I can sleep outside." Yes, yes, it's not even that cold.

"Nonsense," Wulf says, but then his face softens. He looks deep into my eyes. "You don't like being underground, I take it?"

"There's no light. No air." And I need both to survive. I need the wind on my skin, the soil under my feet. I need the wide-open world, not this… prison.

Wulf nods thoughtfully. "Tell you what, it unsettles me quite a bit as well."

I latch onto his words as if they're a fishing rod. "It does?"

"I spent almost two months inside a volcano." He chuckles a little, but it sounds strained. "And…" He needs to take a deep breath. "I wasn't entirely sure I'd ever find a way out from under tons of rock."

Nausea floods my body. At least the trapdoor can be opened again. We're not stuck inside. "I'm sorry."

There's a gentle smile on his face, but it vanishes way too fast. Instead, he offers me his hand. "Can we brave this together? It's just a spirit seeker base, after all."

Tentatively, I put my hand into his. Concentrating on the light squeeze he gives me, I manage a nod, which sets the rest of my body into motion. One foot in front of the other. One breath after another.

Together, we face the trapdoor. It's no longer completely dark. The brothers must've turned on the light. I'm incredibly grateful to them for not having to step into darkness.

The base isn't very deep, a maximum of three metres under the former convent, and it's as modern as it gets. There's even some 20th-century art on the walls. When the door closes above our heads, I feel Wulf's hand shake in mine. It gives me something to concentrate on. If he can do this after two months spent underground, I can too.

The corridor leads into a vast, open space that makes me feel instantly better. Partial walls split the room into small alcoves that create little spaces for work, retreat, or socialising. József and Iván stand near the back of the area, facing each other. Something must have happened in the short time Wulf and I took to follow them because both of them are snarling.

"We wouldn't need him if you hadn't fucked this up," József hisses.

"Basszon agyon a kénköves istennyila!" Iván hurls at his brother, then marches out on us, vanishing into the deeper vaults of the convent.

Wulf looks at me in confusion. "What did he say?"

I feel my face flush and let go of his hand. "Literally? Get fucked to death by lightning with sulphuric stones."

"It's just a more colourful version of 'fuck you'. Really drives it home," József explains, coming towards us. He sighs. "I'm sorry, Wulf. He didn't want me to call you. He's such a child."

To Wulf's credit, he doesn't immediately accept his friend's evaluation, but scratches his chin. "What do you mean? I thought you guys wanted my help."

"*I* want your help," József stresses. "Iván thinks he can get it all under control. He's got a plan, he says, but if he has, it's not working. Twelve people died last week in a rare tidal wave that swept down Elizabeth Bridge. Whether he likes it or not, we need your help."

Wulf nods thoughtfully. "And you'll get it."

József's shoulders sag in relief. "Thank you. I knew I could count on you." He waves us along. "Come on, I'll show you where you can sleep."

I'm given my own room underground, but I already know I'll spend next to no time in it if I can help it. Don't get me wrong, it's a nice little room with a comfy bed, more art, and even daylight lamps that are supposed to make up for the lack of windows. However, it's smaller than my room at the citadel, making me feel as if I'm trapped. It's almost a blessing that the bathrooms are down the corridor, so I have one more excuse to get out. Then again, that means I won't feel safe to have more than a quick shower.

As soon as everyone else has turned in for the night, I take my backpack and sneak out. I'm rather sleepy after the early start and late end to this day, but the fresh spring air invigorates me immediately. I can't see much around the convent as there are no streetlights to illuminate the ruins which are black shapes against the night sky. It's even darker in the garden. Even so, I can make out rows of rose bushes, hedges, and a group of trees. Flowers line the roadside.

I can't fathom why spirit seekers would voluntarily live in a lifeless bunker under the earth with so much beauty surrounding them. Maybe it's for protective value. The water is close but can't come near, dryads only like to stretch their feet in soil, and gnomes would have to cross the Danube first. I shrug. That's what they get for being afraid of spirits.

After I've put some distance between me and the convent, I take out the spirit trap from my backpack. Aeola has waited long enough. Hopefully she's okay.

I unscrew the cap and set the tube on the ground. "You can come out."

The wind picks up, rustling through the leaves above me. I pull my jacket closer, shivering. Then, with a gust, Aeola bursts from the trap and stretches out. At first it looks like she'll expand forever, but then she shrinks back to her normal size. "Finally."

"I'm sorry it took so long. It's been a long day." I sit on the ground and let my fingers run through the grass, as if every fibre of myself needs to be exposed to the living world.

Meanwhile, Aeola tests out the winds over Budapest. She doesn't stick around but uses her chance to shoot up into the sky and let the wind carry her through the city. I can't say I blame her. In fact, I wish I could follow, see the city by night, reacquaint myself with the streets, and walk the Széchenyi Chain Bridge, enjoying the sight of its pearls of light strung up across the Danube.

The surrounding trees are almost as good, though. I enjoy the quiet sounds around me, listening to the wind sighing in the trees. The leaves spread the stories of the day among themselves, passing on rumour and fact alike.

"They'll kill us all," one frightened little voice says.

Another one answers, "It's wrong of them."

"They're wrong," a third voice adds to the chorus.

Alarmed, I get to my feet. I know I shouldn't be surprised about the fear in these spirit voices. After all, they live next to the spirit seekers. But the intensity of it makes my heart ache.

I run my fingers over the bark of the next tree. "Who's killing you?" I believe I already know the answer.

Silence.

Even the wind has ceased. Then it picks up with a small whisper, "She let her out."

"She freed the sylph."

"But she's one of them. She lives with them."

My hands start shaking. They watched Aeola and me, though it looks like they misinterpreted my actions a little. I try to make sure my voice carries my honesty. "I'm with them but not one of them." I know at this very moment that's the truth. Until I complete the official training—which I never intend to do—I'll always be just with them, no matter what enjoyable evenings we might share. "Do they kill you? Do the spirit seekers kill you?"

"When have they not done that?" comes the prompt answer. It hurts me physically.

But another one speaks up, "Long, long ago."

Before I can dwell on the surprising advocacy, the frightened one speaks again. "It's not them. It's the nymphs."

"Be quiet."

I draw my hand back in shock. Spirits fighting among themselves? I shouldn't be too surprised, I guess. I've yet to meet any intelligent species that doesn't. Still, I've never encountered such unbridled fear in a group of spirits. Not even when the Erlking forced his own people into battle. Something is terribly wrong.

"Why would they do that?" I ask, but there'll be no answer. A rustle of leaves tells me that the dryads have hidden.

The reason becomes apparent immediately when I hear footsteps coming my way. The light of a cell phone flashlight blinds me, so I can't tell who it is.

A husky female voice speaks to me in Hungarian. "Who are you? And what are you doing talking to the trees?"

Raising my arm, I try to shield myself from the light. I still can't see her, but I can see that she carries a staff. Another spirit seeker.

"I'm with Wulf Bachmann. I mean, I'm Rika. Could you please turn that light off?"

She only lowers it, so it illuminates the ground instead. Now that I can see again, I notice she's about my size with hair on the lighter side. Dirt smudges half her face. "What are you doing out here, then?" Her voice has lost none of its aggression.

I'd rather not tell her about the dryads, though I'm itching to discuss it with somebody. From what I've gathered, these spirit seekers are just like everybody else. Stubborn and blind to the spirits' true intention. "I was taking a stroll but I got lost, and now I can't find the entrance." She doesn't move, so I add, in what I hope is a sufficient show of embarrassment, "I tend to talk to myself when I'm worried."

"Don't you have a phone?" I notice she still hasn't introduced herself, but at last she accepts my explanation and shines her light the other way. "Come with me. We'll see if you're telling the truth."

I have no choice but to follow her, leaving the dryads behind.

9

It isn't until next morning that I learn who my involuntary late-night guide was. Her name is Rebeka and she went to the academy with Iván. Oh, and she's his girlfriend, which she makes very clear at a PDA-filled breakfast. There are four other spirit seekers Wulf and I are introduced to in the morning because they were patrolling by night, though none have caught a spirit. They all look exhausted and thus grateful when Wulf suggests we investigate the nymph problem alone since I speak enough Hungarian to get us through the city.

I don't know why he doesn't want any help from the Varga brothers, but it's fine with me. Maybe this way I can sneak in some subtle detours to look for my mother. We arrive at Elizabeth Bridge just after the morning rush. The giant white gates gleam in the sun, guarding the entrances to Buda and Pest. A fleet of small and large boats drift through the waters of the Danube while cars swoosh by above.

We take the pedestrian walkway on the northern side and walk up to the middle. Flowers are laid out for the victims of the drowning, an all too stark reminder that not all spirits are friendly. It's several metres down to the water surface, large enough for even the biggest ships to pass through smoothly. How any nymph could reach this high and sweep away twelve human lives is incomprehensible to me, and maybe the greatest testament to the spirits' power.

Wulf watches the water beneath us for a whole ten minutes without saying anything. People walking by point at him. I assume he looks rather impressive with his old-fashioned seeker staff that seems more like a wizard's staff than a weapon.

"Can you see any nymphs?" he asks after a while.

I look into the water—not that I hadn't done so before, just not for ten minutes straight. "It's too deep down there. Nymphs like shallow water. We'll probably have better luck on the banks if you want to talk to them."

"Talk to them?" He turns to me with his usual frown. "Why would I want to talk to them?"

"To find out what happened?" I mean, what does he expect? That the nymphs will show up right now to re-enact their attack?

He studies me for a moment, then shakes his head. "You're weird."

"So, what's the plan, then?" I ask, maybe a smidgen grumpily.

Wulf shrugs and starts walking towards the Pest end of the bridge, forcing me to keep up with him. "There's some truth in what you said. Nymphs usually stick to the banks of the river, especially when they try to kill people. It's much easier to drag someone off the side than produce a tidal wave high enough to sweep over one of these bridges. So I'm interested in why they changed their behaviour so much and how they managed it."

I still think asking the nymphs would get us answers to his questions, but I won't suggest it again. Instead, I tell him, "I talked to some dryads last night..." Uh-oh, big mistake.

Wulf stops short and turns around. "You did what?"

"I talked to some dryads." He opens his mouth, but I'm quicker. "They had something interesting to say. And I'm sure they would've said more if Rebeka hadn't appeared. In any case," I say louder, because he's just about to speak again, "they're afraid of the nymphs, more than they are of spirit seekers."

Now he can talk or tell me off. Instead, Wulf closes his mouth and actually thinks about the information. "So, there's infighting between the spirits?" he asks at last.

"No, I mean, I wouldn't really say the dryads are fighting back. They're just afraid." I'm kind of surprised he hasn't thrown a fit yet.

"Well, as far as I know, dryads are afraid of everything. They're not exactly the strongest spirits." He resumes walking.

I remember how a dryad almost strangled me with its roots less than a month ago. Or how the bushes in Tiergarten gave some creeps hell. "They're not weak at all. They're just... more mellow."

"Either way, the dryads aren't our problem here," Wulf says, slightly strained. "The nymphs are."

Gosh, he's frustrating. "Maybe they could help us figure it out, though."

"I don't work with spirits." Definitely strained now. "*We* don't work with spirits."

"Fine," I grumble. "Have it your way."

The look he gives me tells me he always has it his way and that my way is ridiculous, on top of being wildly inappropriate. I resolve not to help him figure this one out. After all, what could the mighty Wulf Bachmann ever need my help for?

We reach the other side and go down the bank. Wulf opens his backpack and takes out some glass vials, which he proceeds to fill with water from the Danube. I manage to watch him sullenly for almost three minutes before my curiosity gets the better of me. "What are you doing?"

"Testing the water for residual spirit energy." He carefully stows the vials away.

"You can do that?"

Wulf snorts. "There's more to being a spirit seeker than just waving your staff around. You can test how spirit-infested the water or air is. It doesn't work as well for the other elemental areas, but in this case, we're lucky."

I kind of want to know more, but I'm too grossed out by the way he said "spirit-infested". Spirits aren't a pest.

"If you attended the academy, you'd learn all kinds of stuff about spirits—how they affect the world, how to find their strongholds." He stops talking when he sees me roll my eyes. "Seriously, it would do you good."

"I'm sure I'll do brilliantly with my non-existing high school diploma." Seriously, my ass. I can do very well without being humiliated in Spirit Physics or whatever courses they study. "Besides, I know things about spirits they don't teach you."

Wulf presses his jaw together, takes a deep breath, and says, "I wouldn't be so sure about that. The new lecturer for Spirit Behaviour is supposed to be pretty good."

"Too bad they didn't teach you, then." I walk off, only to hear him snort behind me. Whatever they teach them in Spirit Behaviour obviously doesn't change their desire to capture every spirit they encounter.

We walk back to the other side of the river, keeping a one-metre distance between us. Wulf does his thing with the vials again, and I take a little walk along the shoreline, getting my own groove of the river. Grudgingly, I have to admit he's right about the excess spirit energy. The water feels like it's brimming with some sort of power. I hold my hand in it and let it weave through my fingers.

At first, it feels completely normal, but then something oily winds itself around my index finger. I study the water but it doesn't look any different. It's just a distinctive feeling of wrongness. Shivering, I pull out my hand and wipe it on my pants for good measure.

Wulf screws the cap onto his last vial and stows it away. "Let's head back to the base. Do you know which subway we need to take?"

The thought of going back into that hole so early doesn't sit right with me. Besides, I had other plans. "Budapest is a city best explored by walking."

"We're not tourists," Wulf replies.

"Iván was right then," I remember. "They did take fun out of your classes."

In response, the muscles in his cheek spasm. He's either pissed because Iván said something like that or because he doesn't want to be known as joyless. "We've got work to do."

"Oh yeah? What are you gonna do? Analyse those vials all day?" I take a breath to soften my voice. It probably won't help my case by aggravating him. "Please, I haven't been here in such a long time. We'll go back. We'll just do it a bit slower." Then I play my last card. "If you want, I can tell you which line to take and where to get off. I can't help you with the analysis, anyway, so I could go alone?"

Wulf seems to consider it, but in the end, he gives in. "Fine, show me the city."

We could've just walked along the Danube, enjoying the views on either side of the river, including the gorgeous Hungarian Parliament. Instead, I drag Wulf up Castle Hill on the Buda side of the river to stroll through the Buda Castle gardens. It's still early spring, so they're not as impressive as they will be soon. If there are any dryads here, they keep well hidden.

Walking up the Dísz tér, we reach the famous Matthias Church, with its colourful roof and intricate spire, and from there to the one place I remember clear as day from my childhood: Fisherman's Bastion. Seven turrets of limestone, one for each of the seven chieftains of the Magyars that founded Hungary in 896, stand tall over Budapest, creating a viewing platform of the Danube valley.

The wind ruffles through my hair as I lean on the guardrail and take in the beautiful city. We can see the Széchenyi Chain Bridge from up here and the Parliament on the other side, as well as Margaret Island to our left. The city crawls into the valley on the Pest side of the Danube, stretching as far as I can see. On this side, hills like the Gellért Hill to our right, with its beautiful limestone caves, rise among the houses.

Once I've had my fill of sightseeing, I try to look deeper.

Childhood memories suck. You can have some very clear images, unmarred by time, and in between everything's fuzzy or blurry at best. I remember visiting Fisherman's Bastion with my mother, hopping on those marble stairs and trying to climb the statues. I also recognise the City Park and Heroes' Square beyond that. But I have no idea which streets we walked down, and most importantly, where the house we were so often invited into is.

Eszti is the name of the woman whose round, soft figure and wrinkles of laughter are etched into my mind. I don't know her surname or her address. I don't even know why we had such a close relationship with her, other than that I called her Dédi, a loving nickname for great-grandma. But then I called Pavel grandpa, and he wasn't actually related to me. Still, one can hope.

"So are you gonna tell me why you so desperately wanted to come to Budapest?" Wulf asks. He's leaning next to me, resting his elbows on the balustrade.

"I told you: my mum grew up close to here." My voice sounds a bit reserved. There are so many emotions in my mind right now—remembering Eszti and her hearty goulash, being back in Budapest, missing my mum.

Wulf carefully probes a little deeper. "But you also said it's just one of your many homes. That you're not Hungarian yourself. So, why Budapest?" Damn, why does he pay so much attention to detail?

"Part of me is Hungarian," I stress, not daring to look away from the city into his eyes, lest he sees how fragile the front I'm putting up against him is. "I love this city with all my heart."

"It is rather beautiful."

I can't resist him when he agrees with my sentiment and turn to smile at him. The wind steals a tear from my eye, and I quickly return to the city view. Wulf keeps quiet, so after a while, I tell him. I have to. Not because he asked, but because these words need air and light as much as I do. They need to breathe again after being stuck underground for so long. "My mum and I spent many years here. And I miss her a lot."

I can feel his gaze on me, like the sun warming my skin. His voice is very quiet when he asks, "What happened to her?"

"Phew." That opens up a deep cave of feelings. Somehow I find the strength to venture inside. "You ever heard of the Spring Cleaning?"

"I did." Of course he did, living in Berlin and all. "It happened during my last year at the academy, just before I was sent to Berlin."

Or maybe he wasn't living there at the time. "Well, I was fifteen. My mum and I had settled in Britzer Garden the year before. It was a great community. We didn't do any harm. We even took care of the grounds." My voice breaks a little. "So, if you heard how there was waste lying around and not enough hygiene measures, it's a lie. We weren't a homeless camp but Travellers. We respected the spirits, and they respected us." A little bitterness slips into my voice as I look at him. "Fancy that."

There are many different people among the Travellers. You've probably heard of the Roma, Sinti, or Lovari, and then there's us, the ones who chose a life amongst the spirits, savouring the gifts nature provided us with. Sure, we flock to cities in winter—we've got to live, after all—but we spend just as much time travelling through areas of undisturbed wilderness, however rare those places may be. We choose to travel rather than being chased from our homes, like so many of our cousins.

Wulf looks at me with a strange mix of compassion and distaste. I like to imagine that my spirit-loving upbringing is where most of the aversion stems from, and not my ethnicity. Not that it makes it much better. "It seems to have worked for you," he says diplomatically.

Some people wouldn't be so kind. According to them, we attract spirits, indulge them. Some even go as far as to blame us directly for spirit attacks, that we somehow directed them. People haven't really changed that much since the fascist days. But Wulf says nothing like that.

For that reason alone, I keep talking. "It obviously wasn't good enough for the government. They ordered the Spring Cleaning." In my mind's eye I can see the sirens flashing all around the camp. They had us surrounded. "Flush us out with one big strike." I bang my hand on the guardrail. "They arrested my mum and sent me off with the Youth Welfare Office." Even now the memories make me shiver. "I took their bullshit for four months before I had to get out."

"You preferred the streets to a youth home?" he asks, mildly interested.

I guess it sounds ridiculous to everyone else. "I thought I could go back to living in the wild. But it's damn hard if you're alone." My cheeks hurt from trying to seem unaffected. "I stuck around in Berlin because I thought my mum would eventually come and find me. She hadn't done anything, so why would they send her to prison? There's no law against not owning a house. Or not being registered. For a while, I stalked the prisons. I even found a nice officer who looked into the system for me."

"And?" Wulf is frowning now, clearly intrigued.

"And nothing. Not a single entry. I thought maybe she gave them a false name, but if she did, I couldn't trace it. So I waited and waited. And somehow, eight years passed." Thinking back, it seems ridiculous how long I held onto that hope.

Wulf shifts next to me. He's the one looking out at the city now, giving me a few moments to gather myself. "I'm sorry."

"Not your fault." Taking a few deep breaths helps me centre myself. "But when you said you were going to Budapest, I had to come." It hurts so much to say the following few words I almost can't bring myself to do it. "Maybe she just didn't come back for me."

He immediately turns around to protest. "I don't believe that."

It has to be said. Rip the plaster off. "Berlin is big. We could have missed each other. And instead of waiting, she just went back to our travelling ways. I was old enough to take care of myself..." Wulf is shaking his head, which makes me lose my train of thought.

"She's your mum. Why would you think she'd abandon you?" He's visibly aghast.

I shrug, as if it could lift the mountain off my shoulders. "She didn't take things too seriously. Like, for example, I don't know who my dad is. I never really cared, but I also doubt she knows." My mum lived life to the fullest. She never had a proper boyfriend but there were men who came in and out of her life. Or maybe it was her who went in and out of their lives. "She's not attached to any place or anyone. And as I said, I was mostly grown."

"You were fifteen," Wulf protests. "That's hardly grown."

I've only got a weak smile for him. "Thanks, but she never came. I thought maybe she'd return to Budapest. We stayed here for so many years and this is her birthplace, so I'd hoped that I..." Suddenly, all the words fail me. Hope hasn't served me well these last few years. It's such a meagre lifeline, just enough to keep you going, keep you pushing ahead, but not enough to warm you on a cold winter's night, to feed you, to lend substantive help.

Fortunately, Wulf knows how to end the sentence for me. "You hoped you'd find her here."

As I nod, I feel the tears falling. I'm not strong enough to pretend anymore. "Or maybe a trace. Just something."

He looks out at the city, clearly uncomfortable with my stupid breakdown. "So, where do we start?"

"What?"

He turns back to me. "Where do we start looking?"

I can't believe what I'm hearing. "What do you mean? You've got a nymph problem to handle and all this work to do."

My argument makes Wulf snort. Somehow he looks sad. "Rika, I'm gonna help you find her. Or at least look for her."

"But why? You don't even like me. I mean..." Gosh, did I really just say that?

Once again, he scoffs. "I disagree with your attitude towards spirits. That has nothing to do with how much I like you." He sighs, then brings the conversation back on track. "You know what happened to my parents. If there was any chance in the world I could see my mother again, I'd take it and run with it." At that moment, I snatch a rare glimpse of the pain buried deep inside of him. "I'll help you."

He turns his face away, looking back out at the city—or pretending to. I slip a hand around his upper arm and squeeze it lightly. "Thank you."

10

Unfortunately, when we get back to the convent, Iván welcomes us with the words, "Grab your staffs. Let's go. There's some spirit activity around Óbudai-sziget."

"Bloody spirits have the nerve," József mutters.

The Óbuda Island is just north of Margaret Island, connected by the same bridge. "So far the nymph attacks have been removed from our base, but it looks like they're drawing closer," Iván explains as we head to the northern tip.

I watch them stride along the paths purposefully. Wulf hasn't even broken a sweat switching into action mode after I dragged him up and down all those hills. This is what he came for. The spirit seekers have asked for his help, so if he can defeat the nymphs cleanly in one go, we're done. I hope he remembers his promise afterwards and doesn't book the next ticket home.

"What's the intensity?" Wulf asks, bringing himself up to speed.

"4.2 Megajoules," József answers before his brother has a chance to.

If it wasn't for Wulf's mumbled "Scheiße!" I wouldn't know how bad that was. He shakes his head in frustration. "That's at least eight nymphs."

Even I know that that's quite an impressive group. Unless they're having one of their rare group dances, there are usually no more than two or three nymphs in one spot, and humans usually only get to see one—if they can see them, that is.

It's quite hard keeping up with the three men, who seem to have all but forgotten about me as they stride rapidly towards the bridge. I'm not the only one lagging behind, though. Rebeka and two of the other spirit seekers are also coming. Iván's girlfriend is the trapper, while I'm just tagging along, I guess.

We arrive on Óbuda Island, which is a similar size and shape as Margaret Island, but much closer to the Buda shoreline and much less travelled by tourists. A thin arm of the Danube flows between island and mainland, and it's the shore of that arm we're walking along.

Looking into the water, I don't need to stick my hand in to know it would feel slick and oily. It looks like perfectly good water from one angle and horrifyingly muddy from the other. The shifting sight sets me on edge. It's like I can see the pollution in the water, or worse, like all the pollution of the Danube waters have concentrated in this spot.

I'm just about to tell Wulf what I saw when another sight distracts me. The water in front of us is rising, rising slowly but surely, until it becomes one enormous bulge of dirty water, ready to burst at any minute. At first it looks like it'll sweep away the small bridge that connects the island to Buda, but then the water turns around.

"Get back!" Wulf bellows. He saw it at the same time as me, and has already drawn his staff.

His command is so forceful that even the Varga brothers take a step back. But then József draws his staff, and Iván, not to be outdone by his brother, does the same. As for me? I take Wulf seriously and retreat as far back as I can while the water draws nearer, nearer, and then bursts into a massive tidal wave above our heads.

Wulf waits, eerily patient, as the giant wave crashes down on him. At the very last second, he lifts his staff and slices through the curtain of water. The water parts around the three men, flushing up the grass until it pools in front of my feet. In its wake, the nymphs become visible. Or rather, the nymph.

At first glance, she's not very impressive looking. In fact, she looks smaller than the ones I've encountered before, less whole, somehow. Neither size nor impression relates to her power, though. As Wulf said, the energy surrounding her should have been made up by at least eight nymphs, and yet it's just one. One single nymph strong enough to create a powerful wave against the river's flow.

Just looking at her makes me shudder. Nymphs have two faces. I call them the relaxed and the angry face. A relaxed nymph is a beauty to behold, with a long, wavy body, hair cascading down their back like waterfalls, eyes as deep as the ocean. An angry one is the stuff of nightmares. Their face becomes fishier, not the harmless fish you'd find in freshwater lakes and rivers, but creatures from the deep sea with long, thin fangs and huge soulless eyes. The nymph in front of us shows a third face, one I'm entirely unfamiliar with. For lack of better words, she looks like a water corpse, all bloated and pale. Her skin looks spongy, and there's a darkness inside of her that reminds me of an oil spill.

She snarls at the three men in her way, then splashes back into the water, causing a second wave to lap onto land. This time, Wulf is a tad too slow, and the water spills up to his knees. There must be a hideous current, because I see both József and Iván struggling to keep upright. József's knees buckle and he's drawn towards the river. Swift as a snake, Wulf jumps forward, grabs József with one hand and brings down his staff with the other. The grip on József relaxes immediately, and he remains sitting, sputtering and huffing. For now, the water has returned to the river.

"We need to draw her out," Wulf explains sharply. "Retreat!" He makes sure the brothers go first before following, all the while keeping his eyes on the river.

Iván's head snaps around to the rest of us. He orders Rebeka, "Prepare that trap."

"But it's too powerful," she complains. "It'll never work."

"Prepare that trap!" Iván snarls, in a way that's entirely different from the goofy guy I met last night.

I feel sorry for Rebeka because it's clear to everyone that the nymph is in no shape to be caught right now. She's too strong for any of the traps. "Trust Wulf," I find myself saying. I don't even know why since I've never seen him fight until today, but that's why we're here, right? He's the best of the best. "He'll break her down in time."

Rebeka glares at me and starts preparing the trap while muttering under her breath. How she can do any of the calculations Leon showed me while doing that, I have no idea.

Turning my attention back to the guys and the nymph, I notice the water has calmed almost completely. "Did it flee?" I hear Iván ask.

Wulf doesn't answer immediately, but then he looks back at me. "Rika, come here."

My heart hammers in my chest. Hopefully, he won't ask me to fight the spirit. I've already dealt with the Erlking. Surely I've earned a brief reprieve before facing yet another ancient spirit.

Because that's the only explanation I have at the moment. The only explanation that makes any sense.

I step next to Wulf, and he points towards the water. "What do you think?"

As hard as I try, I can't see the nymph. I want to take a step forward, but Wulf's hand wraps around my upper arm like a bench vice and holds me back. He obviously thinks it's still dangerous. And rightfully so. I can't see the wave but I can feel it in my stomach. It's like all the pollution of the Danube is pooling in front of me, hiding under the surface, yet somehow, I feel it seeping into my bones.

"You can feel it, right?" Wulf asks, sounding strained. His eyebrows are deeply furrowed, his eyes flitting back and forth over the surface.

I nod, wanting nothing more than to throw up. "It's so wrong."

He doesn't really hear me, eyes rapidly scanning the river. Then they stop. "There."

A second later, a fountain of water shoots four metres into the sky and twists around itself before taking aim straight at Wulf. Inside, I see the snarling face of the nymph elongating.

I'm rooted to the spot, but Wulf jerks on my arm, pushing me behind him and meeting the water snake head-on with his staff. It hits the nymph right in the face. Water sprays everywhere, splashing into Iván and József and far behind us. I get off remarkably lightly since Wulf takes the full brunt of the hit, acting as a shield in front of me.

A terrible howl rises in the air as the nymph retreats into the water.

"Trap!" Wulf yells.

Before Rebeka can even react, Iván has snatched the tube from her hand and starts directing it at the nymph.

"It's getting away," József shouts, already striding along the riverbank, following the nymph's path.

"It's not working," Iván complains. He throws the trap away in disgust and demands a new one from Rebeka. "Hurry up. I'll do it!"

Wulf has joined József, keeping an eye on the nymph. Again and again, he stabs the water with his staff, trying to slow the nymph down. I bend down and pick up the trap Iván has thrown away. No wonder it isn't working. It's set on a regular nymph with maximum strength. But this nymph isn't regular in any way.

I let the useless tube fall and snatch the one from Iván's hands.

"Hey," he shouts and makes a grab for it. He stops when he sees how fast my hands move around the rings.

The strength stays on maximum, but the type almost leads into gnome territory for all the pollution she carries inside her. A few more adjustments and I'm done. "Wulf!"

He looks around and I throw the tube towards him. It falls short, but he takes one big step in my direction and catches it before it hits the ground. Then he turns back to the river and activates the trap.

I hold my breath. The nymph has almost reached the point where the arm flows back into the Danube under the Ápárd Bridge. She's building up more momentum and I can see another wave bulging. This time it will be directed against the busy bridge connecting Buda and Pest.

The wave is about to break when the nymph is caught in a strong suction, drawing her back, centimetre by centimetre. The trap is working. Wulf's muscles strain as he holds onto the tube. Despite the damage he's dealt to the nymph, she still gives him a hell of a fight. It's only when József steps in and deals another blow to the nymph that she loses, and just like that, the water splashes back into the Danube. I hear an audible popping sound as the nymph is sucked into the tube.

Immediately, Wulf screws the cap shut as if afraid she might escape. Even from this distance, I can hear him huff in exhaustion. He's not the only one who's feeling relieved. József laughs and claps Wulf's shoulder before outright crowing, "Amazing. Gosh, you're good."

Iván isn't that enamoured with Wulf. He seems more grumpy than relieved, but he nods towards me. "Guess he didn't just take you along for your language skills."

I flush, knowing that Wulf would have never considered taking me along if I hadn't practically begged. It feels ridiculous to claim even a tiny part in his overwhelming victory because József is right; Wulf was pretty amazing. The way he stood against the nymph, completely unafraid, each movement so precise—for the first time, I've seen the legend they all hail. It's mesmerising.

11

Wulf's victory is celebrated with a massive party. After weeks of feeling absolutely powerless against the unproportionally strong nymph attacks, it's like the spirit seekers can breathe again. Wine and spirits are rolled out, and Iván orders a tremendous amount of takeaway food. There'll be no one on kitchen duty tonight.

I sit in one of the alcoves by myself, watching Wulf and József in the opposite corner, behaving like the old friends they are. József seems to have blossomed now the danger is under control. He's laughing and joking without care, and to my bigger surprise, Wulf joins in with the merriness, showing yet another side to him.

"Pálinka?" Iván holds a glass filled to the brim with a dark-golden liquid to my face. The fruity spirits inside is so strong it almost burns away the hairs in my nose.

Part of me wants to turn him away, not keen to start drinking now, but the Hungarian part of me knows it would be impossible to refuse. Everyone else around me is already drinking. One drink won't kill me. Or so I think until I take a sip of the home-made pálinka, and it burns away the better part of my throat.

I must look hilarious because Iván is close to wetting himself with laughter. "Oh, my, your face." He gasps for air. "I'll get you a soda."

Leaving the bottle and glass on my table, he returns with a lemonade and bigger glass. He pushes both towards me, then takes my shot glass and downs the rest of the pálinka before refilling it immediately. "Much better," he says, letting himself fall on the bench beside me.

"What's much better?" I ask, pouring myself a soda.

"Watching those two with some alcohol to wash it down." Iván points the glass toward his brother and Wulf. Then he downs that one as well.

I shoot another glance at the two friends, feeling my gaze circling back and back again to the almost triangular dimples that appear on Wulf's face each time he laughs. "You're still bitter your brother asked for help?"

Iván's snort tells me I landed exactly right. He leans forward, his eyes fixed on the two men. "We didn't need help. I was working on a solution. But, of course, my darling brother couldn't wait to see me fail. So he brought in the real seeker." Apparently, bitter doesn't even begin to cut it.

"I'm sorry he makes you feel that way, but at least the problem is solved now, right?" I can understand how hard it must be for him to be compared to someone like Wulf, to be basically shown up in front of his own team, but surely, saving people's lives should count for something. After all, that's what spirit seekers are all about.

Iván tears his gaze away from the two men to face me. "You know what? He would've failed if not for you." He raises a third glass to me.

My immediate reaction is to avoid his gaze and study the graining of the table. "I hardly did anything."

"Nonsense! You smashed the bearings on that trap. You must be some maths genius. I don't even know how you did it." He chucks down the pálinka.

His comment makes me laugh. "Quite the opposite. It's all intuition for me."

Iván tries to whistle, but there's barely a tone coming out between his lips. "Intuition, huh? I've never really asked you, Rika. How high is your NAV?"

"That's like asking a woman how old she is," I answer, batting my eyelids. Truth is, I don't really feel comfortable boasting about a 500-plus NAV. They'd only ask me to fight more spirits. "What's yours?"

Grinning, Iván replies, "389. Exactly six points above my brother." That fact seems to bring him a lot of satisfaction. "He absolutely hates it."

I find the whole rivalry a bit ridiculous. "Does it matter that much?"

"Yes. It's all that matters. Those six points are all that stand between him and the commander position." Iván leans closer to me. "He actually was the preliminary commander, but he basically took the position after learning that I'd be coming for him. Gosh, he hates being bested by me." His eyes flick back to his brother. "He always thought he was better than me, that I was just some child, but I beat him, and now he's just second fiddle to my first."

Woah, that's some serious sibling rivalry. One thing bothers me, though. "How does the SSA pick their commanders? Wouldn't they go with a more experienced one? No offence. It's just weird that they already knew they would replace József when assigning him."

Iván turns back to me. "Oh, well. Of course, they could've sent me somewhere else, but they decided not to. It's solely based on NAV. If you get a high one, you shadow the old commander for a year, and then you take over. Surely they told you that."

My gaze falls on Wulf again. "No, they didn't. So just the NAV. And the error margins?"

"What error margins?"

"Plus-minus whatever." I don't claim to understand them but what did Wulf say? "If they overlap, you couldn't know which one is higher."

Iván scrunches up his nose as if I've personally offended him. "Who cares about the error margins? You get a value, and that's it. Are you saying my brother is actually the one with the higher NAV?"

"No!" I've got Wulf fixed in my stare. "It's just something someone told me once."

"Well, it's utter bullshit." He pours himself yet another glass. "So, what's your NAV?"

Suddenly, there's another reason I can't tell him the truth. Wulf and I are supposed to be a team. If they know we're not, I run the risk they'll rat me out to the SSA. Because apparently, with my NAV, I should be the one leading the Berlin team.

"It's 412." There's no denying I can see spirits after my show on the island now.

Despite my efforts, Iván sputters, then slams the glass on the table, startling me and everyone else. Wulf looks over to check on me, drawing his brows together in question. I glare at him. He lied to me. Or rather, he gaslit me, telling me all that nonsense about how I theoretically could've scored below him when I obviously haven't. Fourteen points. That's more than double the difference between the Varga brothers.

"...thinking?" I hear Iván mutter angrily.

"What?"

He almost snarls at me. "I asked what the SSA was thinking when they put you in his team? Is Berlin that bad? Are people dying en masse there?"

I'm afraid I don't really follow him. "No, I like Berlin. I mean... sure, people die each day, but not from spirit attacks."

"Yeah, well, then I don't understand why Germany should get two seekers above 400. And one that's from Hungary as well." He chucks down the little bit he hasn't spilt on the table. "I've got to pee."

As I watch him stride off, I curse myself for not picking a value closer to 300. Of course the SSA would never place two high-end spirit seekers at the same location. Not if there are so few among them.

It doesn't take long before the seat next to me is filled again. Only this time it's Wulf who slides onto the bench. "You okay?"

"Why wouldn't I be?" There's a turmoil of feelings under my skin.

He lowers his voice a little. "Iván looked a bit intense from over there. Did he say anything, or...?"

"No." He actually said a lot of things, but I'm not in the mood to share them with Wulf. "He just got a little drunk. It was a big victory after all."

"About that." Wulf smiles at me. "That was some outstanding work in the field today. I didn't know you were such a talent with traps."

It pains me to hear his compliment. Not that I don't think it's genuine, but it has so many implications. That I'm like them. That I'm somehow talented when it comes to fighting the spirits. That I could possibly become a valuable part of their team, and thus, society. All that makes me shiver. I don't want to be known for being someone so in tune with spirits that they can bypass all the complicated mathematics and just intuitively sense their way through the trapping. If I ever become a spirit seeker then it'll be because I understand them like no one else does and mitigate the dangers they bear by talking to them, befriending them, and respecting them as much as I'd respect any fellow human.

"Something was wrong with that nymph," I say instead. Her whole appearance and actions still puzzle me.

Wulf nods severely. "It was a lot stronger than any nymph I ever met. Actually, stronger than any nymph could possibly be."

Eager to share my assessment, I lean forward on my elbows. "She felt dirty, polluted. I can't really explain it, but the water around her felt icky somehow."

"Well, that's something for the SSA to deal with. We did our job. We caught the spirit. Now it's their turn." He makes a move to get up.

I didn't expect him to pass responsibility off to someone else that quickly. "Aren't you worried?"

Wulf remains half crouched. "About what?"

"What it could mean? I've never seen or felt anything like what we encountered today."

Leaning towards me, he says, "I told you: that's for the SSA to find out."

"How long will it take them?" In my mind I try to estimate how many days we have between now and the result of their investigation.

Realising I've still got a lot of questions, Wulf sits back down. "I don't know. Weeks. Months."

"Are we gonna stay here that long?" I ask, honestly surprised.

He laughs a little. "No, we're done here."

"But we can't be." Sure, we captured one nymph, but that can't be it, can it?

Wulf puts a hand on my elbow. "Don't worry. I haven't forgotten my promise. We'll take a couple of days to look for your mum."

I hadn't even thought about that, but the reiteration of his promise warms my heart. He really meant it earlier. My lips stretch into a smile before I can remind myself of the topic at hand. "Thanks, but... I mean, I'd love to. It's just I don't think we're done yet."

His hand slips from my arm, and he frowns again. "Why would you say that?"

"Well, for example, the dryads said they were afraid of the nymphs. Nymphs *plural*, not a single one. Furthermore, I'm worried that whatever transformed the nymph into that hideous spirit could affect other spirits in the area. It has to come from somewhere, after all."

Wulf massages the bridge of his nose, and I hear him take a couple of deep breaths. When he looks at me again, I feel like a precocious child. "Have you ever considered that your dryads might not be the most reliable source of information?"

Groaning, I lean back and cross my arms. "For someone so attuned to spirits, you sure dismiss them a lot. The dryads weren't lying or anything. I can actually feel that, you know?"

He places his words carefully, clearly afraid I may blow up otherwise. "Or so you think."

"I know what I feel." He opens his mouth, but I stop him right away. "I don't need you mansplaining my feelings to me."

Wulf raises both his hands in defeat. "Wouldn't think of it," he says in a voice that's no longer trying to hide his annoyance and frustration. "All I wanted to say is that you put an awful amount of trust in these spirits."

"Yeah, well, they've never lied to me. Your kind, though, all the time." And with that, I get up and leave him at the table.

12

It's completely dark when I wake up. Is it morning? Did I wake from a dream in the middle of the night? These chambers underneath the ground really mess with my mind. Usually, I wake at first light, but there's no sun down here. All I have is a digital clock. I stare at the red numbers in confusion until they compute in my head. Somehow, I've slept until 9:20 am. No wonder I feel groggy. In Berlin, I would've already been on my feet for an hour or two.

So much for my plan to sneak out early and talk to Aeola. By the time I get dressed and enter the main room, it looks like everyone's woken up and left before me. Used coffee cups and breakfast plates are piled up on the kitchen bench, silently waiting for someone to wash them. The room is deserted apart from one table, and who else would sit there other than my most precious commander?

Wulf hunches over a laptop in one of the alcoves, thoughtfully staring at the screen while scribbling something on a notepad next to him. He's wearing his glasses again.

I tiptoe over to the kitchen, not really looking forward to confronting him again. But as soon as I pour water into a glass, he looks up.

"Good morning," he says, in that passive-aggressive tone elderly Germans usually use when they're already silently judging you for not saying it first.

Taking a deep breath, I glare at him. "Morning," I finally answer, trying to make it sound as aggressive as his.

He remains unfazed and lowers his gaze towards his laptop again. Obviously he's taunting me, wanting me to ask him what he's doing, but I won't give him that satisfaction. Instead, I grab some leftover bread and salami to go with my water and sit as far away as possible from him.

Whenever I steal a glance at him, he's got his head down, working away. The silence is palpable in the room, lending towards the grave-like atmosphere of the Hungarian headquarters. I wonder where everyone else is but won't ask Wulf to find out.

When I'm almost finished with my sad little breakfast, he looks up at me over the laptop's edge. "So, when did you want to leave?"

"Leave?" What the hell is he talking about?

"To look for your mother? Unless you no longer want me to help you?" His hand on the pen is still, waiting for me to answer.

Right, he's a guy who keeps his promises. He'll lie to you or hide the truth from you, but he'll keep his promise no matter how much he wants to do something else. I decide to call him out. "Looks to me like you're busy."

As if to prove me wrong, Wulf closes the laptop and puts down his pen. "I'm not."

Squinting my eyes a little, I say, "Very convincing."

He sighs as if he holds the sky on his shoulders. "Rika. There's always work to do. I've had to sight some reports from Berlin, sign off on some trap shipments, but none of that is urgent. I can do it tonight or even tomorrow. But if you'd rather not see my face all day, that's fine with me."

Well, too late for that. I won't give him the satisfaction now. I don't want him to think he's got me all figured out. "Fine." I put my dishes together and get up. "Let's go then."

"You're sure?" he asks.

I drop my dishes off on the counter. "Unless you no longer want to join me."

With a snort, he takes off his glasses and puts them away. "Let me get my stuff."

We meet outside the convent about ten minutes later. I wish he'd given me more time alone, but of course, Wulf is never late nor lazy. Thus, I only catch a glimpse of Aeola hanging around at the edge of my sight, keeping her distance from the spirit seeker next to me.

We walk silently next to each other until we reach the Margaret Bridge. Once we step onto the bridge, Wulf stops and turns to me. "So, how are we gonna do this?"

There are two layers to this question. A) What's my plan to find my mother, and B) how are we both gonna stand each other long enough to not make this the most horrible morning in history? I decide to answer the former and leave the latter for him to figure out. "Well, I remember more things on the Buda side than the Pest. So I figured I'd walk the streets until something strikes me as familiar."

I don't need Wulf's raised eyebrows to tell me this is a terribly ineffective plan. It's the only one I have, though, and he either agrees or doesn't really care since he makes an inviting gesture to the hills of Buda, and we set off.

Once again, the silence between us spreads as wide as the Danube behind us. You wouldn't think so, but it's incredibly distracting. I pay more attention to the brooding man half a step behind me than to the surrounding neighbourhoods. By the time we reach the foot of Castle Hill, I'm utterly frustrated.

And so too seems Wulf, because he asks, "Don't you have anything to start off? A name? An address?"

"Sure," I answer, a tad too confronting. "I actually know exactly where we need to go. I just enjoy leading you through the city while you fume behind me."

"I'm not fuming," he bristles ever so slightly. "I'm just wondering how I can be of help?"

I almost believe him. He's got that innocent look down to a T. Just a simple mission where he hasn't been briefed properly. "You wanted to come."

"But you didn't want me to," he replies, his voice slightly off the neutral path.

Part of me wants to agree, mainly because it's true. I'd be much more comfortable on my own. But there's another part of me, which decides that this would be a suitable moment to remind me how sincere Wulf was yesterday when I told him all about my mother.

"Look," I start, slightly more diplomatic. "I was a child. I remember playing on the stairs of Fisherman's Bastion and visiting the caves under Gellért Hill. I remember a hideous couch, which was the best hiding spot ever, but unless you know of some webpage that lists couches of Budapest, I don't know how that would be of any use."

My comment about the webpage makes Wulf chuckle, and I feel the silence fading away. "Can I make a suggestion then?" he asks.

"Sure," I answer, but it comes with an enormous sigh. I can't wait to hear what brilliant idea he comes up with.

"Let's go to the places you definitely remember and see if that sparks a memory that could set us up on a street or subway."

It's actually not a half-bad idea. It definitely beats wandering aimlessly through the city until a house jumps out to me. "Sounds good."

"You really don't like working together, do you?"

"I don't like being told what to do... or who to be." I start moving again. "Relic from my awesome youth home days. I'm sure you actually know better what's good for me, though," I add for good measure.

Wulf chuckles again. "I didn't say that."

"You always say that when we talk about spirits," I point out.

"Yeah, but I grew up among the spirit seekers. I soaked up every piece of knowledge I could find about them." He shakes his head, somewhat frustrated. "I graduated at the top of all my classes, not just fighting. I keep up with all the research results regarding spirits and constantly try to learn more. You've just started out."

Oh, so it's a pissing contest. Who knows more? Well, I can certainly beat him there. "My mum introduced me to spirits before I could talk. She taught me their ways, and we spent hours watching them. You know, actually studying them in their environment, not when they're hurt and torn in your tubes. They talk to me and I listen. You've learned about spirits. I've learned from them."

Wulf looks like he's about to throw his hands up. "How?" Shaking his head, he elaborates, "How can you be the only person in the entire world who knows them better? Spirit seekers have dealt with spirits for hundreds of years. Everyone I've ever met, read about, or listened to says the same thing. Everyone but you."

It's a sobering thought. Of course, I could claim my mother, who taught me all I know about spirits, or the other Travellers who valued spirits are just like me, but I know that they'd still be a minority. I believe in what I know with all my heart, but I understand all too well why he can't do the same.

And what if I'm wrong? What if what my mother told me is just some hippie nonsense? What if we Travellers are all just making it up? I mean, how can we be right if the experts in the world say something else?

"Because I know," I whisper. "I'm higher attuned to spirits than you." Wulf bristles, but I didn't say it to rub it in his face. Not today. "That must count for something."

The fragility of my voice at the end softens his face. He looks to the ground, breathing audibly for a few moments. When he lifts his head again, his voice is equally brittle. "I wish, Rika. I swear, I wish you were right. I wish we could just talk to them. That we could sort out our differences like that. But I've seen too much death. I've seen entire towns laid to waste. I've seen children dead in their mother's arms. I've seen my parents smashed at the bottom of a cliff." He shrugs almost helplessly, breathing heavily. "Maybe there once was a time when talking would have got us anywhere, but that time has long gone. And I can't risk anyone—not even you—on the off-chance you're right."

His honesty is breath-taking. All his arguments make sense. I understand completely where he's coming from. And yet... "I can't do it. I can't follow your lead."

Wulf swallows the bitter pill I've given him. He takes a moment to collect himself, then nods. "Let's agree to disagree for now." Another deep breath. "Shall we go and try Fisherman's Bastion again?"

I'm happy to push the parts we disagree on aside and concentrate on the things we do agree on. Together, we spend the entire day walking through Buda. Nothing speaks to me. There are places I remember, but they stay cold, like images you'd see in a sightseeing video. Remarkable sights each on their own but disjointed as a whole.

By the time we get back to the spirit seeker base, I'm exhausted. I had so many hopes for Budapest. I thought I just had to come here and pick up the threads I'd left. But the city is much larger than it is in my memory, and all my perceived distances are entirely off. Eszti lived in a plain house that doesn't even stick out in my memory. And unless I accidentally run into her tomorrow, I don't know how I'm ever going to find her.

Wulf tries to be optimistic, ensuring me that we'll try again, but I can hear in his voice that, as much as he wants me to succeed, he doesn't honestly believe I will. The probability is just too low.

"I'd like to stay outside a little longer," I say when we approach the trapdoor I've already come to hate.

"Do you want company?" Wulf asks in a peculiar mixture of kindness, wariness, and hope.

I shake my head. "No, I think I need some distance from humans. Just for a few moments. You go, do your work."

He gives me a crooked smile. "Will do. I'll see you later."

After making sure he's gone, I stroll away. It's early evening, and there are still a sizeable number of locals and tourists around. Since I don't have my staff with me, they don't pay me any more attention than anyone else. Still, I seek a spot by the water where I won't be seen from the path.

During the last few weeks of my life, I've had an overload of human interaction. After eight years of going through life primarily alone, it's a bit much. I miss the quiet moments where it was just me and nature, where I could centre myself and pick up the energy to get me through the next few days. Since our arrival here, we've been so busy I haven't even had a chance to talk to Aeola.

Now, the soft breeze bending the grass next to me tells me of her approach. She settles next to me, making the hairs on my right arm stand up in the wind. "You look sad," she notes.

And maybe I am. I look out over the river to my feet, towards the houses of Pest. A passing boat sends waves lapping onto the shore. "I just miss my mum. I miss her so very much."

I told Wulf that she might never have looked for me, but deep in my heart, I don't want to believe that. I can't. "We had such a close bond. Men may have come and gone, but I was her constant. We were a team." Me against the world just doesn't have the same ring to it.

"I never had a mum," Aeola tells me. "My father breathed us out after mingling with particular scents or winds."

I've never considered how sylphs procreate before, but I like it. Studying Aeola, I try to discern what the Erlking mingled with to create her. "You're a summer breeze." Warm in winter, cold in the summer.

Aeola glows. "Yes, I am." She snuggles against me, warming my right side. "What's it like to have a mum?"

I guess, growing up as a daughter of the Erlking, she never experienced parental care. Or at least, the Erlking doesn't strike me as a loving father. "A mum is someone who keeps you safe. Not just physically safe, but safe to be yourself. I could tell her anything, any problem, any worry, ask her any question." I have to take a deep breath. There are a lot of questions I would love to ask her now. "When I was sad, she'd hold me in her arms." I can feel the memory of her touch. "She loved me so much." Blinking away tears, I look at Aeola. "You know, she's that one person who will love you no matter what. Who truly, irrevocably loves you."

Suddenly, I feel Aeola's breeze all around me, but there's more to her. She loves me. Truly, irrevocably loves me.

My tears are falling now, but they're happy tears. "I love you, too," I whisper. "I love you, too."

13

We try again the next day. Last night, I described my mother to Aeola, trying to capture the distinct smell of her. She's flying through the city to look for that particular odour while Wulf and I take a look at the caves under Gellért Hill. They're even more stunning than my memory of them, but they don't lead us anywhere. Disappointed, I return with him to the island.

"When were you planning to go back?" I ask, knowing we can't stay here forever.

I can see in his eyes that he wants to tell me we won't leave until we found her, but when he opens his mouth, reason takes over. "Maybe in a week?"

That's a lot more generous than I could hope for. "Thanks."

"No worries. Things seem to be relaxed in Berlin," he informs me, reminding me of the reports he's received.

"Do you think they'll be all right?" When Wulf was in Naples, the spirit seekers were at a great loss. If they hadn't met me—not that I want to toot my own horn or something—Berlin may have suffered a great tragedy. As it was, the Central Station Disaster was still a tragedy, but it could've been a lot worse if the Erlking had got his way.

Wulf nods. "Yeah, unless there's a new spirit making trouble, it should be quiet for a while. As you said, the sylphs need to regroup. And soon it'll be summer, when they're not as active. I don't think we need to worry about them until the autumn storms."

I don't know if he did it on purpose, but I notice that he said *we.* Could there be a future waiting for me in Berlin?

The Hungarian spirit seekers are on their way out when we return. "Hey," Iván calls. "You guys want to join us at the baths?"

"The baths?" Wulf asks.

"Yeah, we're just heading to the Palatinus Strand Baths here on the island. It's nice having it so close. I'm sure we could lend you some swimwear and towels if you didn't bring any." Iván sounds a little as if he can't really believe anyone *wouldn't* bring their bathing suits to Budapest, a city that prides itself on its many thermal baths. It's said you haven't truly had a bath until you visit the Széchenyi Thermal Bath, a public thermal pool in an actual palace.

Naturally, I don't even own a bathing suit, and it wasn't on the list of things Camille thought to buy in the early months of spring. I look up at Wulf, waiting for his verdict. I notice József isn't part of the group, so he might prefer to stay with him instead. But Wulf nods. "If you could do that, yeah. I guess we could all use some relaxation."

"Alright. Let's get you two outfitted then." Iván skips down the stairs again.

Meanwhile, Rebeka sighs. "I'll see if I have something that fits you."

I blush at her words, glad that she's chosen to speak in Hungarian. Since she's blessed with a curvaceous figure, contrary to my skeletal features, I doubt she'll be successful.

I follow her to her room, and she goes through quite the assortment of bathing suits before throwing a green piece at me. "That should do," she announces. Judging from the rest of her collection, Rebeka's picked the one she was about to throw out. My assumption is proved right when she adds, "You can keep it."

"Thanks," I say, in what I hope was a polite tone.

Rebeka grimaces. "And try to keep away from my man, okay?"

So, that's her problem. I should've guessed. "Honestly?"

"I don't want you to read anything into his interest. Iván's just being nice." Which sounds like the opposite of her, though she looks more insecure right now than nasty.

I remember how he treated her during the nymph attack and allow myself to cut her some slack. "You don't need to worry about it. I'm not interested in him."

"You're with Wulf, right?" she asks, and sure enough, all malice has left her voice.

My face glows as the blood rushes to my head. "No. I mean... no, we're just..." What are we exactly? "Something."

Rebeka grins. "Well. Hopefully, he likes the bikini."

I'm sure my face is bright red as I follow her out of her room. Immediately, Rebeka hangs herself off Iván's arm, all but cooing at him.

Watching them, my thoughts return to what she said. I hadn't even considered that Iván's friendliness could be anything else. It's not that he's bad-looking but he's definitely not my type. Which is primarily due to me not having a type. It's definitely not Wulf, even though my brain keeps wondering what he looks like undressed.

This late, the Palatinus Strand Baths aren't very busy. Most tourists have already left for the day, leaving the locals to enjoy the pools and thermal bath. After Rebeka voiced her worries, I keep my distance from her and Iván, soaking in the opposite side of the bath. The bikini fits rather loosely, even with a couple of extra knots in the string, but as long as I don't go diving in the big pool, I should be okay. I definitely plan on leaving it behind when we leave Budapest.

The heat of the water crawls into my bones, wrapping me in a warm cocoon of pleasure. On the opposite side, Iván and Rebeka are kissing, while the other two spirit seekers who accompanied us are engaged in lively conversation. As for me, I enjoy the solitude.

That is, until I hear steps behind me. Raising my head, I look up at Wulf. Water pearls from his pale skin, running down the lines of his gluteus and calf muscles. I force my gaze to gloss over his trunks, but it gets stuck on his abs and chest before I can drag it up to his face. He's got the audacity to smirk. "Mind if I join you?"

"Sure, I mean, no, go ahead." *Gosh, Rika, get a grip on yourself.*

Still, my eyes return to trailing the muscles on his upper body as he slips into the hot water next to me. He's so close there's barely enough space for the water to flow between us. I draw up my knees and wrap my arms around them while he purrs in pleasure. "Oh, this is good."

It's the heat that makes my cheeks red. It has to be. My gaze wanders aimlessly to the trees on the far side. A safe view, if a boring one.

"Come on, relax a little," Wulf mutters.

Keeping my face turned away, I slowly lower my legs again. "I haven't really done this since I was a child." My Budapest days seem so far away.

"What, swimming?" he asks.

The indignation helps ease my neck muscles. "No! I've been swimming."

For a moment, Wulf is silent. Then he says, almost murmuring, "Relaxing, then?"

I want to tell him no, because that's not what I meant when I said it, but the question strikes a chord deep inside me, and I realise he's right. I haven't really relaxed since that fateful night eight years ago.

"I can't imagine what it's like to live on the streets," Wulf says when I keep quiet. "To have no place to go, always on the move, always hungry, cold…"

"You don't really have to go hungry in Berlin." Maybe I'm focusing on the wrong thing, but at least I'm talking. "There are so many food banks you don't need to worry about that." That is, once you get over yourself and ask for the food. It took me a few weeks to find the courage to enter one. I was too afraid someone would recognise me.

"Hmm." I can feel him shift next to me. "I guess that's why homeless people don't fall over themselves when you offer them food."

I cast him a glance. Wulf is leaning back, eyes closed. "It depends," I tell him. "If you just buy someone a dry piece of bread, then yeah, not much excitement. But it's not like you get used to quality food on the streets." Since he's not looking, I might as well steal some more glances at his chest.

"Makes sense," he answers lazily.

I leave him to relax and study my body instead. It really is rather skeletal. Not much on the chest, either. And let's not even start with the scars on both of my arms. Speaking of scars, there's quite a few on his body as well, probably from his fights with the spirits.

I can't really see them well, but there seems to be a big one across his back.

"What are you looking at?"

Shit! Why did he have to open his eyes now? Flustered, I stare straight across. "I was just... sorry."

"Just what?" Am I imagining it or is he taunting me?

"Just..." Before I can think how to answer him, something catches my eye. Not too far from Iván and Rebeka, a medium-sized salamander crawls through the grass. The spirit seeker commander can't see the spirit since Rebeka is still very much in his face.

It's been a while since I've seen a salamander that big. This one's as large as a beagle, but with a one-metre-long tail that swishes left and right behind them. Under their steps, steam rises in the air. Slowly, they move towards the water.

"Oh, come on." Wulf has followed my gaze and sees them as well.

Did I tell you that salamanders aren't the greatest fans of water? Not even warm water?

"Get out!" I shout at no one in particular, scrambling to my feet. In the meantime, the salamander deliberately dips their claws into the water.

Wulf is slow to rise, but he does and not a moment too late. Already, the temperature is rising.

I climb out of the water, giving Wulf a hand just as the first screams arise. People are scrambling to leave the pool, which is suddenly nearing boiling point. Iván and his spirit seekers have jumped out, though judging by their pained expression, it was a close call. Not everyone makes it in time. More than one person has lost consciousness in the water, and there's nothing anyone can do to save them from drowning. Not without getting boiled as well.

Some of those who made it outside are collapsing on the rim from sudden overheating and shock to their nervous system.

"What do we do?" I ask Wulf, only to find him gone.

I don't spot him again until he charges out of the changing rooms on the other side with his staff. Of course, he brought his weapon to an afternoon of relaxation. He runs to the salamander and stabs them in the back with his staff. Immediately, the spirit bursts into flames, forcing Wulf backwards. As he retreats, though, he draws the salamander away from the pool, leaving the water to cool again.

Instead of joining the fray, Iván slides back into the hot water and begins rescuing those he can get to. He must have given the other two spirit seekers a command because they sprint from the baths while Rebeka helps Iván, pulling people out. Others are starting to provide first aid to the ones who've collapsed.

As for me, I keep staring back and forth amid all that misery. There are children who were hurt. So many people have passed out. Some of whom might be dead. And Wulf is still fighting with the salamander.

Something is off about Wulf. Granted, there's no easy way to fight a ball of literal fire, but he keeps retreating, only occasionally stabbing at the flames, despite them coiling away from the spirit seeker wood. This isn't the calm, collected commander I saw during our fight against the nymph.

And then it hits me. He's afraid.

Wulf fought off salamanders for close to two months. He saw his fellow seekers killed in front of his eyes.

Suddenly, I'm no longer frozen to the spot. Instead, I sprint past the people on the ground, grab a bucket, and fill it with water from the cold pool on the other side. It's harder to move with a heavy bucket, but I hurry as much as possible until I'm close enough to the spirit to splash it.

That thing I said about salamanders not being fans of water? Well, this one really doesn't follow the rules. I manage to douse some flames, but they come back stronger than before, and they shoot straight at my face.

Before I can feel the heat, a wind picks up around my shoulders and blows the fire away. Aeola has come to my aid just in time.

"Are you all right?" she asks, and I nod, unwilling to draw Wulf's attention to her.

It's too late for that, though. He glances at her and frowns for a moment before turning back towards the salamander. "Let's lure it to the river," he says instead.

"Water doesn't help," I shout back over the hissing of the flames.

"Not even an entire river?"

I honestly don't know, so I shrug my shoulders. "Let's give it a try." In my mind, instead of a bedraggled salamander, I see the entire Danube in flames.

Wulf seems to have got over his fright. He's swinging his staff around with such speed and power it's mesmerising. He never actually strikes the salamander, but even the spirit seems to be impressed because they keep retreating now. Slowly, we move away from the baths towards the strand.

I've just decided that this works when the salamander charges Wulf with a speed I've only ever seen sylphs reach. Wulf has no chance other than to use his staff. The wood cuts through the flames and hits the salamander's jaw from below. The impact throws the spirit off course, but they turn back around with a vicious hiss.

Just then, the Budapest spirit seekers led by József arrive. The two with Iván must have alerted them when they went back for their staffs. Immediately, Wulf assumes command, bellowing positions to the five seekers. His eyes meet mine. "Get the trap ready."

Right, I guess that's my job now. Before I can ask which trap, since there's none hiding in my bikini, József throws one at me. I leave the fighting to the others and concentrate on feeling my way through the rings.

They look like a salamander, and they're definitely burning up like a salamander, but as with the nymph, there's something else in them. Something that doesn't belong there.

Water.

The trouble is water and fire are on opposite sides of the spirit-type ring. Putting it between them, like I did with the nymph gnome, will put me squarely into the sylph range, and that's something I'm definitely not seeing in this salamander. To stall for time, I arrange the second ring regarding their strength. While I'm doing that, I notice the lower ring doesn't really make sense. Where are the dryads? There are only symbols for the four main spirit types: nymph, gnome, salamander, and sylph, but there are many more spirits than those.

Come on, Rika, think. The others are already nearing the Danube shoreline.

Suddenly, I have an idea. Maybe the lower ring isn't as simple as setting a spirit type. Maybe spirit types rely on a physical property I have no idea about, a continuous range that translates to fire and water spirits at its opposite ends. Those symbols could just be a visual prompt to make things easier. But just because there's a sylph symbol on the outside of the ring, doesn't necessarily mean it only translates to sylphs. I don't know if any of this makes sense, but I decide to trust my gut.

I turn the ring as far towards the nymph symbol as I dare and let my magic work the third, fine-tuning ring. By the time I'm done, the spirit seekers have pressured the spirit to the shoreline. The salamander's tail whips through the water, leaving it boiling in its wake. If the Danube is cooling them down, they don't show any signs of it. But during their retreat, the salamander has been hit by several spirit seeker weapons, and that has slowed them down.

Time to try out the trap. My heart hammering in my chest, I activate it.

The suction is immediate. Flames shoot towards me, and I shut my eyes tight. Fortunately, I'm not engulfed by fire, but the metal under my hands grows warmer.

Carefully, I open one eye to check on the salamander. Their flames have been extinguished, exposing their scaly skin to the spirit seekers, who strike without mercy. Meanwhile, the trap grows hotter and hotter. Pain sears through my hands, and I all but drop it in the grass when the salamander starts dissolving and entering the trap. I don't know if it's the nymph part of them, but as they do, the metal cools ever so slightly. As soon as I've capped the trap again, I let it fall, turning to Aeola to relieve my hands.

She helps out for about ten seconds before she shies away. I hear long strides behind me. Turning around, I see Wulf approaching with a grim face. He crouches and picks up the trap.

His anger is so palpable I almost take a step back. "I caught them," I explain lamely.

He gets up, glowering at me. "Great, now get a trap ready for that sylph of yours."

Shit.

Not only does he know I smuggled her to Budapest, but he's angry as hell with me. It doesn't even matter that he saw Aeola defending me. For Wulf, she's still a sylph, and thus, not to be trusted. Naturally, Aeola took to the air before anyone could even try to capture her, but that doesn't stop Wulf from being angry, and dare I say, disappointed with me. He doesn't make a scene in front of the others, but I feel his wrath seeping into me like the heat from the salamander.

We don't return directly to the convent but check on the people in the bath. Emergency services have arrived, and the scene bustles with activity. It doesn't distract from all those people covered by white blankets, though. The sight makes my stomach twist around itself. I keep reminding myself what Wulf said to me yesterday. How he's seen so much death in his life.

It seems impossible that one spirit alone could have wrought such destruction, but I can't deny it. I've seen it happen.

Wulf wears a grim face as he strides through the crowd, surveying the place. We find Iván at the end of the pool, trying to tell the paramedics he doesn't need any medical help. The guy has blisters all over his bright red skin, and yet refuses to step into an ambulance. It's only after his brother rushes to his side and has a talk with him that he relents. As the ambulance pulls away, I spot Rebeka nearby, crying her eyes out.

The return to the Budapest base resembles a funeral march. Everyone's looking down. No one speaks.

At the trapdoor, József says aloud, "I'll take care of the press release."

Wulf puts a hand on his shoulder, his voice low. "He'll be fine."

József nods before descending into the darkness.

I want to stay outside, but one dark look from Wulf forces me to follow everyone else. We've barely reached the lower level when he grabs my arm and pulls me into the bedroom they've given him for the stay.

Before I can look around, he slams the door shut and snarls at me, "I told you to get rid of her."

"And I told you she's a friend." I latch onto his anger, drive its teeth deep into my skin to free my consciousness from the shock and terror I've felt ever since the water started boiling.

Wulf paces around the little room. "How could you bring her here? Did she follow you? Did you ask her to come?"

I'm sure as hell not going to tell him how I used a trap to transport her. He'll rip my head off, and I kind of like mine. "Does it matter?"

He keeps fuming. "Does it matter? Does it matter that you never listen to me? That you're insubordinate, in—"

"You're not my commander."

My quiet words stop him in his tracks. He looks at me coolly, as if to claim otherwise, but then his eyes harden. "Very well. This isn't a place for civilians, though."

Scoffing, I shake my head. "You know there's a range between commanding me and pretending I don't exist?" Sure, I could leave the base, stay in Budapest, and try to make a living here. There are certain advantages to the idea. I would have all the time in the world to search for my mother... and waste another eight years not getting anywhere.

"You need me."

Wulf grimaces. "Why would I?"

"Because you don't understand what's going on here." I don't yet either, but I want to find out. "The nymph and the salamander both went against their nature. There was too much gnome in the nymph and too much nymph in the salamander."

Wulf wants to interrupt me, but his mind has picked up my words, and he starts to listen instead.

"The dryads said there were several nymphs to watch out for. I believe we're far from done. Something has changed these spirits, and until we find out what it is, these horrible attacks won't stop."

His anger has been eroded by his professional interest. "What could change a spirit?"

"I don't know. But if I had to make a guess then the answer is usually human activity." The sylphs in Berlin had been so angry because of all the pollution in the air. I have to think of Aeola's creation. The Erlking mingled with a summer breeze, but what would happen if he'd mingled with a toxic fume instead? What kind of monster sylph would have been born then? Could that be what's been happening with these spirits? Are they the children of pollution? "If you want my civilian advice, I'd look for sites of pollution, maybe upriver."

Wulf has calmed to the point where he's breathing normally, but his dark eyes are still glaring at me. "Fine."

I glance at the door handle. "Can I go now?"

"Upstairs to your spirit friends?" he asks sharply. Yeah, I'm definitely not forgiven.

"Into my room," I answer acidly.

Wulf grunts, which I take as approval. I slip through the door and leave him to sort out his feelings about me.

14

Naturally, Wulf holds onto his grudge. Apparently, I wounded him with my "not-my-commander" line, and now he's treating me like some random person who just happens to be in the same place as him. At breakfast, I see him making plans with József, and then the two of them head outside with their staffs and traps. He doesn't look at me, nor tells me to stay put, so once I've finished eating, I set off to do my own thing. It's not like I would want Wulf to join me, sentimental promise or not.

After two days spent in Buda, I decide to try my luck on the Pest side. I take the tram down to the Central Market Hall, a place I remember only vaguely. I knew it was enormous, but I didn't quite expect it to be this big. The building is more than a hundred years old, but modern inside. There are so many stalls here, so much food, local and franchised, a thousand different scents in the air.

Aeola is accompanying me, and she looks dizzy after floating just a few metres into the hall. It smells of fruit and vegetables, of meat and spices, wine and perfume. Every food stand has a tasting plate to help you decide which exact piece of salami you want to buy, or which cheese fits your palate. In between the food stalls, racks of clothes and other trinkets hang. There's a stall that sells crockery and another that sells tourist memorabilia.

I walk through the stalls, slightly intimidated, trying my best to ignore the calls from the salespeople while not offending them. You could certainly get lost in here, drifting from one aisle to the other. I've already forgotten where the entrance lies, and suddenly it hits me.

I got lost here. The memories of it are being dragged out of the depths of my brain like a fish from the river.

"Mama? Mama?" I turn around, looking for her, but there are so many people, some busy, some taking their time. I get pressed into a food stall, and the old woman behind it lowers a plate of cheese to me.

"You want to try these, my dear?" she asks, but I shake my head and retreat deeper down the aisle.

My mum wanted to buy me new shoes, but I can't see any shoe stalls, just dresses, hats, and food stalls. So many food stalls. I find some stairs, but the overwhelming fish smell from downstairs makes me turn back.

There are too many people here and not enough air. Not for me, anyway. I push through the crowd and stumble down aisles until I see the light from outside.

Fewer people walk by outside, and the air is clearer. The smells of Central Market Hall still linger on my skin, but I can breathe again. I sit down next to the homeless guy with his dog and wait for my mum. We talk a little, though I can't remember about what, and after half an hour, I hear her worried tone.

"Rika!"

I'm barely back on my feet when she closes me into her arms, squeezing me so hard my chest aches. Then she kisses my face and repeatedly asks where I've been.

We're outside now, Aeola and I, at the corner where that man sat more than a decade ago. There's no one sitting there now, and my mum isn't here either. I can feel the touch of her hand as she took it to walk me home, but no matter which way I turn, the memory won't tell me which direction we went. I've hit yet another dead-end, and it's so frustrating I almost want to sit down in that old space and just wait there until my mum comes to find me.

Instead, I turn to face Aeola and have to laugh. It smells like she picked up every scent in the market hall, including the heavy fish smell from downstairs. Even funnier, she looks like she's in pure bliss.

"You okay?" I ask when I've calmed down, ignoring the strange looks people give me as I talk to the air, a smile on my face.

Aeola sways happily from side to side. "Best place ever!"

Once again, I have to laugh. "Well, don't go breathing baby sylphs on me. I don't think I could handle a paprika sylph, or whatever that powerful smell in your belly is."

Yep, people are definitely looking now. I grab a strand of Aeola and pull her with me like a really smelly kite. People seem to assume it's me who smells so horrendous and get out of my way, which suits me just fine. Nevertheless, we dip into an alleyway to escape their attention.

Just then, I catch sight of someone familiar. Rebeka and a man who's definitely *not* Iván step out the back of a house and towards a car. Like a gentleman, he opens the door for her first, then goes around the car and gets inside. Neither of them see me, much less Aeola.

"I wonder who that was." Not that it is any of my business who Rebeka sees in her time off.

Aeola floats closer. "I could follow them?"

For a moment, I consider the risks. Rebeka is a spirit seeker. I don't know her NAV, but it must be lower than that of the Varga brothers. She could definitely be over 300, but if so, not by much. My curiosity gets the better of me. "Okay but stay at a distance." As Aeola rises higher, I call after her, "and no baby-breathing."

I didn't know sylphs had tongues until Aeola sticks hers out at me. Then she swooshes down the street to follow the car.

While Aeola follows Rebeka and her lunch date, I keep walking the streets of Pest. As in Buda, all I gain from it is a pair of sore feet. At least I get myself reacquainted with the city. Streets connect with each other in my mind, and though they don't give me any clue as to where the house Eszti lived in is located, I get a much better feel for the city. So much so, I'm starting to think I've must have spent more time in Pest than Buda.

As the afternoon sun drops behind the houses, I make my way back to the island, taking a stroll through the garden. It's there that Aeola catches up with me again.

"And?" I greet her.

She settles around my shoulders, still wearing a couple of faint smells from the market hall. "They had lunch in a restaurant, and then he gave her a present."

Why do I even care about what Rebeka does? If she cheats on her boyfriend, that's their problem. Sure, it strikes me as heartless, especially after Iván was hurt in yesterday's heroics and considering how worried she was about him paying attention to me. I guess the reason I can't seem to let it go is because I feel sorry for the guy. He didn't join the fight, instead risking his health, and maybe even his life, to help other people, probably saving lives. I know technically all spirit seekers do that, but it takes a special person to forsake the glory of fighting a spirit to step into near-boiling water. Nevertheless, I don't have a stake in their relationship, and it feels wrong to act on an assumption.

"It was a miniature spirit seeker staff," Aeola explains.

"Wait. What?" I certainly didn't expect to hear that. "He gifted her a spirit seeker staff?"

Aeola nods. "Yeah, it was about half the size of a real one."

None of that makes any sense. Was it a weird present? Like, is it just a decorative item? Or does the staff truly work? But if so, then why only half-sized? That would turn it into a club, which doesn't sound very appealing in a fight, especially when you can't get close to a spirit.

I decide to file the information away for another time. If Rebeka were a little more approachable, I'd ask her, but I don't feel like she'd appreciate it if I stuck my nose in her business.

Aeola leaves me as soon as we get to the ruins. As usual, I have to take a deep breath before stepping through the trapdoor. I'll never understand how people can choose to live here.

I've hardly reached the open space when I hear a call. "Hey, Rika." Iván is back. "Care to join us for a minute?" I see bandages on his arms running into his sleeves.

He sits between his brother and Wulf. All three men wear severe expressions, but of course, Wulf beats them all with his massive frown and tight jaw.

Gingerly, I step in front of them, unsure whether I should take a chair or remain standing. Standing seems to be fine because Iván starts talking. "So, Wulf told us about your special relationship with the spirits."

Immediately, I look towards Wulf. "You told them?"

He doesn't even look ashamed. "They needed to be aware of the risks."

"Risks? I'm a risk now?" I can't believe this guy. What is this? Spring Cleaning, the second?

"Your relationship with spirits is," he answers drily, as only he can.

József clears his throat. "We should probably inform the SSA."

"Oh yeah, come on, rat me out." I cross my arms as I face József, but my gaze drifts back to Wulf. "I can't believe you'd do that after everything I told you."

He sighs deeply. "Rika, this has nothing to do with your history. We will not inform the SSA. I understand why you wouldn't want to attend the academy. Nevertheless, having you here is a risk."

"How so?" I can't for the life of me think how anything so far has been my fault, or Aeola's for that measure.

"You talked to a bunch of dryads and never told anyone that they were there, potentially leaving the headquarters at risk of an attack," he explains, in all seriousness.

I gasp. "Oh my gosh. When will you finally get it? Not every spirit is aggressive. Nor will they be." His stubbornness is infuriating. I can't believe he can even say that with a straight face.

"You don't know that!" he answers, no less sharply. "They might be peaceful right now and violent and destructive tomorrow. Didn't that salamander teach you anything? Didn't you see all these people it killed? Eight people died last night, two of them children! What do you say to that? That the spirit just wanted to take a bath?"

It's so grossly unfair of him I don't even know what to say. Throwing dead children in my face? Ridiculing the connection I have with Aeola? If Wulf ever had a single redeeming feature, it just went out the window. "You're being ridiculous."

"No, you are."

I'm starting to feel like I'm on trial. A trial I already lost before I was called to the stand. "You just can't handle anyone disagreeing with you. That you possibly aren't the—"

"Oh, stop it," József interrupts, annoyed. "I don't care about your relationship drama."

Wulf splutters. "Józsie, this isn't—"

"I don't care what it is. This doesn't get us anywhere." József waves his hand at me dismissively while looking at Wulf. "In my opinion, you should put her on a train back to Berlin as soon as possible."

"Could you stop that?" Iván asks. "You always tell everyone what they have to do. I'm the commander of this base. And I know you hate it, but I'm the one making the decisions."

Frustrated, József leans back and crosses his arms. "Well, then do it. You send her away."

"You're doing it again," Iván points out. Then he looks at me. "Rika, I don't want you to go. I want you to talk to the dryads again."

"What?" Wulf and I both say at the same time. I can't tell who's more surprised.

Iván nods. "Find out what they know about these eerily powerful spirits that don't fit any of our descriptions."

"You want her to talk to spirits?" Wulf asks. "We don't do that."

"*You* don't do that," Iván says pointedly. "You usually don't *need* to do that. But I don't have a special-issued staff or a 400-plus teammate to help me defend Budapest. If Rika is offering an alternative way, I'm not gonna scoff at it. I don't have that luxury. So, yes, I want her to talk to the dryads. And I want to come with you," Iván adds as he looks back at me. "If you don't mind."

I'm overwhelmed. I've been fighting for this chance to prove we can work with the spirits since I met the spirit seekers, and finally, I've got someone who'll listen. Who wants to learn. "Okay. But you need to leave your staff here."

That doesn't go down well with them. Wulf snorts, taking himself out of the conversation, while Iván looks worried. József warns his brother, "Don't. What if they turn on you?"

His brother's warning is probably what helps Iván make up his mind. "I'm putting myself in Rika's hands. She'll keep me safe."

It would be a big ask if there were any real danger. "I won't need to. The dryads aren't aggressive."

"There you go." He forces his brother to let him through and then slips an arm through mine, turning me away from the disproving looks we're getting. "Let's go."

As he leads me outside, I cast a glance at Wulf. He glowers in silence, staring daggers at Iván's back—or mine. I'm tempted to show my satisfaction that Iván chose my side, but I decide to push the ugly emotion away and concentrate on the task at hand instead.

We leave the convent and step out under the darkening sky. "Thanks for the support down there," I say quietly.

Iván gives me a half-hearted grin. "Anything for you, kedvesem." The endearing term throws me a little, but fortunately, he continues more seriously, "I meant what I said to Wulf. He won't understand. He's the legend, right? He only has to look at spirits, and they fall dead at his feet."

"Well..."

Iván stops me from accidentally defending Wulf's prowess. "I know he's really that good, but a lot of it is all that special attention they're giving him. I mean, he was at the academy longer than anyone I know. Every freaking lecturer toots his horn." He changes his voice. "Oh, let me tell you a story about Wulf Bachmann." According to his impression, all lecturers are well beyond their best years. "Then my brother can't stop gushing about him. And of course they give him one of the ancient staffs. Only the best for Wulf Bachmann. The rest of us can get in line for scraps."

"Are you still mad at your brother for inviting him?" I can't imagine what it would be like to constantly be compared to a single person. The hero worship of Wulf in the SSA is frightening, especially considering his approach towards spirits. If he's the future of the SSA, there might not be any spirits left in a few decades. No whole ones, at least.

Iván scoffs and says, "What do you think? One failure and we can't even discuss strategies. Nope, he calls his buddy Wulf to swoop in and save the day. Too bad Wulf can't be at every seeker base at once, or the world would be saved."

"Or doomed," I mutter.

"You're quite peculiar, you know?" He looks sideways at me. "I've never heard of anyone talking to spirits apart from those spirit-worshipping travelling people."

His comment hurts, even though I'm not surprised. Hungary might have the largest Roma population in all of Europe, but that doesn't mean they're well-liked or respected. I'm not super-keen on antagonising him, but I can't let it stand either. "You still haven't. I'm one of them."

"Are you now?" I hear the sudden distance in his voice. "That makes sense, I guess."

"You want to turn back?" I ask, not sure if I can handle his prejudice.

Iván shakes his head. "No. As I said, I'm desperate. Maybe you folks have it right and talking is the way. If your dryad fans tell us where to find those mega-spirits, I'm on board with whatever."

"Let's see." I'm not that confident they'll tell us anything at all.

We reach the section of the gardens where the trees grow. I put my hand on one of the ones I saw being used by a dryad last time and speak softly. "Please show yourself. We need your help." I let all my sincerity flow into the bark, hoping it'll be enough to draw them out.

The wind rustles through the leaves as we wait. I know Aeola must be somewhere nearby, cautiously watching us. Then the bark under my hand shifts. I step back to watch the dryad step into the open. One minute, she's just another knob in the tree. Next, she's standing on her own two roots, brushing a swath full of white poplar leaves from her face. She looks warily at Ivan, who raises his hands in response.

"We're just here to talk," he says.

Three other dryads step from their trees. They crane their long wooden necks to see what's going on. I smile at them in what I hope is encouragement. "Thanks for showing yourselves."

"Who are you?" The dryad from the tree I touched asks.

"I'm Rika. I'm a Traveller." I don't know if spirits know that term or if I've just confused them, but I hope we carry a bit of a reputation in the spirit world, one that tells them they can trust me. "This is Iván. What's your name?"

She bends the knuckles of her spindly fingers. "Szirom. What do you want?"

"We need your help," I repeat. "There are spirits along the Danube that feel wrong. Unnatural." I hope I'm not offending them.

"The nymphs," Szirom says.

I nod. "And the salamander."

"Yes, they were like the nymphs."

"So, it's mostly nymphs who are affected?" I ask. Talking to dryads can be quite straining. They are so sedentary that they rarely understand the need for action. But they see a lot, and they know even more, using their fungal networks.

Szirom sways in the wind, rustling her leaves. "Affected? You think something made them the way they are?"

"I don't know," I reply honestly. "I've just never felt any spirit like that. They are dangerous."

"So you want to catch them." The statement is full of accusation.

I shake my head quickly. "Not if we don't have to. I'd prefer to talk to them, understand what has been done to them. There might be a way to help them." I haven't thought about it yet, but if pollution is why these nymphs are so aggressive, then it's something we humans might be able to fix. Surely that would be more effective in the long run than battling them each time they decide to attack the city. "Do you know where they live?" Like the dryads, nymphs are impossible to find if they decide to sink into the water.

Szirom turns around to check with the other dryads. If they talk to each other, they do it secretly. At last, she says, "They're not from here."

"What does that mean?"

"They don't belong here," Szirom explains. "So we don't know anything about them."

It's a lie. I can feel that much, but I know what it means. They don't trust me—or us—enough to tell us more. "They're new to the area?" I want to confirm at least this little tidbit since it's essential. Of all the different spirits, sylphs and nymphs are the most likely to travel, but it's not done a lot. Salamanders certainly don't travel long distances.

Szirom nods, her sap-like eyes boring into me as if trying to tell me more than she does. "That's right. They don't belong here."

There are at least two possibilities here. The foreign spirits could have moved here from an area unbeknownst to humankind, at least in regard to its spirit population. In that case, the spirits here are just as wary of immigrants as most humans. Or the term "belonging" goes deeper, and these unknown spirits are upsetting the balance of an already fragile ecosystem.

Iván and I return to the base as the dryads are unwilling to tell us anything more. At the trapdoor, he shrugs. "It was a good try." What he really means to say is: *That was a waste of time.*

15

I've never really attempted proper research, but walking the streets won't help me figure out this problem. The spirits who attacked Budapest are different from any I've seen. They could be spirits from a place I don't know, but that doesn't explain why they feel so wrong to me. I pride myself in knowing what spirits are and what they want, and I couldn't read the nymph or the salamander at all. I couldn't tell what made the salamander so nymph-like, apart from their water affinity, but the nymph looked polluted to me.

So, I'm sitting in that stupid underground base with the daylight lamps on, hunched over a map of the greater Budapest region, looking for possible sites of pollution, such as factories or boat rental places that might flush their oils into the Danube. Reading in Hungarian makes my brain hurt. I must have learnt it when we still lived here, but I've forgotten most of it, and though I know the words when spoken, I can't always decipher them in writing. Hungarian is such an isolated language, none of my other languages can help me.

"What are you doing there?" The last person I want to see has crept up on me. Wulf stands behind me and peers over my shoulder.

What does he care? I thought he wasn't speaking to me. "Work-ing."

"You don't have a job," he says flatly.

Asshole! "Way to rub it in."

I can hear him taking a deep breath. "Are you gonna tell me?"

"Do I have to?" I swear if he's pulling the commander-card again, I'm gonna throw the map at him.

Instead of going away, Wulf takes a seat. "What are those circles?" He points to my scribbles on the map.

I glare at him, but apparently, he's here to stay. "Places I want to check out."

"You should get provisions then," he says in that same unaffected tone. "Some of those will take you a good day's walk."

Now I'm glaring at the map. How can all of this be so far away if it fits right on this map?

He shrugs casually. "You could use a car, of course, but I'm gonna guess you don't have a license or the money to rent one."

I fold my arms under my chest and turn to face him. "Do you want to make a dig at me for not being able to read a map or ridicule my lack of a well-fitting bikini while you're at it? I'm sure you can find some more things you don't like about me." Seriously, he's never been this offensive before.

Wulf sighs. "The only thing I don't like is how stubborn you are in terms of spirits and how blindly you trust them."

So that's the only thing, huh? "What do you want from me?"

"You said I'd need you." He points at my circles again. "Looks to me like you need me, or in other terms, that we have to work together if we want to get to the bottom of this."

"How do you know it's about the spirits and not places I remember from my time in Budapest?" I could be looking for my mum this way, after all.

With a snort, he explains, "Half of those circles are way outside of Budapest, so I doubt you remember them from your childhood." A sheepish grin fights its way across his face. "Besides, my internet search for potential polluters in the area came up with most of these spots, as well as some you missed."

"You know you could have led with that instead of being an asshole about it?" I say, folding the map.

He shrugs. "Sorry. It's not like I want to work with you," he says, not even attempting to mince his words. "But you were right. I need you and your attunement. Iván had the right idea. We need to use all tools available."

His words don't really endear him to me, so I reply with enough acid to spare, "Then I hope I'll be a useful tool to you."

Right now, Wulf is proving a bit more useful than me, because yes, he can drive a car and read maps. It's the most awkward car drive, though. He's concentrating on the road, and I never take my eyes off the landscape to my right. Gentle hills make up most of the area around Budapest. As with everywhere, there's barely a stretch not covered by houses or fields. Humanity has left its mark everywhere but in the most inaccessible areas.

Every time we pull up to one of the spots, Wulf tests the water, in addition to looking for obvious signs. I also hold my hand in the water, remembering the sliminess I felt when we first fought the nymph. So far, we've been unlucky. The water doesn't look any different from how it should be. Which, in itself, is a good thing.

After a while, Aeola joins us. She had to catch up with the car so is a bit late to the party. Naturally, Wulf's face darkens. "Seriously?"

"You got a problem?" I'm done catering to him. As if there weren't tangible tension between the two of them, I introduce them. "Aeola, this is *the* Wulf Bachmann, legendary spirit seeker. Wulf, this is Aeola, daughter of the Erlking."

He's been gritting his teeth ever since I said legendary. "What's she doing here?"

"She's helping," I say innocently. "You know we need to use all tools available."

You wouldn't believe how hard someone could bite down on their own teeth. If his tongue had been in the way, it would no longer be attached. With a grunt, Wulf turns away and returns to the car. Once there, he hollers, "Are you coming?"

"Aeola and I will walk a little downriver, see if we can find some spirits here," I say, making my voice sound insufferably cheery.

If aggravating Wulf is my plan, it's working like a treat. He slams the door shut and locks the car. Then he stares daggers at both of us and trails us with several metres to spare, which is perfectly fine with me.

"Why are you still working with him?" Aeola asks.

"Lack of choices," I answer truthfully. "He's the only one with spare time." I would've much rather done this with Iván, not because I'm into him, but because he responded positively to my abilities. Unfortunately, when I asked him this morning, he apologised and said he was busy, but encouraged me to do it anyway.

Aeola flows backwards, so she can keep an eye on Wulf. "He wanted to hurt me."

"I haven't forgotten, but he won't get another try. Not while I'm around," I promise, glancing at the staff he carries everywhere.

With a smile, she turns back to me. "You protected me back then."

"And I'll do it again and again."

The Danube flows steadily next to us. There's so much traffic on the river, I wonder how anything could be alive in there, much less a spirit. All that combustion waste from ships would be enough to turn off any living creature. But that kind of pollution has been going on for decades if not centuries, and it's never produced overpowered spirits before.

We get out of the industrial area and into a more natural environment, with trees by the river and long grass on the shoreline. Some water from the Danube pools in a little inlet before being swept back into the river. It's there we see our first proper nymphs.

Two of them sit on the shore, their long legs splashing in the water as they chat. When they see me approaching, they both jump headfirst into the water and vanish beneath the waves.

Nevertheless, I kneel at the same spot, waving off Wulf with his stupid staff in case it's him they fled from. "Don't be afraid," I tell the water. "I just want to talk."

The water stays still.

Wulf doesn't say a word either. He's leaning against a tree nearby, watching me with open mockery on his face. I realise I need to come up with results. Now.

I take off my shoes and roll up my pants to my knees. "Hold me, just in case," I whisper to Aeola, who immediately slings part of her body around my arm as she did back at the Central Station.

"Be careful," she says. Meanwhile, Wulf has lost his pseudo-relaxed stance and looks ready to jump into action at any given moment.

Weirdly enough, knowing he's getting ready to save me is the push I need to get over any second guessing and brave the water. Nothing spectacular happens at first. I wade deeper into the river until my rolled-up pants brush the surface. My fingers fin through the water as I call out to the nymphs. "I just want to ask you a question. I'm—"

Something slimy, like a water plant, wraps itself around my ankle. I want to step back, but by then the grip is inhumanely strong, and the ground is sucked away from me.

I can't help but let out a yelp. Aeola pulls against the nymphs, threatening to rip my arm out of its socket. Then Wulf is there, slinging one arm around my waist while stabbing downwards with his staff. In a fit of suicidal stupidity, I lunge forward to grab the staff before it can penetrate the surface.

"Rika!" he shouts, more than annoyed, but I keep hold of the staff until my knuckles turn white.

All this back and forth between the nymphs, Aeola, and Wulf has destabilised us so much that Wulf and I crash backwards into the riverbank when the nymphs suddenly let go. He half lands on my back, his arm still around my waist. In an instant, Wulf is up again, trying to stab the nymphs once more, but he's forgotten that I'm still holding onto his staff for dear life. He slips and crashes into the water once more. The impact drives a sharp pain through my hand, and I let go of the weapon with another yelp.

Alarmed, he looks back at me. "What is it?"

"You!" I shout, surprised at my own anger. "It's you."

Cradling my hand, I sit up in the water, which has completely soaked every piece of fabric I'm wearing. My eyes scan the river for a sign of the nymphs. Nothing.

"They're gone. You spooked them," I tell him, feeling all of yesterday's frustration well up again.

Wulf stares at me, looking absolutely horrified. "I spooked them? They were dragging you underwater!"

I know he's right, and yet those nymphs were our best chance. "Well, now they're gone, and they won't be back."

My words leave him utterly speechless. He kicks the water and then stomps out of it, leaving a trail of wetness behind him. Just perfect.

I pull myself backwards until I can sit on the grass. When I try to support myself with my right wrist, pain shoots through the joint. Great, now I'm wet *and* injured.

"Are you all right?" Aeola asks and blows her warm wind over my face and through my hair.

"I think I twisted my wrist." I look across the water, hoping that I'm wrong, and the nymphs decide to return. No such luck. "Let's go."

Wet clothes are the worst. If it weren't for Aeola, I'd be freezing by now. As it is, each step feels like I'm walking through mud. The fabric sticks to my skin, stretching whenever I move, while Aeola tries to blow me dry.

In front of me, Wulf is still stomping, hitting the ground with his staff with every step. I feel bad for him. He only wanted to help me, and instead of thanking him, I blamed him. With an enormous sigh, I resolve myself to make it up to him and hurry after him.

"What now?" he barks, long before I've reached him.

I close the distance between us. "I'm sorry. I totally overreacted there."

"Oh, did you?" It's not as sharp as it could be. Apparently, my apology has thrown him a little. "What you did was dangerous."

"I needed them to trust me," I try to explain. "Stepping into their territory gives them the advantage, which makes spirits more likely to be open for talk."

Wulf snorts. "Brilliant plan. And it worked splendidly." He wrings out the hem of his shirt, taking a moment to calm himself. "You could've at least warned me before jumping into the water."

"Sorry."

"Whatever." He gives up on his clothes. "I didn't bring any spare clothes."

Well, if that's his biggest problem right now, I'm out of the woods. "Maybe if you ask Aeola nicely, she could give you the blow dryer treatment." I'm already half-dry as it is.

Wulf stares at me as if I asked him to strip. Then his brows soften a little, and he snorts, irritated. "Are you for real?"

"It works for me."

He stops and turns to look at Aeola, clearly weighing his options. I can't help but smirk while he tries to build up his courage to ask a spirit for help. In the process, I spot something else. The river behind him is bulging.

I grab his arm and throw myself to the ground. He stumbles on top of me, and not a second later, a huge wave washes over us, destroying all Aeola's progress. The water washes the soil away from under us, creating a drag on our bodies. I take a panicked breath and raise my head to get a better look.

It's another of those polluted nymphs. Greedily, he reaches for us, and a second wave comes crashing down before either of us has a chance to process the attack. I brace myself for the water, when Aeola swoops in and blocks it, like a giant umbrella made of air.

Wulf gets to his knees and takes a moment to assess the situation, glancing back and forth between the ghastly nymph, Aeola, and the water clawing at the surrounding land. Then he makes a decision.

"Protect solely Rika, not me, when I tell you," he says to Aeola as he pulls himself up to stand.

That doesn't sound good. "What are you doing?"

He doesn't answer me, just grabs his staff tighter, eyes fixed on the nymph. When the nymph opens his mouth, exposing no less than three rows of long sharp teeth, I'm all for letting Wulf have a go first.

With an unearthly scream, the nymph rolls a third wave onto the shore, this time one twice as high as Wulf. Aeola struggles against the onslaught and I fear for her, but then Wulf jumps forward. "To Rika, now!"

Aeola springs back, enveloping me in a tight bubble of air and leaving Wulf to carry the brunt of the attack. His ancient staff only has to pass through a thin layer of water before connecting with the nymph's throat. Wulf's arms shake under the impact. The nymph retreats with another howl, abandoning control over the water. I catch a glimpse of blue sky before the mass of the wave crashes down on us.

Wulf is knocked to the ground. I squeeze my eyes shut, as if that helps anything. The pressure is immense for a few moments, then it weakens, and the water drains back into the Danube. I haven't even missed a single breath, thanks to Aeola.

As soon as the water retreats, I sit up, looking for that vicious nymph. If Wulf had a trap with him, it's been washed away. Fortunately, the nymph leaves us alone for now, and we can only hope we weakened him enough to no longer pose a danger to unsuspecting walkers.

"Wulf?"

He's moaning softly into the ground. With difficulty, he rolls himself onto his back. "Fucking nymphs."

For some reason, I start laughing. Nothing about this is in any way amusing. All three of us are aching, completely soaked, and exhausted. Yet I can't stop laughing.

After a while, Wulf joins in, though the pain makes him wince throughout. He's moaning and wheezing and laughing all at once.

"You know, you could've at least warned me before pulling such a stunt." Am I impressed by his mindless self-sacrifice? Yes. Was it scary? Hell yes.

"Sorry. My self-preservation skills are about as good as yours," he replies flatly.

There's a distinction, though. He did something heroic. I've just been stupid or naïve, if you want to be nice about it. I don't know whether the nymphs alerted their cousin or whether it was just an accident, but I feel bad about the entire trip.

Wulf pushes himself up on his elbows. "So, Rika. Reckon your sylph can give me that blow dryer treatment you promised?"

My immediate reaction is to tense up. Wulf's track record with spirits is abysmal, but I can't ignore the momentous step he's taken in asking me. Maybe Aeola stepping in front of him to preserve both of us has changed his attitude ever so slightly. I bite my lip, then try to test him. "You need to ask her, not me."

"Right." It's clear he'd hoped for an easy way out. Nevertheless, he turns his eyes upward to where Aeola hovers, just as strung up as I am. "Aeola, right?" Wulf takes a deep breath. "Thanks for saving us just now. I know you didn't have to do that, so thank you."

Oh, wow, looks like I'm getting a lot more than I bargained for.

"Would you please help us get our clothes dry?" He actually asked her. And so politely. I'm amazed.

Aeola settles on my shoulder, whispering in my ear, "Do you think it's safe?"

I make sure my eyes are locked with Wulf's. "It'll be safe for you."

Wulf understands immediately. He sits up straight and rolls out his hands. "You have nothing to fear from me."

"That's quite a change of heart," I say when Aeola blows the wind through us like an alpine foehn.

Wulf gets up to his feet and extends a hand to help me up. "Yeah, obviously, there are some exceptions."

16

Aeola's warm breeze doesn't dry our clothes completely. They're still damp by the time we get back to the car, but at least they're no longer dripping. I take off my shoes and socks and leave them in the back. Judging by Wulf's look, he wishes he could do the same, but driving barefoot is probably not a good idea.

Our drive back is distinctively different from the drive here. We've hardly pulled back out on the street when Wulf says, "I guess I owe you an apology."

"Is it my birthday today?" I ask and frown.

Wulf smirks. "Don't be like that. I know how to admit when I'm wrong."

"You're just not wrong most of the time." I know I should stop teasing him before he gets mad again.

"What if we're both right?" He looks at me for a second. "I still think most spirits are dangerous and can cause absolutely devastating catastrophes. But there are obviously exceptions to the rule, and maybe... maybe, some grief can be avoided if we can work with those."

When he says it like that, I can't keep myself from beaming at him.

Wulf glances at me and quickly returns his eyes to the road. "Say something."

"I think the exceptions are the rule, but otherwise, yeah, maybe, we both have a point." I mean, it's proven that some spirits can wreak havoc for literally everyone in their way, spirit or human. I wish there had been a way to talk down the Erlking, but he'd clearly been beyond that. "What made you change your mind? Apart from Aeola proving herself to you?"

He inhales deeply. "That's certainly the biggest part of it. I couldn't get Iván's words out of my mind. How he said that we don't have the luxury to turn down help from the spirits. I thought that if another commander could bring himself to let go of his reservations and attempt a novel approach, I should at least give it a chance."

"That's why you wanted to come along," I conclude softly.

"Yeah, that and what you said about polluted spirits struck a chord." He frowns slightly. "There's something severely wrong about these spirits."

"I know!" I exclaim, a little too excited. I'm just glad he picked it up, too. "They don't feel natural."

His frown deepens, but he nods. "Yeah, I think that's it. I've never heard of a polluted spirit, though. It's weird they're only appearing now."

"You mean when we've been polluting this Earth for over two hundred years?" I think about oil leaks in the ocean or the catastrophes of Fukushima and Chernobyl. If neither of those changed the spirits' essence, then what the hell is turning these around?

Wulf nods. "Yeah, pretty much. You said that the effects we have on natural places are what make spirits so angry. There have been natural disasters since the Earth was young. Pompeii just to start with. But extreme weather phenomena have increased in the last hundred and fifty years, so there definitely seems to be a correlation. Still, angry spirits I can deal with. These monster spirits are nothing like that."

I think of the Erlking and his powers, and rub the lightning scars on my arms in response. "No, they're nothing alike."

After another glance, Wulf clears his throat. "Why did you choose to help my team in Berlin? Against the spirits? Especially considering Aeola is the daughter of the Erlking."

"It's a long story."

"We're still on the road for another hour or so," he offers innocuously.

With a tiny smile on my lips, I start recounting how I met Aeola and how I accidentally faced the Erlking in such a way that he marked me with his words long before he marked me with these scars.

"He must've been afraid you'd ruin his plan," Wulf muses once I've finished, and we're already navigating the streets of Budapest.

To imagine a powerful spirit like that could be afraid of me is a stretch. I remember something else then. "You knew about him."

"No, that would have been reckless. I mean, leaving my team without a warning or protection would be unthinkable." He shakes his head. "No, I had an idea. At best, I was wondering whether it was possible that someone like the Erlking was staking a claim to Berlin."

"Well, I wonder if he was afraid of you, then." It makes sense to me. "You would've been able to see and stop him fairly quickly, probably, but you weren't there." I notice him tense up a little. "And according to Camille, things started as soon as you were gone."

Wulf rubs the wrist of his right hand, which he keeps on the wheel. "It would be freaky if he knew."

"Sylphs make awesome spies, right?" It comes out sharper than I intended it to. I guess I'm not entirely over his previous animosity.

Wulf winces. "They certainly have the ability to, even if not all... or even most do it."

"Thanks."

We take the exit from the Ápárd Bridge down onto Margaret Island. The car we're driving is actually József's, so we don't have to worry about bringing it back to some rental place. I look at the beautiful scenery on both sides of the island. It's like a green oasis between the cities of Buda and Pest.

The trees give way to a flower garden. Then it's forest again, or it should have been.

Instead, I see workers taking down the trees the dryads have claimed. Iván and his team are patrolling the area.

"No, no, no!" Panic overwhelms me as I try to open my passenger door, despite the fact Wulf is still driving.

Tyres screech as he pulls the car to a stop. "What are...?"

Whatever he wants to say to me, I don't wait for to hear. I jump out of the car, running at full speed towards the workers. "Stop that! You can't take the trees! You—"

Iván catches me before I throw myself onto a chainsaw in my panic. "They're already gone, Rika."

"What do you mean, they're gone? Their trees are right there!" I point to where a worker is cutting down Szirom's tree. Several others are already down. "Dryads need their trees. They..." The realisation hits me like another polluted wave from the nymph. I feel the blood drain from my face as I turn around in Iván's grip. "You caught them."

He doesn't even have to say it. I can see it in his eyes. No regret, just a *"What did you expect?"* kind of look.

"We were talking to them." I'm still struggling to believe it.

"And they told us everything they knew, or rather what they wanted us to know," he replies in a detached voice that doesn't really suit him.

I give my wrists a tug, and Iván lets go of me. Apparently, I'm no longer at risk of hurting myself. "How could you do that?"

"What happened here?" Wulf is striding over.

I spin around to him. "Did you know?" A terrible thought crosses my mind. Despite insisting we go together, he hadn't seemed enthusiastic this morning. "Did they ask you to distract me?"

"Nobody needed you to be distracted," Iván interjects, sounding annoyed. "Sure, it made things easier with you going on your little trip, but we don't exactly need the permission of a civilian."

Once again, I stare at him. I can't believe this friendly guy who invited me to Budapest and had been so selfless just days ago could be callous enough to catch the peaceful dryads I introduced him to last night. The very thought that I led him to them makes my stomach turn. I look at Wulf again. "Did you know?"

"I did not," he says at last, and it's enough to keep me breathing. "I get why he wouldn't want spirits living next to his base." *Oh gosh, no, stop talking. Please stop talking.* "But to betray them like that? That's quite something else." He actually looks disgusted with Iván.

The Hungarian commander snorts. "Seriously? I didn't betray shit. How can you betray a spirit? They're not human." My knees feel like jelly at this point. "You're gonna tell me that you would've left them alive after you knew where they were?"

"I wouldn't have talked to them," Wulf answers, and it's terribly noncommittal. But I can live with that. I already know how mercilessly he deals with spirits. But even he wouldn't have earned their trust only to slaughter them.

And that's what's happened here, I think as I turn to face the devastation. This is slaughter. Those trees were more than homes to the dryads. They were a part of them. And I betrayed them.

The shock of what's happened stays with me throughout the evening. The spirit seekers are celebrating as if they claimed some colossal victory. I can't even stomach a single bite. The only thing that keeps me from drowning in despair is Wulf's grim face. He's not joining in the jubilations. All his claims in the car weren't just empty talk.

Trouble starts when he retreats to his room. Suddenly, I feel all alone in a sea of enemies. Iván, who is so busy celebrating himself with shot after shot of pálinka, has betrayed my trust. It's even worse than when Fez did it to me—seriously, why does this keep happening to me? As a result of Fez's betrayal, I might have lost my life, but I didn't cause innocent spirits to be hurt and caught.

The weight of the betrayal I was made an accomplice of bears down on me with such force I want to throw up. No, this sickness goes so much deeper. I could spend the entire night in the bathroom and still not shed it.

Once again, they're toasting each other, and I can no longer stand being in the same room as them. I push away from the table and all but run outside, ignoring the rows of traps packed for shipment in the corridor. Stumbling on the last set of stairs, I fall to my knees on the sandy surface covering most of the ruins. Now there's a matching set of ruins next to them where a forest stood this morning.

Aeola comes down to dry my tears, but I shoo her away. I don't want the comfort. I haven't deserved it. Instead, I stumble to the forest grounds, now an eerily quiet ground of tree stumps.

"I'm so sorry," I say to the dead plants. "I'm so, so sorry. I didn't want this to happen. I—"

"It's not your fault," Aeola whispers, but I don't want to hear it.

I can't even discern which trees belong to which dryad anymore. There are no shapes to guide me, no leaves to whisper to me. Every tree I touch is still in shock. They haven't realised they're dead yet. I mourn each of them as if they were my own. It's the least I can do for the dryads who put their trust in me.

When I reach the last one, I'm exhausted. Aeola dries my tears, and this time, I let her. I sit down with my back against one of the stumps, the one I believe belonged to Szirom.

I don't know how long Aeola and I sit there in silence, but we're startled by the sound of the trapdoor sliding open. Rebeka comes out, huddling a total of three spirit traps under her arm. They're some of the traps containing the dryads. At first, I think that she wants to let them free, since the look on her face almost mirrors my dismay. My heart thumps faster at the thought, but then she walks down the road at a brisk pace.

"Let's follow her," I whisper to Aeola.

We keep our distance, just close enough so we don't lose her. Rebeka keeps up her pace as she traverses the island's length, gets on the bridge, and enters the subway station. I follow her, even though the descent via escalators is so insanely deep I feel the earth closing in on me. I've always hated the Budapest Metro. It might be the oldest metro system in continental Europe, but it's certainly the most oppressive.

We barely make it in time before the train arrives. Getting into the same wagon as Rebeka is a risk, but one we have to take if we don't want to miss her stop. At the moment she's too busy on her phone to notice anything. I would've expected her to be drunker after all the celebrations, but if she is, she doesn't show any sign.

She gets up just before the Aquincum stop, and I manage to follow her unseen. Few people get out at this time of night, so it's pure luck she never looks over her shoulder as we ascend back to the surface.

The old Roman settlement, predating the arrival of the Magyars, is located across the street. The museum is closed for the night, but that doesn't stop Rebeka from approaching the side gate. Apparently she has a key, because she slips through and threads her way through the ruins.

Okay, if her behaviour wasn't suspicious before, it definitely is now. Obviously, the spirit seekers really like their ruins, but why would she bring three traps that have been packaged for delivery to the SSA to Aquincum?

To find out the answer, I climb over the fence and follow her, trying my best not to make a single sound on the gravelly paths of the old Roman city. Rebeka reaches a modern house at the back of the ruins and steps through the door. From the looks of it, it's a research facility. I can't follow her inside, but I can see a single window alight and creep under it, hoping to be able to listen in. Fortunately, it's slightly ajar, and I hear Rebeka's knock on what I believe is the doorframe.

"I hope I'm not too late?" she says.

"Never for you." You'd think they're having an affair, but with the traps under her arm, I no longer believe that. "I heard you had a good day."

"Yeah, I guess so." She doesn't sound half as happy about it as I expected her to. "We caught enough dryads to spare, thanks to a little tip." My heart aches at her sharp words. "Most of them aren't too damaged."

"Well, I hope you brought me the good ones," he says.

Aeola looks absolutely horrified. She's risked floating up and takes a look inside.

Rebeka says, "Of course. The most powerful for you. Did you manage to get anything from that salamander?"

So, this isn't the first time this has happened.

"Not yet. I've managed to melt it down, but I'm struggling to join it with the metal. They're opposing each other like oil and water."

I bite into my hand to stifle a gasp and stop myself from retching. Did that guy really just say he *broke down* a spirit to use it on some metal object?

"Well, these are dryads, so it should be a lot easier to make something useful out of them," Rebeka explains. She sounds disgusted, but I doubt it's because of what this researcher does with spirits. "I need your payment upfront."

The rustling of paper money can be heard through the window. Not long after that, they say their goodbyes. The guy promises to share his results as soon as he obtains some. I slip around the corner of the house before Rebeka comes out to avoid running into her.

I don't follow her to the metro station. It's an hour-long walk from here back to Margaret Island, but I need at least that much time to process the horrible things I've learnt.

17

I've spent most of the night outside in Aeola's comforting embrace, but in the morning, I'm bursting to tell a human soul. Thus, I find myself slipping into Wulf's room the first chance I get.

"What are you doing?"

Boundaries are something that becomes very diffuse when you're living on the streets. Regular people don't sleep in their street clothes and generally assume they've got the privacy of their own room to change. In short, I've walked in on Wulf getting dressed for the day, and he's only halfway there.

I watch as the tips of his ears become even redder than my cheeks feel. The whole situation is ridiculous. Why am I even bothered—or why is he, for that matter—when I saw him in bathing shorts only a few days ago?

"I need to tell you something." For lack of a place to sit, I lean against the door.

Wulf snaps his belt closed, then bends forward to pick up a T-shirt. "It can't wait a second?"

"It has to be in private." I hope that explains why it has to be in this room.

"I see." He pulls the T-shirt over his head. "Is this about yesterday?" His dark eyes look at me, full of concern. "I'm so sorry. This is not how we normally deal with things."

Just the reminder is enough for my chest to tighten. "I know. Normally, you don't bother talking to them first."

Wulf comes closer, gently putting his hands on my elbows. "I mean it. I'm sorry." There's no further explanation. He's not trying to weasel his way out of this. He just looks into my eyes until the pressure around my chest eases.

I clear my throat, and he steps back to grab a fresh pair of socks. "That's not what I wanted to talk to you about," I say.

"What was it then?" He sits down on his bed.

"I saw Rebeka sell filled spirit traps to a researcher at Aquincum." He probably doesn't know what that is. "It's that old Roman settlement north of here. Anyway, apparently he does experiments on them. He melts down spirits." I notice Wulf's face has darkened severely.

"Are you sure that's what you saw?" It's like he's moving in slow motion now, almost forgetting how to put on his second sock.

"Well, I didn't see it happening, but I heard them talk about it." Gosh, I'm making a mess of this story. As I realise that I can't even convey the necessary details, my throat starts to swell and the pressure around my chest returns. "She's selling them to be experimented on. They already broke down the salamander."

Wulf gets up again, looking worried. "Okay, okay, we'll figure it out. Look!" He grabs his phone. "I'm actually good friends with someone working at the SSA warehouse. I'll text her to check what's been logged by Budapest since we arrived here, and if any spirits are missing, we'll know."

As I watch him writing the text, I feel a little better. At least he's taken immediate action. "Thanks."

"What's your plan for today?" he asks.

"Plan?"

Wulf puts his jacket on. "Well, we've got to get you out of here." It says something that even he knows I can't stand being down here. "How about we try to jog your memory again?"

I'm not really in the mood to walk the streets in another failed venture, but it beats staying at the convent. "Sure. Why not?"

"Did the vials ever tell you anything?" I ask Wulf as we interrupt our walk once again to test the waters of the Danube.

He raises the glass vial from the river and corks it. "They did, actually. I took some yesterday, and according to the data, the spirit energy is less up-river than it is in the city."

"Does that mean those polluted spirits are located in the city?" It's a chilly day, and I fold my arms under my chest to keep warm.

"It looks that way. Though it beats me why. Usually, the spirit energy is far more concentrated in rural areas." Wulf stows away the vial. "Problem is, we know that one got away, and I'm afraid it's not the only one left." Neither of us mentions the dryads who told us that more than one nymph was making trouble.

I can't really muster any enthusiasm for the hunt. I know that the polluted spirits pose a problem, but at the moment, I have such an aversion to the Budapest team, I don't want to help them.

"You look cold," Wulf notes, his voice surprisingly gentle. "What do you think about finding a restaurant and having one of those hearty soups? My treat."

"Goulash?" I'm not really in the mood for the fatty stew. My stomach reminds me that I haven't eaten anything since lunch yesterday, though. "I don't want to sit inside. But I've got an idea. Follow me."

I lead Wulf back through the streets. We keep walking until I spot a street vendor. "Have you ever had lángos?"

Wulf shakes his head. "I've seen it at a Christmas market but never tried it."

"Oh, then you're in for a treat." I love lángos. It's a very simple dough deep-fried in oil, which makes it golden-crusted and puffy. It's then basted with garlic oil, topped with sour cream and lots of grated cheese—like a mountain of grated cheese. That's the traditional way, at least. Nowadays, you can order it with all kinds of toppings. Since the traditional version is still the cheapest, and in my opinion the yummiest, I order two.

There's no way to eat lángos gracefully. The bread is so wide you can only bite into it and hope for the best, while smearing your mouth with sour cream and trying to stop the cheese from falling off. But my gosh, it's delicious, hot, and filling.

Ravenous, I all but devour mine. Despite that, Wulf finishes his sooner, claiming it's the best thing he's eaten here so far. When I laugh, he points at my face. "May I?"

Told you there's no way to eat this without getting messy. I hold still for Wulf to wipe off a blob of sour cream. His finger is just about to touch my face when a memory drifts to the surface.

Her face full of laugh wrinkles, Eszti leans over to me and dabs the cream from the corner of my mouth with an embroidered handkerchief. "Look at this mess, édes kicsikém."

I'm a little annoyed having to hold still as she wipes my face since I still have more than half of the delicious lángos in my hands to go. But once she's done, Eszti is happy to watch me eat, even though it takes ages for me to finish.

When I'm finally done, she wipes my face once more. Then she takes my hand, and we walk back home.

As I get up, I take Wulf's hand in mine. "Bear with me," I say, trying my hardest not to let go of the memory.

Take a left, walk past the little supermarket, then a turn to the right and past the park, the house at the corner. That's where she lives, the third floor on the right.

My finger hovers over the doorbell until it comes to rest next to one of the buttons. Juhász. Was that Eszti's last name? I can't remember.

"Is this it?" Wulf asks quietly. He hasn't said a word since I suddenly got up, respectfully letting me find my way.

I nod. "I think so." My finger is shaking. What if I'm wrong? What if I'm ringing some stranger's door and embarrass myself? What am I even supposed to say? *Remember me? You might be my grandmother?*

Suddenly, I feel Wulf's hand steadying mine. He looks at me and nods once. Then we turn our eyes back on the doorbell and Wulf's finger pushes down mine.

The person who opens the door upstairs is not Eszti. For one, he's a man, and second, he's not even close to her age. It's been how many years? Fifteen or more? In my memories, time stood still, but that's not reality. In reality, people move away. My mum and I did, so why not Eszti?

I'm so disappointed I don't even know what to say to his expectant face. He needs an answer fast or that door will be closed forever.

I start by repeating his polite greeting, then I swallow. Wulf gives me a little nudge, unable to help me out with his lacking grasp of the Hungarian language. This has to come from me. "Hi, uh, we were looking for an old woman named Eszti?"

Surprise softens the man's facial features. "My mother was called Eszti. She lived here until her death ten years ago." He studies me sceptically. "You know her from back then?"

Oh dear, it's even worse. Eszti never moved. She died.

"I think I lived with her for a while. My name's Rika." I bite my lip, waiting for his instant dismissal.

But the man's face lightens up. "I remember you. You were that little Traveller girl." He steps back and invites us inside. "Come on in. Let me get you some pálinka." As he walks into the flat, he says, "Oh, by the way, I'm Imre, Eszti's son. I took over the flat after... I'm sorry. I know you probably weren't expecting her to be dead."

I nod, still unable to process. Not only is that kind, loving woman of my memories long dead, but it also buries the chance that my mother checked in here. She wasn't even missing yet ten years ago.

The flat has changed surprisingly little. Some of the furniture has been updated—the ugly couch is gone—but it's still a similar set-up and style, with big cushy chairs a child could vanish in and a lace placemat running down the long wooden table. On a wood-panelled wall, painted plates are hung. A shelf shows a collection of unique, handmade vases, and I remember being allowed to pick one for the flowers we bought on our walk.

Imre asks us to sit down and busies himself in the tiny kitchen. Wulf puts his hand on mine and says in a low voice, "What's happening?"

I hear myself explaining that Eszti died and this is her son, but it sounds like someone else is speaking through my lips. As Imre serves us clear-coloured pálinka, I can't help but wonder about him. He seems to live alone here, judging by the lack of diversity in the shoes at the front. Was he the reason Eszti took me in for whatever time she did? Could he be my father? He's old enough for sure, and Eszti always called me "édes kicsikém", her sweet little one.

He finally sits down opposite us. "Look at you, all grown up. Marika, was it?"

"Yes, but everyone calls me Rika." Everyone but Eszti.

"I think I only saw you a couple of times when I visited home," Imre explains. "I was studying in Prague at that time." He regards me again. "She missed you."

The pálinka burns in my throat, but there's no way to refuse his hospitality. "She did?"

Imre nods, a sad smile on his face. "Oh yes, you were her sweet little girl. When I asked where you went, she told me that you can't keep the birds from flying south, and you can't keep the Travellers from moving around. But she missed you." He picks up his glass. "Her memories were failing her at the end, but she'd always ask me if I'd seen you. If you were coming back soon."

His words leave me with an enormous lump in my throat. I'd never even thought of Eszti all these years. As she said, Travellers move around. We meet people along the way, and if they're family, we return to them. But we don't follow a schedule, something that's hard to grasp for those settled in their homes.

"Do you... do you know why she took us in?" I can't ask him directly whether he's my father, that's for sure.

"Oh, gosh, I asked her that." He sets down his glass, looking sheepishly at me. "You know, when you're young, you're full of opinions. When I heard that my mother was taking care of some random child she found on the streets, I tried to talk her out of it." He's obviously feeling bad now. "She told me, 'Imre, when you see someone in need of help, you help.' Apparently, you begged her for money that winter when we had a thin sheet of ice on the Danube for a couple of days. Instead of giving you money, though, she took you and your mother in. Then in spring, your mother took you away again, but she brought you back in autumn for two or three years."

That sounds like my mother, always moving, never staying too long. "Did my mum ever come back?" I force myself to ask directly, "Did she come by in the last eight years?"

I'm not terribly surprised when Imre shakes his head. "No, not that I know of."

Wulf gently squeezes my hand. To be honest, I'd forgotten he was there. He hasn't understood a single word of what Imre told me, but he obviously gets my disappointment. This is not the news I'd hoped to hear. His presence gives me the strength to smile at Imre. "Thank you so much. I'm sorry we intruded. We'd better—"

"Drink your pálinka," Imre laughs.

The glass isn't even half-empty yet. "Right. Sorry." It's a good one, if I can say so with my limited experience. Very fruity.

"I might have something for you," Eszti's son says all of a sudden and gets up.

While Imre is gone, I fill Wulf in on what I've learnt.

"I'm so sorry, Rika," he says as Imre comes back with an old flat box that he puts on the table.

Inside are several old photo albums filled with primarily black and white images. There are a couple of coloured ones from more recent years, the years I lived with Eszti. Imre flicks through them until he finds a couple that he passes to me.

I've never owned photos before. My memories have all the pictures I need, or so I thought. Now, looking at these photographs of me, I wonder how I could've ever gone without. They're pictures of me, little Rika with her long, brown hair in two braids, and Eszti. There's one where I'm sat on her lap, and we're reading a book about the Magyars together. It's beautiful, like from another life, but the image that takes my breath away is the next.

It shows me in a beautiful dress, almost entirely white with blue stitching, puffy short arms, and a lacy skirt. I remember how much I loved this dress. I wore it until its hem rode up the middle of my thighs, and I couldn't possibly squeeze into it without tearing it. In this picture, the dress still falls to below my knees. My hair is braided and tied with long blue ribbons. And around my waist, two arms are holding me. My mother's face looks at the camera from where her chin is nestled against my neck.

She hasn't done her hair like mine. Instead, her blonde locks curl onto her shoulders. Her eyes are the same as mine, blue as the sky. And she's laughing, not just smiling, but outright laughing as she holds me tight.

"You can keep them if you want," Imre says.

I nod at him, unable to say anything.

18

Wulf leaves me time to process as we walk back to Margaret Island. I hold my treasured photos in my hands, flicking through the pictures every so often as I come to terms with the fact that the trace I was hoping to find went cold long ago; has never existed at all. If I want to find my mother, I'll need to go back to Berlin and pick up the ends there. I've got a picture of my mum now, which could help. Maybe Wulf could help me get access to places where an underaged homeless girl couldn't go.

"Thanks for coming with me," I mutter softly. He didn't have to do it, but he kept his promise.

Wulf glances at me, a gentle smile on his lips. "Don't worry about it. I'm glad we were able to find something at least." He looks at the pictures. "So, you're a brunette?"

The comment is so out of place it makes me chuckle. "Did you think I had natural blue hair?"

"It wouldn't have surprised me," Wulf says, playing along. "It's a bold colour."

I wonder how long he must've wanted to talk about my hair but didn't because he was too polite to do so. "Well, I generally consider myself bold."

"I agree."

We walk down the ramp to the island. I take a glance at him, shoulders hunched a little, hands in his pockets, the ever-present staff on his back. I wonder if he goes anywhere without it or if he always expects to be attacked. "Would you now?"

I love how his ears turn red when he's flustered. He probably got a lot of grief for it during school, but it's cute now. Wulf clears his throat, getting a bit caught up in the cough. "I—"

"You don't need to elaborate," I say, letting him off the hook with a laugh. "I'll just take it, maybe frame it, and put it up in my room at the citadel." I mimic the picture by waving my left hand. "'I consider Rika a bold woman,' quote by Wulf Bachmann." I giggle.

"I never said that," Wulf protests, but he can't help the grin slipping onto his face. "I said 'I agree'."

Playfully, I frown at him. "But that's a shitty quote. You sure you want to be immortalised like that?"

Instead of answering, he bumps his elbow against my arm. He's still grinning when he gets a text. As he looks at his phone, though, I see the grin slipping off.

"What is it?" I try not to crane my neck and check for myself. You know, being polite and all.

He puts the phone away, back to a frown. "That was Carmen, my friend at the SSA office. You're right. Budapest never logged the salamander, and only eight of the eleven dryads they caught yesterday. I assume Rebeka is the one responsible for the shipments. She's their trapper, so there's the possibility it's her side hustle."

We don't discuss it any further as we go down the stairs. Once we've found the others, Wulf asks the Varga brothers to speak with them alone, and Iván leads us into an adjacent room containing an electronic map of Budapest and several spare staffs. As he closes the door behind him, I notice a particularly short staff among the others, and a queasiness settles over me.

Wulf starts by showing Iván and József the records of the missing shipments. "As you can see, several spirits have been unaccounted for in the logged trap shipments. Last night, Rika followed Rebeka to... What was that place again?"

"Aquincum. She met with someone from the museum there. Or lab. I didn't get a proper view," I explain.

"Right." Wulf nods to me before he continues, "It looks like Rebeka is selling off spirits to civilian researchers, which, as you know, is a gross violation of the SSA code of conduct."

The brothers stare at him, caught in surprise. Then Iván clears his throat. "I take full responsibility for this... digression. Rebeka acted on my command."

"What?" József looks at him, aghast. "Have you gone mad? You can't sell spirits like that."

Wulf crosses his arms, his frown deepening. "I need to report this to the office." He's not happy about it. Iván's confession clearly caught him off-guard, and as usual, he hides behind regulations and proper conduct to deal with it.

Iván scoffs. "Of course you do. Gosh, you're such a rule-stickler. That's what you get when you're a German, I guess."

"Iván, he's right," József says. "This isn't just some stupid prank. Do you know how dangerous it is to give away spirits to untrained personnel? That researcher is lucky to be alive."

"Oh, shut it, Józsie. I don't need you to lecture me." Iván shakes his head. There's still so much frustration he's keeping in. "Go ahead, Wulf, report me! Then my brother gets the position he's always wanted, and everyone's happy."

I can see how overwhelming the direct confrontation is for Wulf. He's a good man, not a snitch, but he believes in those rules with all his heart.

József has less patience with his brother. "I don't want your position!"

"Yeah, right."

"Seriously," József is angry now. "I was happy for you when you got it. Yes, it's weird. I would've preferred to work in another team..."

"Like in Berlin," Iván mocks.

József's face darkens. "You always pull this bullshit. What is this, Iván? A stunt for attention? What's the money for? Parties? Drugs?"

Wulf looks like he'd like to be anywhere but here as we watch this brotherly feud play out. However, he doesn't step in, leaving it to József to bear down on his little brother.

Iván scoffs again. "You want to know what I do with the money?" He takes a few steps, fuming. "I use it to update our equipment. I use it to make Budapest just a little bit safer."

"If you needed extra provisions, there are official channels to go through," Wulf starts to explain, still working his way through the issue at hand.

"You think I didn't do that?" Iván laughs, before mimicking, "*I'm sorry, but we can't extend your budget this year. Or the year before or any given year, as a matter of fact.*" With each word, he becomes louder. "You don't get it, do you, Wulf? The SSA isn't some big wish-fulfilment machine for the rest of us."

I'm contemplating whether I can slip out of the room without being noticed. Clearly, there are some high-level issues here that I shouldn't be privy to.

Wulf shakes his head. "I'm sorry if you think your headquarters is underfunded. That's an issue you should raise with the officials, but you can't sell spirits to civilians to make up for it."

"He's paying us for the privilege to work on them. We get the results, not that it's been worth it so far." Iván picks up the miniature staff and throws it on the table. "Useless shit."

József steps forward and runs his hand over the staff. "You're commissioning him to build weapons?"

Cockily, Iván leans against the table, taunting Wulf to throw a fit. "There aren't enough ancient staffs to go around. There's surely no way Budapest will end up with one. So, what if we try to do our own research? If we sent them off to Rome, any successful weapon would go west, I'm sure. We get to catch the powerful spirits, and you get the powerful weapons. Doesn't sound fair to me."

I feel like a stone has just dropped into my stomach.

"Again," Wulf stresses, slowly losing his patience, "this is an issue you should raise through the official channels."

"Oh, come on," József says, suddenly taking his brother's side. "They won't change anything. Yes, what Iván did is wrong, but I get where he's coming from. The distribution of funds and weapons is grossly unfair."

"Always goes west, never east," Iván adds bitterly.

Now having to deal with both Varga brothers, Wulf shifts his feet. Usually, he thinks quicker on his feet, but this time, he's weirdly stoic about it. Even I understand that there's something fundamentally wrong with an unequal distribution of funds.

"I'm sorry to hear that," he says. "I really am. If you want, I'll lend my voice to the complaints. Nevertheless, the risk in dealing with spirits is too high."

"The risk is that people are dying!" Iván shouts. "People are dying, and they're dying on my watch! And there's nothing I can do about it, not because I'm not a good fighter or as well-educated as you, but because I don't have access to the proper equipment. You come here and think you're such a big hero, when the only reason for your success is that ancient staff in your hands. Oh, look at you, cutting straight through an A-class spirit wave."

I guess I completely misjudged what the battle staffs can do and what they can't. Which is weird because I damaged the Erlking with Daisy's certainly-not-SSA-issued staff. Iván seems to think Wulf's success against the polluted spirits largely hinges on the ancient staff he received as a reward for stopping a volcanic eruption. And neither of the others moves to correct him.

Wulf is at the point of growling now. "You can't blame me for your failures."

"I'm blaming the system," Iván clarifies. "It's just that the system is so far up your ass, it's hard to separate the two of you."

"Sorry, Wulf," József says, "but I have to side with Iván on this. The system is skewed towards the big money-makers, and we all know Germany is the biggest of them. I guess it doesn't hurt to be raised by the Vallescos, either," he adds in a murmur. Wulf is staring at him, but József seems oblivious. "What I did wasn't too different from Iván's approach. Instead of asking for funds, I asked for the one getting the funds. I couldn't see how we could possibly stand against those powerful spirits with the means we have."

Wulf looks from one brother to the other, his jaw so clenched I fear for his bones. At last, he speaks. "So, one of you uses his personal connections to order reinforcements, while the other blames me for having similar connections." As József lowers his eyes, Wulf looks to Iván. "And you issue your own spirit weapon experiments by selling the SSA's secrets."

Iván nods. "As I said, go ahead and report us. It's not like it can get any worse."

"I have to," Wulf says, his voice distant and detached.

József steps in. "Don't do it. Please. We'll get those spirits back. I mean those that haven't been used yet. We'll stop the arrangement, pay that researcher off, draw up an NDA. Let us take care of it, and maybe we'll get lucky and receive better weapons in the future."

"You know I can't look away and pretend it never happened." Wulf takes a deep breath. This doesn't seem to be easy for him.

Iván looks ready to murder him while József shakes his head in disappointment. "I thought our friendship was worth more than that."

It's the wrong road to take with Wulf. Even I could have called that after this brief exchange about familial allegiances. His dark eyes are blazing. "You've abused our friendship, and now you're doing it again. I normally like you, Józsie, but I won't have you making me an accomplice to this travesty. You don't get to use me like that."

"Guess we're not really friends then," József replies coldly.

I'm usually not rule-abiding and think the German obsession with bureaucracy is comical at best and annoying at its worst, but I'm entirely on Wulf's side here. "He's turning spirits into weapons, for fuck's sake!"

They'd genuinely forgotten about me until then. József glares at me. "So?"

"So?" My gaze shoots from him to Wulf, who's taking another deep breath, to Iván, who shakes his head in amusement. "That's disgusting!"

József snorts at me, "Hey, Wulf, why don't you educate your little girlfriend a bit?"

"She's not my girlfriend," Wulf says with a face like stone. Yes, that friendship is well and truly over. Then he grabs my arm and opens the door. "Come on, you shouldn't even be in here."

He's so distant it sends a chill down my back. The Varga brothers don't get another look from him, and he drags me all the way to his room.

"You're going to report them to the SSA, right?"

Wulf closes the door behind him and takes a deep breath. "I will, but not for that." He takes his staff off his back and puts it into my hands. "Feel it."

Confused, I run my fingers over the wood. As before, the staff seems to come alive under my fingertips. "I don't understand." My mind doesn't want to understand.

Wulf sits down next to me. "All spirit seeker weapons are made from spirits. It's the only thing that can hurt them. Take a gun, and you might as well try to shoot water. Spirit beats spirit."

The staff in my hands suddenly feels like it's turned into a snake. I drop it on the ground, recoiling from it. "No."

"Yes." Wulf's voice is merciless. "The first spirit seekers were much better at it than us, though. We know that they used dryad wood, which is why I assume Iván leaped at the chance to secure a bunch of dryads."

Don't defend him, I want to say, but my tongue is a heavy, furry stranger in my mouth.

"All the others... There have been experiments with using salamanders in forging, but it doesn't work. Did you never wonder why such a high-profile organisation issues their seekers' wooden staffs instead of modern weaponry? There's a trick the old spirit seekers knew, but it's lost to us. And so far, nobody has been able to replicate it."

I bend down like I'm in a trance and pick the staff back up. Once again, I look at it, truly see it. When I finally do, a whimper slips from my throat. "It's not dryad wood. It's part of a dryad," I hear myself saying. Everything clicks into place, but the sound of it makes me sick to the stomach. "You can't replicate it because your armourers don't see it."

Wulf cocks his head. "They don't see what?"

My index finger runs along a groove in the wood, a rune of some sort that accentuates an old muscle of the dryad. "They don't see the spirit." I force myself to speak, though all I want to do is to tear my eyes out and scream. There's no way to unsee this. "The dryad in your staff is whole. When you make those standard staffs, you take away all that makes them who they are. It's like trying to capture a spirit by only using the first two rings." I shudder at the thought of those smooth, polished staffs the spirit seeker use for fighting. Not staffs, but mutilated dryads.

"If you're right..." Wulf takes the staff from me to run his own hands along the shaft. "Rika, you could've advanced our weapon-making by light-years. We just need to get some dryads and—"

I slap him so hard his eyes fly wide open. His head jerks in my direction. Tears are burning in my eyes as I try to stare him down. "Listen to yourself!"

"Rika..."

"Stop it!" My head is shaking under the force of my own anger. I have to get some distance between us. "This is unspeakably cruel, even for your kind." I retreat to the far wall.

His concerned look turns into a glower. "My kind? It's yours too."

"Never!" I struggle to hold myself up, my knees as weak as jelly. "I will never set foot in an organisation that supports such cruelty. That's based on such a disgusting practice."

Slowly, Wulf gets to his feet. He puts the staff on his bed beside him. "What we do ensures the survival of the human race. You might not like our methods, but they've been proven time and time again."

"Oh, it's that *'the end justifies all means'* speech." My wrath keeps spilling out of me. It's like my entire mouth is filled with bile. "You're such a hypocrite, Wulf! You've eaten up their bullshit all your life. Who cares for a few spirits, right? We're saving the world."

His face grows darker. "Well, if you have a better idea, go ahead. I want to hear it. Tell me how we can fend off the next typhoon that rips a million houses apart. Tell me how we can protect the thousands of people dying in mega earthquakes every couple of years! Tell me how we should have dealt with that salamander that boiled people alive!"

"There have to be other ways." My voice is shaking like the rest of my body now. There has to be at least one. "We can talk with them, we can—"

"Don't kid yourself!" Wulf interrupts me. "Just because you know one sylph that's not trying to drop you down a cliff doesn't mean you can negotiate with a volcanic eruption or a forest fire. You can't talk down a flood. You can't stop a landslide by asking nicely."

"Did you ever try?" I hurl back at him. "Did you ever consider not chopping up spirits and turning them against their own kind?

How would you feel, huh? How would you feel if some spirit cut off your mother's arm to come at you? You don't think they've got an excellent reason to be angry? Don't you..."

Wulf's face has turned ashen. He raises his arm and points toward the door. "Get out!" The vein in his neck is pulsing wildly.

No, I'm not going to stand down now. "Wulf, we take away their living spaces, we pollute their environment, and then we chop them to pieces? Experiment on them?"

"Get out!" he snarls.

"This can't—"

I don't get any further because, at this point, Wulf's fingers wrap themselves around my upper arm, fingers digging into my skin as he drags me to his door. Once there, he almost rips it out of its hinges and pushes me out. "Get out of my sight!" Then he slams the door shut with such force, that a crack appears at the top.

I feel like he's punched me in the face, and my stomach, and my chest. My mind circles around our argument, faster and faster. He was on my side just minutes ago. But he isn't. He never was. The things standing between us aren't just a difference of opinions. We're fundamentally opposed. No compromise will ever be able to bridge the chasm between us, and I knew that. I knew it from the day I stared into his eyes as he tried to go after Aeola. Without hesitation, without even considering asking first. I thought I could change his mind. That eventually, he'd have to see my truth. I thought he did after yesterday, but I was kidding myself. I let myself be blinded by his good looks, his empathy, and, most importantly, by his stupid promise.

Now I know I won't ever be able to look him in the eye and not flinch at the horrors he's so willingly part of. I can't stay here, where they sell spirits to be turned into weapons, to destroy even more spirits.

Blinded by my conclusions, I return to my room. I pack all the essentials, which takes me fewer than ten minutes, and then I'm out. I don't know how I'll get back to Berlin yet, but I'll find a way. I'll walk if I have to. I survived eight years on the streets; I can do it again. Anything will be better than this.

19

I can't run away from this. There's no going back to my aimless wandering on the streets. Sure, I could pride myself in the genuine spirit relationships I would build and how I'm doing the right thing. But running away isn't the right thing. It's the cowardly thing. After learning what I have, I'll have to spread the word. I have to get my story out. I have to find ways to stop the cruelties. I have to try, at least.

As I walk out of my room, my gaze falls on the spirit traps in the hallway. They haven't been shipped yet. Looking over my shoulder, I check whether anyone's paying attention to me. There's no one in sight. I make a quick decision and grab the box. Then I get the hell out of there before anyone can stop me.

Outside, I look over my shoulder until I'm well past the recently deforested area. Under the trees on the far side of the island, I kneel and take out the traps. As Leon taught me, I deactivate them and open all of them. As I do so, Aeola floats down to me.

"What are you doing?"

"I'm freeing the dryads." Anxiously, I watch the opened traps. No spirits have materialised yet.

Aeola comes closer. "You can do that? Won't you get in trouble?"

"Let me care about that." My mind pulls up a fantasy of breaking into shipments for the SSA and freeing all the spirits the seekers have captured. "Come on, you need to get to safety," I tell the dryads. The spirit seekers will never be able to convince the city council to take all the trees on Margaret Island down. At least I hope they don't have that much of an influence.

Very slowly, the spirits creep into the open air. It tears my heart apart to see how broken some of them are. I know they'll recover in time, but it'll take many years, decades even.

My tears fall on the grass. "I'm so sorry. I didn't know any better." I know that my apology will never be good enough, but it's all I have to offer.

Aeola gently blows my tears away. "This isn't your fault, Rika."

"I feel like it is. I never wanted to hurt anyone." There are three dryads I won't be able to release back into the wild. They'll never be allowed to recover. A shudder runs through me as I remember the little salamander I once caught with Camille. I wanted to believe her when she told me he'd be sent to Iceland. But it was Miriam's reaction that told me the truth. *A perfect spirit?* She was so excited someone would examine it... and then try to turn it into a weapon.

My stomach can't take it anymore. It brings up the lángos and the pálinka I consumed what feels like years ago.

As I rid myself of my lunch, retching and crying all at once, I feel something soft brush my cheek. Looking up, I see Szirom. She's not the same as before. There are deep scars around her face, and half her leaves are missing. The left side of her is charred. And yet she looks at me with gentle amber eyes.

"I'm sorry," I whisper, then wipe my mouth.

Once again, Szirom's leaves brush my cheek. "I know," the spirit says in a voice that sounds hollow. She's lost so much of herself.

"It wasn't you who did this." She regards my tears on her leaves. "You're not like them. You actually care." She lets the tear drop to the ground, her gaze intensifying. "Do you still want to know about the nymphs?"

I hadn't even thought about them yet. What are they but another group of spirits that have been altered by human greed? "If there's a way to save them, I need to try. I want to talk to them." I might as well start with them if I want to expose the SSA for its wrongdoings.

"They nest in the Danube inlet on Óbuda." Szirom retreats a little. "But be careful. They are angry. Very angry."

I know by now that the anger of spirits is often justified. "Thank you."

It's late at night when Aeola and I reach the long Danube inlet on Óbuda Island. Since its mouth is located downriver, the water inside is like a lake. It doesn't flow but just sits there. I know why the nymphs have chosen it as their nesting spot. It feels as artificial and wrong as they do.

I leave my backpack with the precious pictures near the path and approach the black water, arms raised. "Don't slip away. I just want to talk. I know you're here." Softening my voice, I add, "I want to help."

Unlike the nymphs further upriver, these ones don't shy away from me. Instead, three of them float to the surface. My stomach turns at the thought of what power these three could wield together. But that's okay. Just because they're powerful doesn't mean they'll use it for destruction.

"I'm Rika," I tell them. "I'm a Traveller. We care for spirits."

All three nymphs look like something left too long in the water. Their skin is blotchy and bloated. Oil shimmers in their veins. Their eyes are swollen. I'm kind of glad that they're water spirits and not earth spirits, or I'd probably see maggots creeping through their flesh.

"Do you now?" one of them asks, her voice a slimy liquid that seeps into my ears.

"I know someone did this to you," I tell them, sounding much braver than I feel. Aeola presses herself against me, carrying a waft of the same fear I feel deep in my bones.

A fourth nymph appears from further downriver. "You did this." I know this one. It's the nymph who attacked Wulf and me the day before. My feet feel like jelly now.

"No, it wasn't me."

"You're with them. You're one of them," the nymph says, causing the water of the inlet to lap at my feet. I can see where Wulf hit him in the face. Something like pus is flowing out of that hole, washing down his face before it gets swept up in his body again.

I shake my head, trying not to grimace in disgust. "No, I'm not. I thought I was, but they're wrong. They're wrong about you, and what they do to you is... It's unspeakable."

"Do you now?" the slimy nymph repeats like a broken record.

Another one seems to be more whole, since she actually manages to string coherent sentences together. "They did this to us. They turned us into these abominations of ourselves, and we hate them. We hate them."

The formerly still water is getting choppier by the minute. Hopefully, the raised energy won't alert the spirit seekers. "I know.

I hate them too." Clenching my fists, I speak on, "But we can do something about it."

"Yes," the nymph on the far right says, her voice gleeful. "Do something about it."

Her enthusiasm makes me queasy. The last thing I want is to provoke another battle and get someone else hurt. "I will. There are avenues we can take." My mind is moving fast, going through all the different possibilities of how I could make people aware of their plight. "Maybe I could get a news reporter to cover your story." And they'd likely call me crazy for claiming I can talk to the nymphs. "We need to get other Travellers involved." Maybe together, we can change the public's perception bit by bit. *Because that worked so well for us all these centuries,* a snarky voice inside of me says.

"Yes, get others," the nymph on the right says.

They are coming closer now. Two of them are stepping onto land. I have to fight my instincts with everything I have to remain where I am.

Aeola whispers, "Let's leave. Please." She floats a little higher.

One of the nymphs comes closer. Each step ends in a reeking puddle until she stands right before me, teeth bared. "Are you gonna help us take revenge on them?" Her long, webbed fingers run over my temples, leaving behind gooey streaks.

My heart is hammering in my throat. Her rotten smell is over-powering. The touch of her is so disgusting the bile rises from my stomach. Foul water seeps under my collar, trickling down my back. My breath catches in my throat.

"I'll help you," I whisper, returning the look from her bottomless eyes.

Her hands move to my hips, leaving wet patches in their wake. "Good."

Before I can even begin to understand, the nymph grabs hold of me and throws me into the water.

20

Cold waves crash over my head. I clamp my mouth shut and try to swim to the surface. I've just managed to break through when something wraps itself around my thigh and pulls me back into the deep. I know somewhere in my mind that this inlet can't be terribly deep, but gosh, it's dark.

Panic makes it impossible to think. I thrash around, unable to tell where up and where down is. I just know that I need to breathe. I need to...

Aeola wraps herself around my face, bringing with her much-needed air. My mind clears a little, enough to know that she can't sustain this for long. The water pressure will eventually be too much for her. Nevertheless, her presence lends me a sense of direction as we float up a little.

More hands grab for me, tear at my arms, my legs, even my waist. I can't possibly fight them all off, not in their own element. Not anywhere. Only spirits can hurt other spirits, and I'm not one of them.

Long fingers close around my neck, choking me until I have to gasp, and water fills my mouth. I try to spit it out before it runs down to my lungs, but the pressure around my neck intensifies, and I see stars dancing in front of my eyes.

Yet another hand grabs my upper arm, just where Wulf's fingers left their mark earlier, and I'm ripped in another direction. This one brings me back to the surface. Instantly, the pressure around my neck disappears. As I cough up the water, I see a wooden staff flashing in front of my face. Again and again, it stabs the waves around me until the nymphs let go.

I find myself being dragged back to shore by Wulf. He's only got eyes for the dry ground, onto which he pushes me before returning to the river.

Aeola is right beside me, making sure I get all the water out of my lungs. "Are you all right?" she asks, visibly worried.

I nod at her, unable to speak. Wulf is not the only spirit seeker who's come to my help—or rather, who responded to the heightened spirit energy. The entire Budapest team is present, trying their best to fight the nymphs, who are rapidly retreating. No one tries to capture them.

By the time Wulf gets out of the water again, I've managed to get back to my feet. He immediately has a go at me. "What were you thinking?"

I swallow. "I was talking to them."

"Underwater?" He spits out some of the water he swallowed. "What's wrong with you?"

"What's wrong with me? You're the ones that experiment on spirits. That twist them into something unnatural!" I gesticulate in the direction of the river. "This is your fault. It's not pollution. It's you!" Wulf shakes his head and walks off, but I'm not done with him. "What if everything you do is aggravating the situation? If you would talk to them instead of fighting even the most peaceful spirits in your vicinity..."

He spins around, snarling at me. "Talk to them? How long have you been without air? They were trying to drown you!"

I notice faintly that the other spirit seekers have gathered around us. "Because they're broken. They're no longer whole. The only thing they know is anger and hate." It clings to me, even now.

"So, like all spirits then." Wulf has crossed his arms, daring me to disagree with him.

I do him the pleasure. "No. No, not like all spirits. Most spirits aren't anything like that. You can talk to them."

"No. You. Can't," he spits out each word individually, then throws his hands up in the air. "Gosh, you're so gullible and naïve. I can't anymore with your hippy attitude."

"Hippy attitude?" Did he really just go there?

Wulf nods grimly. "You're endangering yourself and everyone else if you keep pretending all spirits are just lovey-dovey, waiting for us to embrace them. There wouldn't have been any spirit seekers for hundreds of years if spirits were harmless. Don't you think someone would've tried talking to them at one point if you were right?"

"Travellers did." Before he can protest, I continue, "Oh, I forgot, we don't count because we don't belong anywhere." My voice gets sharper with each word. "I mean, how could people who live outside with the spirits know anything about them, especially when there are much more experienced spirit seekers sitting behind thick walls and killing every spirit that moves—or doesn't." I glare at Iván for good measure.

"You're so ridiculous." Wulf sneers at me. "Józsie was right. I should have sent you home straight away. Forget about that. I should have never brought you along."

It's the cherry on top, the one bit that pushes me too far. "You know that I should be the one calling the shots."

Wulf frowns. "What?"

"My NAV is much higher than yours. Fourteen points, probably more, because—knowing you—you underscored my last test. So, according to your stupid rules and conventions, I should call the shots." My breath has quickened. I don't even know what I'm doing here. Claiming command of the spirit seekers? Have I gone mad?

Wulf certainly stares at me as if I have. He's so perplexed he even forgets to shout. "I told you, the errors—"

"Are bullshit," I blurt out. "Iván told me they don't matter. You're under 500; I'm over. Case closed." There are some gasps from the other spirit seekers following my outrageous claim.

"No!" Wulf's face turns an ugly shade of purple. "No, Rika! This is not how it works. The SSA didn't introduce the NAV ranking just so you could spit on our values and traditions. The highest-ranked spirit seekers are ranked that way so we can lead our teams to victory. You don't want to fight spirits; you want to pretend you're friends with them." His spittle covers my face, he's snarling that much. "You want your own command, Rika? Fine! Go to the academy! Go and get yourself properly inducted. They'll give you a command. I'm sure of it, but it won't be over me." Abruptly, he turns away, telling the others, "We're done here."

What I mostly hear is that he's done with me. Which is fine, because I'm most certainly done with him, too.

"Over 500." Iván whistles softly. "What a freaking waste."

He and the others follow Wulf, leaving me to shiver in my wet clothes. A waste of a good NAV, that's all they can think. It's like I haven't uttered a single word. Iván joked that they took the fun out of Wulf's and József's curriculum, but it looks like they took empathy out of all of theirs.

Aeola tries to warm me up with her breeze, but the cold in me goes far deeper. "You did well," she whispers.

"I failed," I say.

"But at least you tried," a new voice says. I peer into the darkness until Rebeka steps out of the woods. "Look at you. You're soaked."

If she's come back to mock me, I'm not in the mood for it. "I'll be fine."

"Will you?" Rebeka comes to a stop five metres across from me, as if she's unsure how close she's allowed to come. "I know a place where you could get changed."

Is she kidding? "I'm not going back there."

"I figured as much." One step closer and she begins to knead her hands. "Look, I think what you did was incredibly brave. I... I wish I had the guts to stand up to them like that."

"Them?" I'm a little confused now. Is there more to this than gleeful gloating?

Rebeka shrugs with a small smile. "Guys with a high NAV, you know, the big jocks. But I guess it's easier when you're actually more talented than them." She takes a deep breath. "I've got a cousin. She lives not too far from here. You could stay the night. Have a shower, get some dry clothes, and then think about your next steps."

"And what would those be?" I don't want to be trapped in yet another bad situation.

"Let's discuss this over some food, okay?" She cocks her head like an invitation. "Please."

I'm too tired and wet to refuse. Where else do I have to go? "Okay."

21

Maybe I'm too tired or just plain exhausted from everything that's happened today—Eszti's son, Iván's betrayal, the fight with Wulf, and those broken spirits—but I've taken Rebeka up on her offer, and now she, her cousin Szonja, and I are sitting around the kitchen table of the small flat with soup in front of us. The walls around us are a garish yellow, and there's a terrifying metal heater from another century under the ceiling right above the couch. A faint cigarette smell hangs in the net curtains, though neither Rebeka nor Szonja smoke.

As promised, I've been able to take a hot shower and put on some dry clothes. Szonja took my wet clothes down to the drying room in the cellar while Rebeka whizzed up the soup. After throwing up earlier, it's probably the only thing I can stomach.

We don't really talk much over dinner. Szonja and Rebeka are covering the basics, how they've been and whether they've heard the newest of this or that relative, but even they stick to the superficial, never acknowledging my glaring presence at the table. I assume Rebeka must've filled her in with the bare minimum while I was showering because Szonja never questions my right to sit at her table.

"Well," she says, after finishing her bowl, "this has been lovely. I have to get up early for work. So, I'm gonna get the bed ready for you, and then I'll put my mattress down in the office. You two stay up as long as you want. Get yourself something to drink."

It's such a thinly veiled attempt to give us some privacy that I have to chuckle softly. Rebeka smiles at me. "I know, she's making too much of a fuss, but she can keep a secret. You're safe here."

"I'm not making a fuss; I'm being a good hostess!" Szonja complains, but she smiles warmly at me and starts converting the sofa to a bed.

I wait until she's busy in the office next door before I ask Rebeka, "Are you gonna tell me a secret?" I'm still trying to figure out what her game is. I haven't forgotten that it was she who sold the spirits to the researcher.

"More like a warning," Rebeka says, her eyes faintly glistening. She takes a moment to gather herself by turning out some pálinka and glasses for the both of us. Once she's filled both and taken a sip from hers, she looks at me. "Run, Rika. Don't ever set a foot in the academy."

Now I'm intrigued. Not that I planned to join the SSA—not after everything I've learnt about them—but I wouldn't have expected a spirit seeker to warn me off. I take a small sip of my pálinka and lick the fruity taste off my bottom lip. "Why?"

Rebeka's shoulders sag. This seems to bring up some old memories for her. "I got drafted into the SSA during my bachelor's. I studied Archaeology here in Budapest, and we learnt all about spirit activity in prehistoric times. It was fascinating. I learnt that some people feared the spirits. Others thought they were messengers of the gods. And yet others hailed them in their own regard. We learnt that some of the first spirit seekers appeared in Ancient Rome.

Most of the history is classified, so for all public purposes, the spirit seekers didn't officially band together until the late eighteenth century. But you can read between the lines, and there definitely were some sort of spirit seekers in Ancient Rome. As usual with the Romans, they sought to conquer the spirits."

I wonder where this history lesson is going, but I don't dare interrupt her. Despite my reservations, I'm intrigued. Things weren't always like they were today. No matter what Wulf claims.

"A friend and I... Sebestyen, the guy you saw me with in Aquincum, were intrigued by the Roman's spirit weapons. We both did our bachelor theses on them. Somehow, that triggered a response from the SSA. Sebestyen and I got tested for our NAV. He scored below 50 and continued on with his master's and PhD, until he recently got a research position at Aquincum, still specialising in ancient spirit weapons."

I pull a face. After what I've learnt about spirit weapons and hearing Sebestyen talk about the salamander he broke down, spirit research doesn't sound one iota better than spirit seeking.

"I know," Rebeka says. "It's despicable." She sighs and runs her hands over her face. Then chucks back her pálinka. "I can't believe I was actually taking part in this." She shakes her head, once again looking close to tears. "That's what you get for joining the SSA, I guess." Her voice chokes on the words.

Gently, I pour her another glass. "Why would you say that?" As heart-breaking as it is to watch her, I believe people are responsible for their own actions. No one walked her to Aquincum and forced her to keep that relationship with Sebestyen alive.

"Because it changes you." She straightens her back after a more measured sip from the glass. "I tested above 200, which saw me strongly invited to the academy. And if I say strongly, I mean there wasn't really an option to say no. Because I certainly didn't see the appeal of becoming some sort of soldier." She suddenly grows passionate. "I wanted to study and learn all I could. Spirits were intriguing, but Roman life was more so. I never shared Sebestyen's enthusiasm for weapons, despite my thesis."

Add another argument against the SSA: forced recruitment. "I'm sorry they didn't let you choose."

Rebeka draws her shoulders up and drops them again. "They won't let you choose either. You're lucky Wulf hasn't contacted the SSA yet. If they find out your NAV is above 500, they're gonna come for you. They're gonna hunt you down."

A shiver runs down my back. *Don't tell them about the spirits,* was the last thing my mum said to me, and I suddenly realise that she knew. She knew that I would draw the attention of the SSA and warned me against it. "Lovely." I hate how my voice shakes when I say that.

"I joined the academy without really knowing what I was in for," Rebeka explains. "Some of it was exciting. I learnt more about the history, but whenever I asked a question that leaned towards a more pro-spirit direction, it was shut down. The research at the SSA is deeply flawed. Most people don't care, or they don't notice, but you can't ignore critical questioning. I'd be very surprised if any of the current research passed a peer-reviewed study."

Whatever that is. Though, I have an idea of what it could mean. "You mean it's biased."

"Exactly. Results need to be reproducible, and as a researcher, you need to accept that your working hypothesis might have been wrong," Rebeka explains. "That's why you do the research. You have to interpret the data you get; not get the data you want. The SSA only wants one result: that there are absolutely no redeeming characteristics in a spirit. That we must fight them. When you hear that every day, you find yourself believing it." She points both her index fingers at herself. "Point in case. And I considered myself smart. But once I graduated, I'd gobbled it all up." Her voice is somersaulting once again.

For some reason, my thoughts wander to Wulf. Can I really blame him? The SSA took him in as a nine-year-old. A nine-year-old who had just watched his parents die. That he hasn't reported me to the SSA but respected my decision not to join them might be the only hope he's not a lost cause.

"What happens to those who don't believe?" I can't imagine ever swallowing that bullshit, even if I was exposed to it for three years.

Rebeka mindlessly swirls her pálinka. "They disappear," she says at last. When she looks at me, her eyes are full of tears. "I had a friend like that. We roomed together, and at night, we'd discuss our lectures. She kept saying how the SSA was wrong, pointing out all the inconsistencies. She was very smart, emotionally as well as intellectually. Then, one day, we were separated. I was assigned another roommate, one I'm pretty sure was given to me so I'd take on her views, which were as anti-spirit as they get."

"And your friend?"

"She continued her studies, and then she graduated ahead of class." Rebeka smirks in a decisively ugly way. "But you can't find her in the database. She never got stationed anywhere. She's not working for the research facilities either. I checked. She completely disappeared."

The hot soup in my stomach has turned to ice water. My eyes flicker to the door. It's past midnight. If I run now, I could hide. If there's one thing I know about more than spirits, it's people disappearing. Homeless people disappear all the time, until they reappear face down in the Spree. And let's not even think about my mum.

"You're safe here," Rebeka says, grabbing my hand. "Nobody would suspect me of helping you, right? I'm Iván's right-hand woman. His girlfriend. A good and proper spirit seeker."

"Why?" Even for cover, I'd never sink that low. "Do you sell spirits to avoid suffering the same fate as your friend?"

She withdraws her hand with a sigh. "As I said, you get bombarded with anti-spirit propaganda until you believe it. We were separated during our second year. Shortly after, I got together with Iván. Like my new roommate, he had completely swallowed their beliefs, priding himself in the future that awaited him. I mean, his mother was a spirit seeker, so there's that. I wish I could tell you I held onto my beliefs, but they faded before I even knew what was happening. By the time I graduated, I thought I was doing the right thing. Saving the world from spirits."

Just as Wulf does. And Lukas, and every other spirit seeker I know.

"He knew about my connection to Sebestyen," Rebeka continues. "I introduced them to each other. It was Iván's idea to sell off the occasional spirit. He hoped it would help us defend the city when the SSA wouldn't step up their game."

Annoyingly, I get where Iván's coming from. While he has absolutely no regard for spirit lives, he cares for this city, for his people. In the end, he's much more like Wulf than he'd be able to stand.

"Sebestyen was all for it, delighting in the chance to get his hands on some actual spirits. I didn't feel comfortable at first, but Iván convinced me it was necessary. We had to do everything in our power to stop the spirits."

"So, what made you change your mind?"

"That first night I saw you, I heard you talking to the dryads. It reminded me of my friend. But then you said you were with Wulf Bachmann, and I know better than to confide my doubts in one of his seekers. I didn't know what to make of you until your breakdown over the dryads. That's when I knew you were just like her. And still, I was wary. Could you really be so naïve as to hang out with the SSA's poster child, or what was going on?"

My cheeks are burning, and I quickly down some pálinka. It *was* naïve of me to believe I could change him.

"And then you gave that speech to Wulf today. You reminded me of everything I used to believe in. Everything I knew!" Once again, Rebeka grabs my hands, her eyes burning with passion. "I believe you. I believe that there's a better way. Because there was. It's in the research. There have been people who revered spirits."

I wouldn't call my relationship with spirits reverence, but it's comforting to know that, contrary to Wulf's beliefs, I'm not the first—much less the only one—who's ever seen spirits for what they are. People know. The SSA knows. They just decided to keep it a secret.

Well, I'm ready to expose them. I won't disappear.

22

I feel like I've barely slept at all when Rebeka shakes me awake again. Her eyes are wide with fear. "We have a problem," she says when I moan in response.

My mind instantly jumps to our previous conversation. "Are they coming for me?" In my dream, Wulf and his entire team were hunting me all through Berlin.

Rebeka shakes her head. "No. It's worse. I mean, maybe not for you, but for Budapest. I just had a call from Iván. The nymphs are taking down the bridges."

I sit up and rub the sleep from my eyes. "What do you mean?"

"There's an immense wave coming in from the South, and it's building up. It swept under the Rákóczi Bridge, washed over Petőfi and hit Liberty so hard it took down some of the crossing cars. Right now, it's on its way to Elisabeth Bridge." Rebeka is shivering, and so am I. If you know anything about Budapest or the Danube, you'd know how wrong this wave is. It's not just some freak flash tide from the melting snow; it's a wave that's going upriver, against the current, the work of something disturbingly unnatural.

The polluted nymphs.

"So, what's going to happen?" I ask. "Do we need to evacuate?" I'm already getting dressed.

Rebeka rocks back on her heels. "They're evacuating the houses closest to the river. This one's not in the zone, but if this wave continues to build up, it will rival the destruction of the Second World War. To stop it, the spirit seekers will meet it head-on on the Széchenyi Chain Bridge."

"What?" This is ridiculous. Fighting an enormous wave of dirty, spoilt water? "They can't possibly hope to defeat it." Then I remember Wulf is with them. The man fought a volcanic eruption; why not the Danube?

Rebeka looks like she's going to burst into tears. "I know! We'll have to try, though."

"You're going?" I can see how much this frightens her, and after everything she told me about the SSA last night, I thought things had changed.

"This is my city. If we don't stop the wave, it'll destroy parliament. It doesn't matter whether the SSA sucks, this about our people. But maybe... Maybe you could do something? Talk to them."

The hope in her voice tortures me. What did I do to inspire that in her? And how can I possibly disappoint her now?

You can't talk down a flood, I hear Wulf bellowing in my head. Part of me wants to prove him wrong, but there's a bigger, wiser part that knows it's in vain. These aren't ordinary spirits. They aren't even angry spirits, not like the Erlking. They are so destroyed internally they only know destruction now. "These spirits are different. I'm terribly sorry, but they don't listen to me."

Rebeka closes her eyes for a moment, breathing flatly. "Then run. Run as far as you can and stay away from the SSA." Then she grabs her staff and hugs her cousin. Tears are streaming down both their faces. A few hushed well-wishes, and Rebeka is out of the door.

Her cousin looks at me, clearly struggling to breathe. "I don't claim to understand why you're not going with her, but you can stay until tomorrow morning... or longer if needed."

Yeah, I'm not going to impose on this poor woman who might lose her cousin tonight any longer than I absolutely have to. In fact, I need to leave right away. "Thanks for everything, but I have to go."

I might not be able to stop a tidal wave, but there's something I *can* do.

By the time I come down the stairs, Rebeka is already long gone. It must be four or five in the morning. The sky is still dark, and the streets are mostly empty. The closer I get to the river, though, the more activity buzzes around me. People are leaving their homes, only a few bundles in their hands. Children are crying in their parents' arms. The police are instructing people to get into the hills.

The flashing lights of the police cars meld with those of my memories. The cries of the strangers around me become the cries of the people I loved. When somebody grabs my shoulder, I almost hit the guy in the face. It takes every fibre of my being to not give in to the panic attack building in my chest. This guy might be a policeman, but he's not the one that put me into his car, then arrested the rest of my friends and family.

"You can't go to the Danube. You need to evacuate." It takes a moment for me to realise he's just trying to help.

Fortunately, my mouth works quicker than my mind. "SSA. I'm with the SSA."

He lets go of me, studying me with curiosity. "Right. Well, in that case, you might want to head to Széchenyi. I heard that's where they're making a stand." Then he salutes me. "Thank you for your service. Good luck!"

Managing not to roll my eyes at him, I slip past the barrier the police have built and head down Margaret Bridge. I'm not stupid. I know that this isn't the Széchenyi Chain Bridge, but I'm not here to fight. There's no staff for me, none that I would willingly touch, and I don't see any point in getting in the way of the spirit seekers.

Instead, I'm here to evacuate the dryads. If an upriver wave can sweep away the bridges of Budapest, it will completely devastate Margaret Island.

Aeola joins me as I run across the empty bridge. "Are we going to fight?" she asks.

Between huffs, I explain my plan to her. "We need to warn them, at least." The dryads are still weak. Most of them won't have found a tree to bond with yet, and I'm not sure any trees will survive the water.

"What about the spirit seekers?" Aeola asks. "What about Wulf?"

"Wulf made his choice," I say pointedly. "This is what he signed up for. He lives for these catastrophes." And after tonight, he might be dead. Despite all our differences, I find I still care. Everything I said is the truth. He's a spirit seeker through and through, and for him, that means risking his own life to save thousands of others. And though he infuriates me more than anyone ever has, I still admire him for that.

I shake off the undeserved adoration. "He could save so many more if he wasn't at war with the spirits." I have to say it out loud to get over my doubts.

Aeola sighs a little. "He's like my father. The anger has made him blind to the world."

"And righteous and overbearing and... just an all-around idiot." Will I ever get over him? Now, don't get the wrong idea. I'm not in love with the guy. I've just got to know him too well to simply put him in the people-to-avoid drawer he belongs in.

We arrive at the park, and I instantly pick up the panicked whispers between the trees. There are so many of them I can't understand more than a few words. "...flee..." "...what do we do?" "...don't want to die."

"Quiet!" I shout, and the leaves around me fall silent.

I turn around, trying to face all of them, though most of them are still hidden in the trees. "Panic won't help us."

"Us?" an old voice asks.

"Yes, us. We can only survive this if we work together." My voice is surprisingly calm although I haven't planned any of this speech. "The spirit seekers are making a last stand on Széchenyi Chain Bridge. They won't succeed, but they'll buy us time. While they fight off the nymphs, we can leave the island."

Naturally, there's protest. "Without our trees? We can't leave the trees behind."

"I understand that." Great, now my voice is on the verge of breaking. "Leaving behind a part of you hurts." In my mind, I see myself hugging Eszti goodbye, not knowing it would be the last time I'd see her. "But you will survive. You will grow new roots." The citadel of Spandau somehow sneaks into my mind. "They'll grow stronger, and you'll grow stronger. But if you stay here, you'll drown."

The protest is softer now, more defeated. "But what about our trees?" The trees are more than just their home. They're a part of them. They're their parent and their child. Some of the dryads have cared for these trees since they were saplings.

A dryad steps out in front of me. She doesn't have a tree, not anymore. "We cannot run away, Rika," Szirom says.

But I want them to. I want them to be safe. There are more parks in Budapest, up on the hills of Buda, further inland in Pest. "I don't want you to die." Tears are streaming down my face.

"Then we must fight." Szirom nods. She turns around to face the rest of them. "These nymphs don't belong here. They have been introduced. Introduced to bring horror and death to everything alive. We are dryads. We live. We grow. We die, only to give new life. Today, the spirit seekers and we have a common enemy. Let us fight. Not for them, but for us, and everything that lives."

"Elisabeth Bridge is down." That's the call I pick up as we move along the shoreline. I swallow at the thought of how powerful this nymph-forced wave is to tear down a fortified bridge with giant white gates.

Luckily, none of the police officers has a high NAV, or they'd be freaking out about the two dozen dryads following me toward the Széchenyi Chain Bridge. Things will change when we get to the bridge, but I'm hoping the spirit seekers will be too occupied to worry about the dryads making a stand next to them. And if we somehow survive this and Iván takes down the rest of the trees, I will personally skewer him with his staff.

When I step onto the bridge, Aeola and Szirom at my side, I can see the wave. A giant bulge of water moves towards us in a slow creep-like fashion, more like a dune shifting with the wind than water flowing. In the early morning light, it looks grey instead of blue. Behind it, I see Elisabeth Bridge broken in two. The white gates have fallen inward, still precariously perched on steel ropes. Water flows into the city from the sides of the wave. It sweeps away cars and streetlamps, crashing them into each other or the nearby buildings.

The lions of Széchenyi welcome me with their stone eyes. They've guarded this bridge for so long, but there's nothing they can do tonight.

The spirit seekers are spread across the bridge, each with ample space around them. The first, Zsuzsanna, notices me, but she doesn't see the dryads. From her frown, I can tell that she knows something is up. I ignore her as I do Rebeka's widening eyes. József is next, but he's so focused, eyes fixed on the approaching wave, his fingers clenching around the staff, that he doesn't even hear me pass behind him.

Like the spirit seekers, the dryads spread out along the bridge. I slip next to Wulf, who has naturally taken the centre spot where the brunt of the wave will hit.

"Try not to kill our allies if you can," I say softly as I take my place next to him.

He nearly jumps out of his skin. "Rika?" Then he looks behind him and pales. "What have you done?"

"Surprisingly, nothing. They wanted to help." I skip the part where the dryads couldn't care less about the spirit seekers and are here because they want to protect their trees and whatever they include in *"all that lives"*. "Where's your staff?"

The one in his hands is a standard-issue staff. Wulf doesn't answer, so I look around and find it in Iván's hands. "You've got a serious hero complex," I tell Wulf. Of course he'd give away his powerful ancient staff and prove he can still kick ass with one that doesn't even come close to the original.

"Says the woman who turns up empty-handed to a battle," he mutters, still not looking at me.

Noting the slight undertone of concern, I smile. "I'm not empty-handed. I've got Aeola."

For a moment, Wulf doesn't say anything. His eyes are fixed on the wave that's now only one or two hundred metres away. When he speaks again, his voice sounds pained. "Rika, leave, please."

"It's too late for that," I whisper.

I'm right. The wave is speeding up. It's growing in size, as high as the bridge, then higher, much higher. It's not just water that's coming at us, but a wave of pure hate. It may very likely tear us apart.

"There's five of them," I say, noticing the bloated shapes of the nymphs.

Aeola wraps her lower body around my hand, and I squeeze her tight. There's no going back now.

For a moment, it looks like the water is just going to move over our heads, curling into itself like a wave you could surf. Then it crashes down on us, grasping at the stone gates and tearing at the steel ropes.

Wulf raises his staff, but it's the dryads that launch themselves forward, cutting through the water and slicing it to ribbons.

I scream at the top of my lungs as I watch a dryad drop into the river, only to be swept away from us. The Danube will take him down its course, further away from his roots than he's ever been.

A nymph lunges at us, and Wulf steps forward to meet her, spinning his staff around to hit her left and right. Though each hit is placed near perfectly, the staff barely cuts into the water-filled form. I can see Iván further down, fighting on the slippery railing of all places, smacking Wulf's staff into another nymph.

Water sweeps at us from all directions. Instead of flowing on, it keeps enveloping us, greedily reaching for our lives. Within seconds, I'm drenched from head to toe. Aeola makes sure I've always got enough air, but apart from that, there's not much I can do other than watch seekers and dryads go down under the onslaught.

The smell of the foul nymphs is overbearing. Their oily touch makes me want to scream, while the hate makes me want to curl up and cry. But I can't do that. Everyone's fighting for their survival, and I have to do my part. One look at Aeola, and she knows what to do.

"József, hit the water where it shimmers black, four steps to your right." Aeola's wind carries my words, and the spirit seeker follows them, driving his staff into the oily gleam I know is there. The pressure of the water lessens a little around him.

Turning to the Pest side, I shout, "I need three dryads down at the lions. Hold there."

I no longer see the individual nymphs but the wave as a whole. It's not perfect, just like the nymphs aren't perfect. There are many spots that seem less dense than the rest. If we hit those, we can lessen the hold the nymphs have over the water. I keep moving up and down the bridge, directing spirits and seekers alike as the wave continues to build around us, frozen in mid-air. I don't know whether the seekers know who gives them the impressions or whether they think it's their own doing, but they're hitting the wave exactly where they need to.

The nymphs themselves are still a big problem. Iván has weakened his one enough to assist his teammates at the Pest side of the bridge. Meanwhile, Wulf is managing to keep the nymph at a distance. I can see the frustration grow on his face. He's not used to his blows having so little effect. He's got the strongest, most complete nymph in front of him, and I worry he'll exhaust long before the spirit will.

"Rika, quick," Aeola alerts me to a problem on the Buda side. There, Rebeka and Zsuzsanna are fighting against the nymph that attacked Wulf and me on that day at the river. Two dryads are also involved in the battle, and yet the nymph bears down on all of them. He's sunk his needle-like teeth into Zsuzsanna's thigh and is threatening to drag her down the bridge, but the seeker's other leg is jammed in the railing. No, a dryad is holding onto her, wrapping her roots around her leg and railing to save her. I need to get them a break, or the water will wash them both down the bridge.

"Rebeka, strike where the spray hits! Aeola will show you!" Aeola speeds away from me, leaving a spray of water in her wake. The spray shows Rebeka exactly where Wulf hit the nymph before, and only seconds later, Rebeka's staff hits the same space, widening the ugly hole in his forehead.

The nymph loosens his jaw, and the dryad manages to pull Zsuzsanna back onto the bridge. She lies there, disoriented and clasping her bleeding leg. Meanwhile, the two other dryads hit the nymph with their spindly fingers in the exact same spot as Rebeka, until his entire forehead cracks open, spraying water like a mouldy fountain.

I'm still grossed out by it when something hits me so fast I can't even scream for help before my body slams into the railing on the far side of the bridge. Pain explodes in my back, making me gasp. But there's no air to breathe, only water. Foul water. Slimy oil fills my mouth, causing me to gag instead. Clawing at the railing, I try to get to my knees, only to have them knocked out from under me.

Then someone grabs me. At first I think it's Wulf because the grip around both of my arms is as firm as his, but it's twigs that hold me, not fingers. Szirom pulls me to my feet and steadies me, helping me breathe through the pain. An instant later, Aeola is at my side, brushing my face with her warm breeze until I can think straight again.

As soon as I can, she tells me, "Wulf is in trouble."

My head whips around to the left. For some reason, there are now two nymphs attacking him. It looks like József has abandoned the one he had engaged in a battle and joined Rebeka and their hurt teammate instead. With his back against the railing, Wulf is hard-pressed. The moment he concentrates on one, the other tries to get on his undefended side. One of the nymphs spits foul water into his eyes, and the reflex causes Wulf to jerk his head to the side. Immediately, the second one lunges forward, plunges her teeth into Wulf's lower arm, and drags him over the railing.

"Aeola!" I watch in horror as he falls backwards into the tumultuous waves. Aeola dives after him in a flash.

The second nymph begins tearing at the steel cables until one of them snaps loose and smacks a dryad in the face, flinging her far into the water. The spirit seekers are still fighting up and down the bridge, but they're losing the battle.

I try not to think about Wulf and take a deep breath, ready to do my part. Just before I step forward, Szirom puts a hand on my shoulder. When I look at her, she's concentrating so hard the knots of wood in her face pulsate. One of Szirom's long fingers separates from her hand. A knot appears in its place as the finger falls into her hand. She passes it to me. "Stick her where it hurts."

My fingers close around the piece of living wood in my hand that's barely long enough to be a dagger. "Thank you." Facing the nymph, I take a deep breath, then I holler with as much taunting as I can manage, "Hey, you slimy puddle."

The nymph reacts instantly. "Who are you calling a puddle?" Water splashes over my knees, threatening to wash me away.

"Would you prefer stinky swamp face?"

Nope, she doesn't. With a snarl, the nymph splashes herself at me. I try to sidestep her but get swept into her wave instead. She would've flushed me over the railing like Wulf if Szirom hadn't rooted me to the spot. I can hardly thank Szirom before she moves forward and entangles the nymph in long vines. The nymph expands and expands with an unearthly scream until Szirom's vines snap in ear-splitting thunder.

"No," I whisper, realising how badly hurt Szirom already is from her fight with the spirit seekers. Now she's writhing on the ground and still trying to pull the nymph down with her.

Her former finger in my hand pulsates with her life force, reminding me what I have to do. Using the opening Szirom's sacrifice gives me, I jump onto the nymph's back. Just before I crash through the wave, I drive the dryad wood through her head and back out her mouth, tearing my wrist on her teeth as I fall through the water. My knees hit the ground, and I howl with pain as I fall on my side next to Szirom.

But it worked. The freely given dryad wood has torn the nymph open from inside, and now she is nothing more than what I'd already called her—a sad little puddle. All around me, I feel the wave losing its force and the water changing direction, flowing back downriver as it's supposed to.

"Szirom, we did it! We—" My jubilant cries are quickly stifled when I look at the dryad. The oil has seeped beneath the cracks in her bark from the earlier fight with the spirit seekers. Already, her remaining leaves are turning brittle and grey. "No, no. Szirom, we did it. We saved the trees."

She raises her hand to my cheek, and I grasp it with mine, holding it close. "Plant me one, will you? A white poplar." I feel something round taking shape between my skin and her wood. A seed.

"Don't die," I beg her. She just saved my life, saved everyone's life. Even those who sought to capture her.

"We live," Szirom whispers, her voice as brittle as her leaves. "We grow. We die, only to give new life. That's the dryad's way of life. Remember that." As she turns entirely rigid, a light wind blows her leaves away. All that's left from her life is the dryad wood in my hand and the seed in my other.

Gently, I brush her face. "I'll plant you an entire forest, my dear friend."

"Oh, Rika." Suddenly, Aeola is there, wrapping herself around my body and offering me solace.

With a start, I remember why she wasn't here in the first place. "Is Wulf—"

I haven't even finished the sentence when I hear his soggy steps on the bridge. There's a gaping wound on his arm and another on his thigh, but the water has washed away the blood. He looks tired enough to drop right here and sleep through the next day and night.

His gaze drifts from me to the dead dryad, then back to me again. I hold my breath, waiting for his verdict.

"I'll see if the others need my help," is all he says, before dragging himself down to the Pest end of the bridge where the water hasn't quite calmed yet.

"He thanked me for saving him," Aeola says, trying to cheer me up.

I don't know what I expected from him. If Aeola saving him didn't change his mind, a couple of dryads joining forces with him wouldn't do it either.

My jaw is set. "As he should." It's the least he could do after the spirits gave their lives for him.

23

After what happened at the Széchenyi Chain Bridge, it didn't take much to convince the Budapest spirit seekers to replant the forest. Not even Wulf argued against it, though he shook his head when I demanded it and stayed at the base. Although the dryads saved everyone's lives, he remains stubborn. Fortunately, the others have had a change of heart, especially after the notice Iván received this morning.

"They're defunding us," he tells me as I dig a little hole for the white poplar seedling I've managed to find. "A sixty-per-cent cut to all funds because we had so much before."

You'd think after saving Budapest from a bunch of monster nymphs, the SSA would be a bit more forgiving, but no. Wulf's report has rendered the Budapest base practically defenceless.

"And of course, they ordered me to step down for Józsie." There's just a hint of bitterness in his voice. It's clearly not the worst consequence.

His brother won't have any of it. "You've got the higher NAV. You'll always be the commander in my book."

Iván smiles, and I'm glad that, at least these two now seem to be on the same page. "But what are we gonna do now? My team will have to get part-time jobs so they can afford to risk their lives. How am I supposed to protect everyone?"

I carefully lower Szirom's dryad seed into the ground before I plant the seedling on top. "There could be a way." I look across the meadow at Rebeka, who nods to me.

"Spill, Spirit Girl." After the bridge attack, Iván has adopted a new name for me. I don't really mind as long as he doesn't pass it on to the SSA.

"Well, you could start cultivating your relationships with the dryads." Patting the soil around the seedling, I try not to sound too giddy. "You'd have to make amends first, but I'd say they've proven themselves immeasurably valuable."

Iván and József share a look. The older brother shrugs, deferring the situation to Iván. When Iván turns back to me, it looks like he's set his mind. "If that's what we need to do to keep people safe, I'm all in. I just... I wouldn't know where to start." He takes a deep breath. "What are your plans?"

"My plans?" I get up from the ground.

"I'm assuming after the fight you and Wulf had, you're not so keen on Berlin anymore." He looks sheepishly at me. "Rika, you belong here. You're one of us. And we want you here. You could help us establish this unique collaboration. You could see it come to fruition. I mean, the dryads already trust you, and you know what they need."

It feels good to hear Iván appreciating me. When he's done, I smile. "You have to learn how to listen to them. Your NAV is almost at 400. You just need to open your heart to them. And you'll have to earn their trust. It's not gonna be easy. That said, I can't be your easy way out." I look over to Rebeka, who is directing two of the workers. "If you need help, I'd suggest listening to your girlfriend. She knows more about spirits than you think."

Iván follows my gaze and swallows. "So, where are you going?"

Staying in Budapest is tempting. It definitely feels more like home, and now that the spirit seekers are inclined to work with the spirits, I'd love to stay and watch my vision come to life. But I'm a Traveller. Settling isn't for me. Maybe I'll come back one day, visit old friends, and look after Szirom's tree, but for now, I need to move on. "There are things I have to take care of in Berlin, and then... I don't know." I look up at Aeola, who is drifting with the clouds. "Wherever the wind takes me."

"Well," Iván says, the disappointment thick in his voice. "It's not like I can pay you anything."

I can't bear seeing him this defeated. While I'm still angry about what he did to the dryads, I understand that it was born from desperation. He truly cares about the people here, and it breaks his heart that he can't defend them as he wants. I look at the white poplar seedling. It's just a tree now, but there's a dryad seed underneath, and though it hasn't sprouted yet, I know she would agree with me.

I take out the dryad wood Szirom gave me so graciously and put it into Iván's hands. "Her name was Szirom. She fought at your side, even though you hurt her. She died because of it." The oil wouldn't have got into her if she'd been whole. "This is more powerful than any spirit seeker staff you'll ever have because it has been given freely. I'm lending it to you until you've earned it."

His fingers curl around the wood, and I feel him shudder in reverence. "Thank you."

"Thank Szirom." I point to the seedling. "She'll bloom one day. You'd better treat her right from now on."

Iván nods, unable to speak, then he pulls me into a hug. "Viszontlátásra," he whispers. He pats my back before stepping backwards. "I'll take care of her."

I leave him with his brother and go over to Rebeka. She opens her arms wide and greets me with, "Don't worry. I'll keep him in line from now on."

"I'm counting on you." I hug her dearly.

More earnest, she adds, "And I'll make sure Sebestyen does no more research with spirits without their explicit consent."

"Thank you." It eases my heart to know I've put an end to the gruesome experiments here, at least.

"You're going back to Berlin with Wulf?" she asks, pulling a face.

"If he'll take me." He's still not talking to me, though he hasn't protested, either. After being such a presence from the first day I met him, he seems like a ghost now.

Rebeka looks worried. "Be careful, Rika. Wulf might be a good guy, but he has connections to the SSA that run deeper than anyone else's. Duty will call, and he'll answer."

"I know." It's a risk, but there's more in Berlin for me than Wulf.

Wulf keeps his distance on the ride back to Berlin. I thought we could discuss what had happened, but as soon as he stows away his luggage, he's off to the diner wagon. I spend the entire trip alone, thinking about what I'll do in Berlin. The picture of my mum is in my hands. Maybe Miriam can help me log into some database and look for her. Or I could post pictures of her around town. I'd need a phone for starters. Maybe I could use some of the funds I received for helping with the Erlking to buy one.

As we travel through Bratislava and Prague, I try to imagine my mother walking through the city. She could be literally anywhere, and my chances of finding her are incredibly slim. But then again, I found Eszti's home and this picture of the two of us. If nothing else, I'll always have that.

Wulf returns about five minutes before we arrive in Berlin to retrieve his luggage. He still doesn't look at me, treating me just like any other random person on the train.

Once outside, I immediately free Aeola, even though it's in plain sight of him. I can tell from the contraction of his shoulder muscles that he notices, but thankfully, he keeps quiet. I remember Rebeka's words about Wulf's ties to the SSA. He's already proven that he will report violations of the code of conduct despite all reason. Instead of improving the situation for Budapest, he's made it worse because duty told him to. I doubt it will be much longer before duty tells him to report my NAV to the agency. When he does, I need to be long gone.

Despite treating me like I'm invisible, he doesn't object to me returning with him to the citadel. By the time we reach the colossal grey walls, I'm low-key pissed about it. What I did in Budapest saved his life. Aeola actively saved his life. She told me how she'd kept him breathing while he fought off that nymph underwater. Without her, he would've drowned, and still he acts like I committed an unspeakable crime.

The others are in the hall when we arrive. They've already learnt we'll be returning and have waited with dinner. It's not a big bash like the Hungarian welcome, just some crumbed zucchini and schnitzel, but it tastes delicious after an entire day of travelling.

There's surprisingly little talk at the table, which makes me wonder whether Wulf already sent them a report or called them from the train.

"So, how did you like Budapest?" Camille asks as we finish our dessert, a raspberry jelly.

Before I can answer, Wulf dismisses the question. "She's been there before."

Camille frowns a little, clearly picking up on his vibe. For now, she decides to ignore him. "Have you?"

Despite his passive-aggressiveness, I answer cheerfully, "My mum and I lived there for a couple of years. It was amazing to be back. I missed the food, the people, the language."

"You can speak Hungarian?" Lukas asks, sounding as if I just claimed to be the daughter of the Pope.

"Természetesen." I grin at him. It pleases me to see him roll his eyes. Gosh, I've missed these guys.

Before I can answer any more questions, Wulf gets up, putting his hands on the table. At last, he's looking at me. "Rika will leave us tomorrow. She will pack her bags and go."

"What if I don't want to?" I ask, my heart fluttering in my chest. I expected something like this, but it still hits me like a splash of cold water.

His eyes narrow. "Then you leave me no choice but to report you to the SSA for engaging with spirits on a non-combat basis."

The remarkable thing here is really that he *won't* report me if I leave.

Camille puts a hand on my arm. "Wulf. I think you're overreacting." Yep, she definitely knows what happened. "Rika has a unique way with spirits, I know, but maybe that's what we need."

It's the straw that breaks the camel's back. "We need people who fight spirits," he snaps at her. "Rika won't do that. Rika wants to talk with them and play house. There's no place for her among us. So, tomorrow, she'll leave."

"Then I'll leave with her," Leon says, in a voice as calm as if he's just announced tomorrow's weather.

Everybody stares, even me. Wulf's nostrils flare. "What?" It's a question I would've asked more nicely, but I certainly want to know the answer. I've never had anyone step up for me. Not like that.

Leon takes a deep breath. "I'm sorry, Wulf, but I think you're wrong about her. And about spirits. While you were gone, I opened myself up to them. Rika wanted to show me how to do that, but she wasn't here, so I tried on my own. I stopped seeing them as the enemy and instead accepted their presence. I invited nature into my life. And you know what? I felt a spirit yesterday. I *felt* him."

This is such a big deal for him. His low NAV has always prevented Leon from becoming aware of the spirits around him. That a change of attitude, even without my guidance, would have such a huge effect on his abilities is breath-taking. It opens up so many possibilities. "I'm so happy for you," I tell him.

But Wulf's face has darkened. "I hope you caught him."

Leon shakes his head. "He wasn't aggressive." He smiles at me. "I believe you."

"Well, if we're taking sides now..." Lukas starts.

"We're not." Wulf's voice is shaking in disbelief.

Lukas sneers at me. "I'm on Wulf's. He's the best spirit seeker there is. His methods have been proven time and time again. I'd follow him into any battle." No surprise there.

Miriam raises her hands. "I'm not taking any sides. Scientifically, though, I find Rika's approach fascinating." Her eyes lock into Leon's. "And I want to retest your NAV. If you can actually improve your attunement by adjusting your attitude, I want to document it."

She's exuding so much excitement, Camille reaches over the table to squeeze her hand. Then Wulf's gaze finds Camille. He's this close to losing it all. His whole body is trembling, anger flashing in his eyes. "What about you?"

Camille sighs. "I love you, Wulf. You're my best friend, but you're also as stubborn as stone. And you don't veer from your path, which is commendable in most situations, but a weakness in others. You can see the spirits as well as Rika. You've seen what she can do. What she hears. If you're really honest with yourself, can you confidently say she doesn't have a point?" He opens his mouth, but Camille isn't done. "Because I can't."

"This is ridiculous," Lukas mutters. "Guys, we're spirit seekers, not spirit... friends?"

But it's Wulf who has all eyes on him. His gaze flits from one to the other until it lands on me. There's so much pain in his eyes, and it's all my fault. I've ruined it for him. His vocation, his team, his whole life! Without another word, he marches out of the hall.

Lukas is quick to follow while the rest of us let go a collective breath of relief.

"Well, that was fun," Leon says, loading his plate with more jelly.

"Did you really feel a spirit?" I ask him.

He nods. "Yeah, a nymph down the Havel. Camille confirmed it for me."

The thought of nymphs makes me shudder, but I must remind myself that not all nymphs are corrupted and foul. "That's amazing." It's even more amazing that they didn't decide to catch him on what must have been a patrol.

Camille sighs again. "I'd better check on Wulf."

"Good luck," Miriam tells her.

Camille squeezes her hand again, then smiles at me. "I'm glad to have you back, Rika. I'll fix this somehow."

I wish she could, but I can't bring myself to believe it.

24

Awkward doesn't even begin to describe it when I meet Wulf the following day. Despite his wishes, I have not packed my things, and he knows with one look. He takes his bread roll and leaves the hall, Lukas on his heels.

I ignore both of them, pour myself some coffee, and sit down with the others. "No luck yesterday?" I ask Camille.

"Not yet. He's agreed not to throw you out, so that's a start," Camille says. She tries for a smile, but it falls flat.

I sigh into my coffee. "It's not gonna work. I love you guys, and I'm glad to hear that you believe me, but I can't stay here. We're just polar opposites."

"See, that's where I think you're wrong," Camille points out, handing me the basket with the bread rolls. "You are both passionate about your beliefs, but you're also compassionate. If you two could work out your differences, you could change the world."

Picking a poppy seed roll, I shake my head. "It's not just differences. He thinks all spirits are evil and should be killed. He's happy to use them for science or their weapons. He doesn't question any of it. And I'm sorry, but there's no compromise. Unless he changes his mind, I don't see how we can even be in the same city." Or world.

"He's questioning," Camille says quietly. "You can see it in his face. He's struggling a lot."

"He wants me gone. Better yesterday than tomorrow."

Camille shakes her head. "Because that's the easiest way. If you're gone, those questions will go away. He can't ignore you forever, but he can try to forget you."

She knows Wulf better than me, so I stop arguing. The problem is, I don't know what to do with the information. Should I provoke him by staying around in the hopes he'll see the light one day, and risk that the next easiest way for him to deal with this situation is to report me to the SSA? I don't want to disappear tomorrow. I want to be able to act, to reveal the truth about spirits and the SSA. But without others on my side, do I even stand a chance?

"What happened in Budapest?" Miriam asks. "Wulf mentioned that the dryads helped in the battle? I've checked the official report, but there's nothing about dryads."

Wulf never made the official report; that was Iván's duty. I'm amazed he didn't amend it right away. Maybe he does have a conscience and knows the dryads will all be hunted down if the SSA knows. Or maybe he decided not to look at it. "It's a long story," I say, then decide that they need to know if I want them on my side.

"The dryads wanted to fight. Their trees were also in danger from the water, not just human buildings. Some of them had actually been captured by the team there—I freed them—but they were still willing to fight at their side to defend what's dear to him, and so they did." I'm still amazed by the dryad's ability to look past the hurt that had been done to them. "They could've just fought against the nymphs, but they went out of their way to keep the spirit seekers alive. I saw one of them pull back a seeker who had fallen over the railing. She'd be dead now if not for them." For now, I keep to myself that Wulf himself would've died without Aeola.

"That's amazing." Leon's eyes gleam with excitement. "I've never heard of anything like that. Gosh, guys, just imagine what we can achieve if we work with the spirits."

I want to kiss him for those words. Camille still looks a bit wary about it, though. "I think there's no harm in exploring that possibility a little more."

"Ask Wulf about that one. He thinks I'm endangering myself and everyone else by dismissing the danger some of them pose." I don't know what's more bitter, the coffee or the bile in my mouth. I quickly replace both with a bite from my roll.

"Did you?" Camille asks.

The question makes me stop in my tracks. "Well, maybe that one time." Or twice. I did go in the water with the natural nymphs, after all. Now that I'm thinking about it, I might have been a little too eager to prove my point. "I was distraught. I'd just learnt what your weapons are made of, and Iván had betrayed the dryads, and it was all my fault. I wanted to do something that would make up for it." Shrugging, I concede, "So, yes, maybe I ignored some obvious warning signs. Trying to talk to the polluted nymphs was stupid. I knew there was something wrong with them. They weren't natural, but I wanted them to be. And I still don't know what made them like that. I mean, I've got a theory, but Wulf would never let it fly if I blamed his precious SSA."

"It is concerning," Miriam admits. "I've had a look at the nymph data. Of course, they're not properly processed yet, but as you say, they're all wrong. Their energy potential is way above a normal nymph, and their classification doesn't even say nymph."

"I know. They're closer to gnomes than nymphs," I say, after finishing my bread roll. "Someone has run some experiments on them, and since I'm pretty sure they were damaged before, that only leaves the SSA."

Miriam frowns deeply. "But why would they be roaming around Budapest, then? There's no SSA research facility in Hungary they could've escaped from."

That's not what I meant, but I don't have the energy to pursue this yet.

"It's disconcerting," Camille agrees. She looks at me. "Wulf is worried about that as well. Said he's never seen anything like it. Maybe this is something the two of you agree on and could use to build on."

Leon groans. "It's not happening, Camille. Rika isn't the one who should make the first step."

"Well, somebody has to," she argues.

"I'm with Leon," I declare before this can go any further. "I've tried to see it his way and tried to explain where I'm coming from. I've done enough. The ball's in his court now."

I wish he'd hurry up, though, because he's literally everywhere in this citadel. I can't even spend time outside with Aeola to enjoy the nature that has sprung into full bloom while we were gone without seeing him. Right now, Wulf and Lukas are sparring in the courtyard by the big oak tree. The first time I watched them, Wulf had been training Lukas, holding back where needed, pushing when Lukas made a mistake. Now he's beating Lukas, no lesson included.

But the younger spirit seeker laps it up. He's so eager to prove himself to Wulf that he pushes himself way beyond his capabilities. Sweating like a pig, he holds up a hand at last. "Break. I need a break. Please."

Wulf steps back immediately, grabbing his own water bottle. As he drinks, his gaze falls on me. "I told you I didn't want to see that sylph of yours inside these walls."

Oh, so we're talking again now. I'm not sure if that's progress. "This sylph saved your life."

"This is no place for spirits," he answers, ignoring what I said and turning back to Lukas. "Ready for another round?"

Lukas looks at him, wide-eyed. He's barely had a sip of water and is still breathing hard. "Okay." It doesn't sound terribly convincing.

Fortunately for him, all hell breaks loose.

Across the entire courtyard, seedlings pop out of the ground, shooting into the air until several young birches, oak, and chestnut trees have transformed the courtyard into a forest. At the same time, the thick branches of the old oak tree in the middle take a swipe at Wulf and Lukas.

Wulf jumps over the branch trying to knock his legs out from under him and hits it with his staff. But it's only a practice staff and not nearly as forceful as his ancient one, or even a standard one. Lukas is less lucky. In his current constitution he's too weakened to evade the branch that knocks him over the head, and he falls to the ground like a stone. Wulf sees it, and for a moment, it looks like he rather wants to continue to attack the powerful dryad in his backyard, but then his real self kicks in. He evades another branch by sliding under it and gathers a semi-conscious Lukas under the arms, looking for a way to drag him to safety.

Meanwhile, Aeola has shot into the air, worried, while I'm still trying to assess the situation. Is it another polluted spirit? Because dryads don't act that way. They don't regrow trees in fast-forward, and they don't suddenly decide to resettle in the middle of a spirit seeker base.

The small trees are swaying, trying to whip their thin branches at Wulf as he drags Lukas towards me. They don't belong to individual dryads. No, the trees are all connected to the oak tree, which is slamming his thickest branch into one of the sheds in the courtyard, crushing it. Slowly, I come to see him for what he is. He's an old dryad, ancient, really, and not polluted at all. This is a pure force of nature.

"Get inside!" Wulf barks at me. "Or help me."

I decide to do the latter, picking up Lukas' feet and helping to lift him through the door, which Camille holds open for us. She's got her staff in her hand but doesn't dare go outside.

Wulf and I lower Lukas on the couch. He's already moaning, which means he's coming to. Miriam hurries to his side and starts checking his head injury. Meanwhile, Wulf strides out the hall.

I follow immediately. He grabs his proper staff and turns toward the door. Quickly, I slip in between. "Don't fight him."

"Get out of my way, Rika!" His eyes are blazing, and he's breathing hard.

I don't budge a bit. "No, there's a reason why he's here. He's not like them."

"I'm warning you…"

Camille hurries to our side, coming from the hall. "Wulf, let's make a plan first. We're safe in here for now."

Looking out the window, I see that the trees have calmed down. I have no doubt they'll start again as soon as Wulf sets a foot outside.

"Let me talk to him." A spirit as ancient as the oak dryad must have a good reason why he suddenly turned on us.

Wulf stares at me, nostrils flaring. "Absolutely not!"

"Wulf—"

"You cannot talk down an enraged spirit." He almost hits me in the face with his hand as he points to the oak tree.

I cross my arms. "That's what you think. You've never tried it, though."

My answer has rendered him speechless. For a few moments all I hear from him are the huffs of exhaustion from barely escaping death by falling branches. Then he takes a step back. "Go!"

"Wulf, don't," Camille warns, but he holds her back.

"Let her go. I can't protect someone so eager to get themselves killed," he says.

Camille looks absolutely terrified for me. I wish there was something comforting I could tell her, but I don't even know if this will work. So instead, I focus on Wulf. On the pain in his eyes, the thinly veiled worry, and the very well-hidden plea for me not to go.

"I'll be all right. You'll see." And with that, I step out the door.

25

Aeola comes down to my side, her face full of worry. "I don't think he'll listen to you."

Right now, the big oak tree is still, as if he's never moved at all. But all the new saplings in the courtyard remind me of the outburst. What I'm about to do is incredibly dangerous, and it has nothing to do with proving my ideas to Wulf.

"I have to try, Aeola. Didn't you feel his hurt and pain?" There is more to the dryad's presence than a sudden wish for revenge. Something big has happened.

She sighs, deflating a little. "I felt it, but he won't listen to you. And to be honest..." her voice is as low as a whisper now, "I'm scared of him."

I reach out to brush her. "You should stay back."

"Rika..."

"I mean it. He'll rip you apart, and I don't want that." My sylph friend is no match for this ancient dryad. His branches will tear into her fragile body.

She slowly takes flight. "I'll help from above."

I have no idea what she plans to do, but I believe in her. Aeola has my back, and I have hers.

Taking a deep breath, I step into the courtyard, empty hands on display. I get to the first trees, so thin they're still swaying in the wind.

Nothing moves.

A little more confident, I keep walking. I'm now in the middle of this newly grown wannabe forest. A look over my shoulder tells me that Wulf and Camille are watching through the window, though I can't read their faces from this distance.

My next step is my last. I'm now in reach of his powerful branches, and sure enough, the tip of one of them slams into the ground next to me, its leaves and twigs brushing my arm. I nearly jump out of my skin, heart hammering in my chest, but I manage to stay on course.

"I'm here to talk," I say, but the draft from another branch barely missing my head makes it inaudible. He's not gonna hear me, not from this distance.

My pulse is racing, and still, I keep going. Again and again, the dryad comes for me, lashing out in anger and pain. But he keeps missing me, and it's not because I have such amazing evasion skills. In fact, the only time I get hurt is when I see the branch coming and try to avoid it.

Twigs scrape over part of my face and rip out some strands of hair. A scream escapes my lips, and I want to cower, but that will only spur him on, so I take a few seconds to calm my breathing and press on, exuding calmness around me.

It doesn't help. The closer I get to his trunk, the more violently the branches come at me. He wants me to go away and bring back the spirit seekers he hates so much.

"I know your pain," I say, though he's still not willing to listen.

I'm now too close for his branches to whip down on me without them snapping in half. I've barely exhaled in relief when a sudden hail of acorns falls from the tree. It feels like an entire autumn's worth of acorns is coming down on my head. I yelp and raise my arms for cover.

A wind brushes past me, taking the force away from the acorns. Aeola still has my back.

I force myself not to run at the trunk since I don't want to spook the dryad any further. Instead, I place one foot in front of the other until, finally, I'm there. Raising my hand, I gently place it against the bark. "I'm here," I whisper. "I'm here to listen."

Suddenly, I feel myself pulled forward, but it's not my body that's taken somewhere. Instead, the dryad pulls me into his own mind, showing me his pain, and I gasp as I realise who he is.

Grune.

The dryad who guards Berlin's largest forest, the Grunewald.

He's lived there since the first seedling put down roots in the glacial valley of Berlin. He watched each tree grow and saw many dryads among their leaves come and go. Then the humans came. First, they only passed through the forest along the rivers, but then they cut the trees down and made space for their fields. Several groups came and left, each taking another piece of the forest but ultimately vanishing again. Then the Saxons came, and with them Albrecht, the Bear. At that point, Spandau and its wall, which predates the citadel, already existed. The Saxons founded Berlin and its twin city Coelln. The cities grew, and the forest shrunk until all that was left of the Grunewald were the trees along the Havel in Southwest Berlin and the surrounding area.

My heart aches for all the loss Grune bears so deep inside him. There are far fewer dryads now than there were before, but he's stayed on. He's defended his forest as well as he could and cared for the trees left to him, even when the Erlking and his sylphs settled here and used the trees to wage war against the humans, ripping them out of the ground. He recognises me as the one that brought an end to the realm of terror the Erlking had erected, but he doesn't know where I stand exactly.

"With you," I tell him softly, or instead, I show him how I feel about the spirits, how much I care, and how much sorrow is in me knowing that so many natural places have been destroyed; are still being destroyed.

The following image Grune flings at me is that of a woman with short, blond hair and steel-blue eyes. I don't recognise her, but she carries a staff on her back as she walks through the forest. I recognise a trap in her hands, and at first, I think she's like me, that she wants to free the spirits. She opens the trap, but what comes out makes me recoil. It's a dryad, thin and wiry like ivy vines. Her leaves are full of holes, and what grows inside can only be described as something rotten.

The dryad slithers onto the ground like a snake. The woman leaves, and the dryad remains still for a while. Then she begins to spread. She chokes the sunlight from the small plants on the forest ground before wrapping herself around a tree, sapping its life force out from underneath its bark.

"When did this happen?" I ask, aghast.

And for the first time, Grune answers, "Two sunsets ago."

"That's horrible." My words can't convey what I feel, but they don't need to. Grune can see into my soul. Just as I can read him, he reads me. And as he does, his anger ebbs away.

"You didn't know," he concludes.

It doesn't matter that I wasn't here two days ago. I know in my heart that no one in this citadel knew of this, not even Wulf. "We're gonna get to the bottom of this," I promise. "Do you need help with the..." I don't even want to call her a dryad because she's not life; she's death.

"The abomination needs to be removed from the forest. Your kind has already killed too many of my children. I can't afford to lose any more." There is so much sadness in him I want to reach out and hug him. He seems to know it because suddenly, I feel wrapped in his embrace, leaves brushing over my hair.

And then he says something that knocks the wind out of me. "You're a true spirit seeker. One of the old ones."

He shows me another image: a middle-aged man in medieval garb sits under the oak tree where I stand, his back against the dryad, a hand on Grune's bark and a gentle smile on his face. There's a staff over his knees, but it's like Wulf's, gnarly and whole. A gift from Grune himself.

"They've forgotten." I gasp. "The spirit seekers have forgotten their purpose." The ancient staffs they value so much are the only relics of that time. A time when spirit seekers and spirits worked together. When dryads gifted parts of themselves to friendly seekers so they could defend their people from the wilful destruction of other spirits. I see the complete picture, past and present now.

"They've forgotten so much," Grune says. "Will you help them remember? Will you help the spirits?"

The answer is already written in my heart. "To my very last breath."

I have to wipe tears from my cheek when I leave Grune. He's calm now, and I feel his strength pulsing through me. But there is so much pain, loss, and grief in him it takes my breath away.

Aeola envelops me in a warm hug, and the ache in my heart lessens a little. She understands me more than anyone, with or without words. "You did well," she whispers.

"I haven't done anything yet," I answer, facing the door to the spirit seekers' living quarters. The promise I gave Grune weighs heavily on my shoulders. I can't run away. I have to stay and make them see, whatever it may cost me.

Bracing myself, I open the door. Immediately, Camille pulls me into her arms and hugs me tight, gasping. Then her hands run over my face and my arms, inspecting me with worry. "That was the scariest thing I've ever seen. Are you okay? How are you holding up?"

"I'm fine." I point to the oak tree in the courtyard. "He's not here to fight us." He was. His anger towards the spirit seekers brought him here. They brought something vile into his forest, and he was prepared to take their fortress down in response. "I've talked to him. There's a lot I need to tell you." I wish I could do it like him, just share my memories with them. Right now, I'm exhausted.

Leon looks at me, awe in his eyes. "You calmed him down. I didn't quite get it, but... you're amazing, Rika."

I smile weakly at him. In my opinion, that remains to be seen. My gaze drifts to the one person who can stop me dead in my tracks. One report, and I'll never be able to keep my promise to Grune.

Wulf has stepped away from the door, but his eyes linger on me. I don't know what to make of the look in them. Is it desperation like the one I saw in Iván's eyes? Helplessness? Awe? Certainly not awe. Or is it?

He swallows and takes a step forward, holding his staff out to me. "Your attunement is higher than mine," he says, his voice full of gravity. "You should be the one leading this team."

Please review

Thanks so much for reading Natural Enemies. If you think Rika deserves a little pick-me-up after all that turmoil in Budapest, please consider leaving a review. The Spirit Seekers could really use some good press after the near-disaster in this book.

Want to read more?

Become a Story Seeker and read Wulf's adventure in Naples for free by joining my mailing list! Don't miss another release and get all the spirit intel.

www.janna-ruth.com/newsletter

Want to connect with other readers?

Join my Story Seeker group for sneak peeks, games, events, and book discussions:

https://www.facebook.com/groups/storyseekers

Don't forget to check out book 3

Back to Nature

Where we visit the big library of Dublin.

Nature spirits are known for holding a grudge. Well, turns out they're not the only ones.

I've got the Spirit Seeker team on board with my programme. They finally believe me that not all spirits are evil. We even discovered that spirits and humans used to work together to protect land and people. Wulf decides to launch a secret investigation and invites ourselves to Dublin, the spirit capital.

To our surprise, we're met with instant hostility. The Dublin team doesn't want us there. They've got something to hide. But before I can find out what it is, we're attacked.

Accusations run wild. Someone has betrayed us. The Dublin team blames Wulf. Can I put my trust in a man who once fought to rid the world of spirits? Or do I abandon the family that got my back for greener pastures?

Watch Rika and the Spirit Seekers grow as they travel to Ireland. If you enjoy action-packed urban fantasy with unique supernatural creatures, get your copy today.

Continue Reading

Join Rika, Wulf & Co. in Dublin

**Nature has declared war on us, and we're here to answer that
call.**

Wulf might be the greatest spirit seeker the agency who leads the
war against nature has to offer. A new mission calls him and other
elite spirit seekers to Italy where they face off against an active
volcano. Two thousand years ago, Vesuvius obliterated the city of
Pompeii. Now the fire spirit has set his eyes on Naples.
Leading the spirit seekers into the volcano, Wulf begins to realise
that his biggest challenge might not be the spirits but keeping this
group of big egos in check. Tensions rise as the heat is turned up
and one false move could spell out their death.

**Join the Spirit Seekers in this prequel to meet the greatest of
them all in action!**
**Get this book for free by signing up to my mailing list
www.janna-ruth.com/newsletter**

Magic, Demons and High School Drama

Urban Fantasy with French Flair

About Janna Ruth

Once upon a time, Janna Ruth studied the plate boundaries of this world. Now, she's creating her own worlds. Born in Berlin, Germany, Janna lives in Wellington, New Zealand, writing both English and German books.

Janna's writing career kicked off when she won a writing competition for German publisher Ueberreuter. Her first self-published novel "Im Bann der zertanzten Schuhe" (Melody of Curse, coming in June 2022) went on to win the 2018 SERAPH for "Best Independent Title". She debuted in English with her witchy novella "Witching with Dolphins" in 2020 and has since published urban fantasy, YA sci-fi, and contemporary coming-of-age novels and series.

When Janna isn't writing, she has a plethora of hobbies, such as aerial acrobatics, cake decorating, drawing, reading, and anything crafty you can throw her way.

Find out more about Janna and her books here:

Website: www.janna-ruth.com
BookBub: www.bookbub.com/authors/janna-ruth
Facebook: www.facebook.com/authorjannaruth
Reader Group: www.facebook.com/groups/storyseeker
Goodreads:
www.goodreads.com/author/show/16513923.Janna_Ruth
BlueSky: https://bsky.app/profile/janna-ruth.bsky.social
Instagram: www.instagram.com/janna_ruth
TikTok: www.tiktok.com/@jannaruthwrites
Pinterest: www.pinterest.com/jannaruthwrites

www.ingramcontent.com/pod-product-compliance
Lightning Source LLC
Chambersburg PA
CBHW050244110726
47898CB00007B/2273